The Big Sky

The Big Sky

Gareth Creer

W F HOWES LTD

This large print edition published in 2002 by
W F Howes Ltd
Units 6/7, Victoria Mills, Fowke Street
Rothley, Leicester LE7 7PJ

1 3 5 7 9 10 8 6 4 2

First published in 2001 by Doubleday

A CIP catalogue record for this book is available
from the British Library

ISBN 1 84197 565 6

X000 000 006 7779

Typeset by Palimpsest Book Production Limited,
Polmont, Stirlingshire
Printed and bound in Great Britain
by Antony Rowe Ltd, Chippenham, Wilts.

For Emma

Acknowledgements

Thanks to Trevor Wray for the big skies
and to Brian Durrant for the dogs.

PART 1

HURT THE ONES YOU LOVE

I have felt the warm steel of death's rusting blade on my smooth neck, smelt the clean and chemical smell of it cutting through the bowel stench of its early dispatches. I have seen its snarling lip curl in my direction, heard the broken flap of its wings. And I have tasted its kiss, a fresh gland affair that you might think would be free of disease or other harm.

So I say to you now, with the bidding for my lover's life commenced and an untouching squeeze of fear and life upon my balls, that things must change, that it is imperative to risk everything for perfection. Because perfection is what we all deserve, and if we cannot somehow summon the final drop of fulfilment from our dreams and desires, then we may as well embrace a final throe and stake the chips of being left with absolutely nothing.

The telephone fractures an imperfect and solitary silence in the crouched basement of my office. It tolls for me. It rings Lutine loud, cuts a bad-message swath through the drum-and-bass thud of the club above. Something in me sinks, water in my lungs as I make my silent response, quaking in my heart and belly and boots in ways I knew I would for all of the seventy hours that have passed since Angela slammed the door and went to resume something from which I have tried and failed to woo her.

The frenetic flesh of a human voice shouts down the line, 'Jimmy? Jimmy Mack? Are you there?'

'It's Angela; she's in a bad way,' says Tommy Curl. 'Come quick, Jimmy. I'm in the Whalebone. They've given her bad stuff. They've set her up, and now they're coming for her. Can you hear me? Give me a sign, Jimmy.'

I do the only thing I can: hang up and give voice to my answer with the only means available.

My heart beats fast and out of synch with the dancefloor Propellerheads. I can feel my body shaking as I sink to my knees and fast-dial the code on the chamber of my safe. I wait for the steel clunk as it releases itself, unlocks the bulk of my worldly wealth. Not a vast amount, thirty grand. Not bad: enough to grant a modicum of freedom you might think; but not really, only just enough to clear Angela's debt to Denny Lane, which is now multiplying with itself on the passage of each day. It's a nice wad to hold, has that solid sponge texture of something that might provide comfort. I stuff it into my pockets. Take it back out again, watch my hand place it back in the safe.

It would be the last time I could settle her debt.

Better to invest in something more sustaining. So I rush empty-handed into the night, unweaponed and with distorted notions as to how I can wrest my chosen one from lethal clutches.

I boot the car along fast-trammel 2D headlight tracks that take me from Max, the nightclub I own, to the Whalebone; from the sad seaside of Warnsea to Easport's docks, where the old habit is slowly dying in the Whalebone, like a last gust of methane in a dead-cow culture.

Rabbits and voles and bats scuttle and swoop in and out of the speeding rays. I drive unthinking across the tattoo pattern of routes that score my past and present, with my mind fixed on the up-close frightening future. I can drive sixth sense on the single-track dyke roads which follow the ditched waterlines of this sunk island that we have made home.

When I hit Dockroad going into Easport, the traffic turns maelstrom, flashing and blaring, swerving as I take a second gear blindcorner passage into the narrow canyon warehouse lanes where dockers, sailors and whores have been coming for a hundred years to rendezvous in the night. Except now it's worse, because these are badlands of urban Gothic where modern horrors are screened, night and day.

Angela is my chosen one. We fit, and like mortice and tenon garnered from Dutch Elm, we are probably as good as either of us are likely to get, bound together as we are like vine by our bizarre, mutual pasts.

Trouble scrolls across the night in a slowdrift human passage away from the Whalebone. The seriousness of trouble's subtext is written in the absence of police presence. No flashlight serenade, no siren backcloth. As I handbrake my squealing tyres and leap into the street, I force calm upon myself; stop myself dead, shape a mood that's at one with the eerie tranquillity of felonies being policed from within. I breathe deep and nod '*all right*' to youths I have seen in my club.

'All right, Jimmy,' they reply.

There are two girls outside the Whalebone. One of them is squatting, legs astride and a contortion tuck of arms holding the tiny cloth she would probably call a skirt. In Easport this is norm. In Easport, men piss like dogs and women piss like men, but I try not to break my stride. I continue my passage onward to the saloon doors of the Whalebone, past the kerb cluster of junkies with dead narcotic faces, faces I vaguely know, gathered in a quickfix huddle that confirms to me that law will not be interfering with the airwave message heard by pirates everywhere: that Angela is to be apprehended by unofficial forces.

I intake sharp breath and press open the pub doors which are stain glassed and unspoiled. There are snugs left and right and straight ahead, one horseshoe bar to service them all. The ciggiesmog smoke is thick and they are still serving.

There is no aftermath buzz, no bedlam blemish or blood drying on the tracks. But there's something in the air you might think you could cut with a knife.

'Jimmy?'

I heelspin round with pistons pumping in my blood and nerves, reaching out for the glass whirr weapon of brown Newcastle on the bar, but I see the voice belongs to Deano, more friend than foe, and the nephew of Tommy Curl.

'Tommy's out the back,' says Deano. 'You'd better be quick.' He nods at the landlady and she dials a number into the phone as he turns back to me. 'Sorry, Jimmy. It's Denny Lane, see. He'll know if we don't make the call.'

As I go into the back I hear her say, 'Yes, the Whalebone. It's that girl; the one you said. She's here.'

The back room, which is guarded by another of Tommy's nephews, has been deconstructed by the overturn of tables, the smashing of glass. On the bench seat, with Tommy sat astride her, pinning her hands down and a beer towel stuffed in her mouth, is my lover. My Angela.

'She's been like this twenty minutes – knocked one of my boys out. It's that bastard Lane got her like this. You got to get rid of her, Jimmy. Lane's set her up, you know. He's set her up with a right load a fucking bad shit this time. She owes him a fucking shitload is what I've heard. You got to walk away from this one, lad. Get shot before they come

7

after you. We've got lives to get on with, Jimmy. You know what Lane's like; he carries a fuckin' shooter now.'

'*I know,*' I motion.

'You're not going after him? Not Lane. He's a fucking nutter.'

'*No.*' I walk towards Tommy, motion for him to stand away from Angela and, as he leaps away and she uncoils into me, violent and springing, we smile at each other. In a sweet frozen fraction of a moment, I engage her and she me as we silently agree to embark upon the first stage in the process of rehabilitation. In this wafer-thin and raw carpaccio slither of time within motion, an unpoisoned conviction courses in my blood. I know she can be saved. By me and me alone.

I lash her with a recoil jab behind the ear and she drops like a deadweight to the floor. Sometimes I loathe myself for the things I have to do. The things that describe the plight I have acquired.

I load her into the car, which Tommy has driven round to the back door. I think about what he said, about getting rid. It's something I could never do. I can hear the empty echo of a house, you see. I am deafened by the sound-lessness of a thousand lulls between a thousand commonplace tasks, blinded by the sadness of a single deckchair on a summer lawn, crippled by the weight of an absent arm that doesn't come unannounced on my belly as I wake in orderly sheets on an uncontested bed. All of which are absences I have known too well, too often in my life.

There are fast-car lights coming towards us, so I pull Angela to me. I hold her like an infant. No, an invalid; her head in my lap beneath the sightlines of Denny Lane and his apemen with their black hearts and brown habits. In the false colours of the dashboard lights, in the fast-panning warp of her supplier's 3-series beam, Angela looks paler than white, as if life has really got to her.

SOUNDS OF CHORD AND DISCORD

A fortnight later and we have come to a coastal place fifty miles north of the family home we have manufactured. Barb gorse prickles my shins as I watch Wingnut make his hither-thither hairpin climb up from the shore. The moor edges towards the sea, plunging a hundred feet to meet the waves, and between me and the slow advance of a friend and colleague who gives me voice, you can almost hear the rock breaking down like crumble cheese, giving way to the roar and pound of continental surf.

I grant my fancy a brief flight: think what it would be like to step off. My stomach turns, slow somersaulting, and my balls go light, puffing themselves up with fear. The wind is loud and constant, coming in with salt spray and incoherent stage whispers, but I can still hear Wingnut's huff curses. He is a frail soul who looks up at me with eyebrows raised and a thumb coming up.

I climb down to meet him, listen to him cub report on Angela's tough turkey in short panting bulletin. He tells me that the fisherman we paid to landlub has kept his eyes on the shack, seen that Angela has stayed, not strayed, for two interminable weeks of cold cuts and tins, no smoke and twenty-eight methadone.

She has given temptation the finger, told it to find some other mug because she understood what I was saying when Wingnut messaged her that this was life or death, that if she did leave the shack for any reason what!so!ever! then Denny Lane would surely find her out and there would be nothing I could do to help her. For I have been told by Silverpiece, who is in my debt and also an official of the law, that Lane must be paid this time, that there will be no intervention of malprocess. It has come down from on high.

We sit at the bottom of the cliff, on the huge grooved sediments of fossil pavements, waiting for the tide to pull back and unseal the secret cove where Angela is troved in a shack that was once my home. We are in the fringe of spray from a falling river high above. Rainbows glint all around us and at our feet the sea is fantastic: raging, surfing, swelling. Looking east, with my back to our new and Iberian future, I can clearly see the million fates that bob in the sea's white-knuckle grip, can see how providence will soon put our past behind us – for better or worse. We have hair-triggered the near future, are set upon our marks, ready to go. As if he can hear my thoughts, Wingnut says, 'You worried, Jimmy?'

'*About next week?*'

He nods, understanding my silent signs.

11

'*I'd be a fool not to be,*' I motion in the spray.

'You're not going to tell Angela? You know what she's like.' And in the way he says it, steering his sights unfocused out to sea, I can understand that he might have harboured hopes that she might lapse, because he knows, like all of us, that Angela's presence in our midst sandbags the odds against us.

'*I wish you liked her.*'

I cannot be sure whether he has seen me, but with his gaze still somewhere between beach and horizon he says, 'She's lucky to have you. She takes you for granted, takes advantage. Maybe sometimes I don't like her. Sometimes I think you deserve better.' And, as if he might be on chemical truth, he continues, 'Do you ever think, when things are turning for the worse, like they have been doing, do you ever think what it would be like to have someone to turn to, Jimmy? Someone you know will be there, say things you want to hear, catch you when things get too bad.'

He turns away again, so he can't see me say, '*We've got each other. All of us.*' I put a hand upon his shoulder. His bone feels tiny, as if I could snap it off. He turns round, smiles weakly and I say, '*Come on, the tide's going out. Let's go and see Angela.*'

'You go. I'll stay here.'

'*See you at the car.*'

Walking away, hugging the cliff face as I go, the seaweed beach sponges underfoot. I turn as I hear, 'Jimmy!' Wingnut shouts with outsize semaphore

12

through the rainbow surf, '*You won't tell the boys what I said.*'

'*No,*' I sign, salt spray whipping my face.

I am soon scratching up the gorse hillside which rises from the small cove. The shack is as it always has been, its wood a part of the furniture and derelict for almost all the long years since alum ceased to be mined in these parts.

The shape of Angela is at the window. I can see that recovery is under way, as if a hand has been removed from a shoulder in the way that she moves slowly but certainly between rag curtains as she comes out to meet me halfway.

'Jimmy. Oh Jimmy, thank God. I've been going off my head in here.'

'*You look good.*'

'I don't. I look a mess.' She cannot read me clearly. My signs are bad radio to her, but she can receive most of my everyday drift.

'*Here.*' I dig into the pocket of my coat, hand her a quarter bottle of Bells.

'You're an angel. Come in, sit down.'

She throws a large cushion onto the cold linoleum. The room smells of calor and sea and there are gaps in the wooden walls, but she has put wild flowers in old coffee jars on the plastic garden table; they make the place pretty but whisper a sweet lie to me, for they are water violets, which means she must have climbed up the cliff to where the water is unsalted. Sometimes it is better to let things lie,

13

which I do because, picking up the blister pack of pills, I can see that there are still four tablets left, which is a testament to the chemical control she has exerted over her rebirth. These are bitter pills to have not swallowed.

Angela sits cross-legged on the floor, patting for me to join her and looking up through doe eyes that are bigger and more clear than when I had left her. Her skin is almost translucent. I sit and run a single finger down her cheek, and she turns her face, rotates her head under my touch, like a cat. She takes my finger in her mouth, like a seal plucking small fish. She rolls my finger in her tongue and I feel her hand on me. The wetness on my finger gets cold under a rush of air, a gasp. There is a metal creak in the pure new wool of the trousers to my favourite suit.

'How long do I have to stay here?' says Angela, standing naked above me and too skinny for the goodness of her health. She smells of me, and me her. We have blended a third scent in the still room. I want to weep for her, condemned as she is to be alone in this ramshack, with the constant surf and the slow changing light. Nothing else. But expecting something else.

'*Two days*,' I signal.

'Did you get the place? In Spain.'

I nod.

'Tell me about it, Jimmy.'

I look into the black core of her. With her small

14

and brittle, hard soft, round angle face big in my eyeshot, I transport myself in words she cannot hear but in ways she might partially understand to what we have found in a foreign land: a safe place for us all.

There is a place, built for Castile and taken by Moors, overlooked by many century passages of time and no longer tainted by the blood rivers of reconquest, high above a village of white walls and terracotta roofs, between the mountains and the sea with Africa beyond. It has a luscious desert garden where the air bursts with the smell of lemons, and below this hacienda that we have found and leased there is a village where bars surge and lapse with the rattle and fold of dominoes and cards. Above zinc counters, alongside casks of wine, hangs the scent of leather, smoke, ham. The days are long and swift, empty and full. There is everything to be accomplished and nothing to do. And in a nearby town, on the opposite shore to Africa, is a place where we can make a new life, where I can import my MC soldjuz, as they say, to shout out blue air onto a dry-ice flesh floor.

'Oh, Jimmy. I wish I could understand everything you're saying. I've missed you.'

'I have to go.'

'Stay a little longer. Stay the night. Hold me.'

'I can't.'

'You don't want to.'

And I fall into the trap. I tell her, quite easily, what I had resolved to keep secret. I tell her that I need to visit my mother. She rages that she should come too, that my mother should know about her, and we are into our usual exchange about honesty and deception, trust and suspicion which examines the very nature of this and all relationships until, eventually, Angela accepts, not for the first time, that there is a part of the myself standing opposite her in the place that shaped me for ever that must remain mine, to hide from people whom I love for as long as I choose.

MOTHER AND CHILD REUNION

I have travelled on long wending lines through the limestone, green-grey outcrop heart of the North Moors from Whitby to York – west and south at drive-by pace. I drove high into Esk dale with the sea getting smaller, like dust between a shelf and a wall. I turned my back on that mad and seething force which no longer batters the life of Frances, the mother towards whom I journey.

I left Wingnut at the station after he had called her and she had told him she would love to see me, even though Lydia had just finished her A levels and they were having a barbecue which she, quite accurately, presumed I would prefer not to attend. If I was agreeable, she would meet me at the restaurant opposite the minster at eight thirty.

It was kind of her to reschedule, but a little late to show favours to an elder son at the expense of a younger daughter. In any event, my half sister would understand. She is, from what I can gather, well balanced, with an easy demeanour – which is easier for some than others.

Throughout the drive I have tried and failed, like

a stalling engine, to will myself to surrender to the unearthing of the most natural love of all. I have weaved this way and that on roads that grew narrow and became smothered in hedges, until I am high above the trunk road. York sprawls in the gold and sinking light, stretching out alongside roads like spilt paint.

I have slowed to an almost halt on the outskirts of an escarpment village which could be any of a thousand other English places, going about its unnamed business unreported, with its poppy boxes for post and calls, its spire and pub and shrinking ladies tending their violets, its flaking vicarage and its corporation fringe, its bypass posters and its sell-by fête. This is everywhere and nowhere, and as perfect a place as could be to recover from a past.

I am approaching the bricks and mortar of the reinvention of my mother's life, her home. Two hours remain before I am due to meet her, two hours in which to drive twelve miles, check into the hotel and walk for three minutes across the minster grounds to the restaurant.

My mother has found happiness here, has seemed thoroughly content on each of my six visits in the nine years since I suppressed unworthy instincts and sanctioned reacquaintance. All of which has taken place in the duskless, dawnless wake of her desertion of me, when she left four-year-old me for the starched confines of a sanatorium; left me to the whims of her mad lover, a token parent.

I have sat in a chair by the long windows of her new drawing room and listened to her tearless explanations of why she did what she did, how her love for me has never waned; listened to her explain why she does not cry, how she has come to learn that she was more sinned against than sinner; listened to her new family laugh and play in the rambling garden that runs through a gate into open fields. And I have seen with my own eyes that she reserves no different kind of look for them, whom she indisputably loves, than she does for me, her first-born; seen that she is genuine, sincere in what she says and does, but still I bolster my bitterness at how she seems to have recovered from our joint fates. Bitter because I have never been able to manage such a recovery and feel that perhaps I carry sufficient scars for both of us.

I sit in my car outside the gates to her home in the selfish hope that I will be deigned some sort of relief by an ordinary misery that haunts them. What I wish for, like a child on a festive eve, is evidence that her new life is, at least in part, a happy sham – sufficient grounds on which to found the beginnings of my learning to relove her.

But there is no such evidence in this crimeless scene. I merely hear the onset of barbecue preliminaries, watch a gaggle of teenagers walking towards me from the centre of the village, carrying cider and sixpacks and swinging bags of meat. Life

19

is carrying on. The last drop is being squeezed from the long day. There is a whoosh of smoke, a raucous laugh and Bob Marley's voice sings like sunshine, asking, 'Is this love is this love is this love . . .' I start the engine and begin the slow drive to the hotel, where I will sit in the bar on my own for an hour before waiting for my mother, who will arrive late at the restaurant, weighed down with heartfelt apologies.

'Oh, Jack. Sorry I'm so late. The girls' barbecue. I helped them get it started. Lydia finished her A levels yesterday. What's wrong? Oh, sorry. I just can't get used to calling you Jimmy. Sorry. Let's get some wine, hey?'

The waiter scurries in answer to my mother's wave, says, 'Hello Mrs Lorrimar'.

'I'll order,' she says in a gesture that is both kind and unnecessary, revealing also how little she knows the person I have become, how I allow others to adapt to my limitations, not vice versa. It pays no heed to the ease with which I bear the embarrassments that ride on the back of my over-estimated affliction.

Frances holds the waiter, Carl, by the hand as she goes through the entire menu and wine list. She converses through me with herself and orders for both of us, choosing more or less what I would probably have chosen for myself.

'Now we can relax.' She leans into her handbag and offers me a cigarette. I take one, a Gitanes

Blonde, which elicits disapproving looks from an American couple three tables away, but above which Frances rises high enough for both of us.

'So, tell me, do you have a girlfriend?' she says, as if she might be a normal mother to my normal son. She smiles, seeing through my failed feign of non-response. 'When are we going to meet her? You must bring her to see us, at the house.'

A chink appears in her spirits, a sadness coming to the surface that shafts searing light on my defences, makes me want to reach out, touch her skin which all the void years have mottled and made soft. I want to be held by her. But like a different kind of cancer that blights a fleeting and spurious miracle of recovery, I suffer strength. I feel it surge in me and all I do is message her, transmit gists of what lies ahead.

'You're . . . ? You're going away? Abroad? Why? Oh, Jack. It's been so hard, these last few times I've seen you. But I thought, I thought maybe we might just be getting to know each other again.'

I try to communicate that it is for me to dictate the pace and boundaries of whatever union she might wish us to rejoin. I am dismissive in the shrug and upward-palm *c'est la vie* of my hands. I remind myself of the harshness of the nature and terms of my abandonment.

It was an abandonment inflicted on me by her. Defenceless and four-year-old me had been surrendered into the care of a mad woman – her lover, my would-be parent, who was quite capable of being as big a bastard as any father.

I flail my message lazily. I flick it out for her to take or leave. I do it without concession. '*I have a life of my own. You have your own life.*'

'You've every right to be angry with me, I can see that much. But I've tried to explain.' The Americans lay down their silver, stop eating and intrude upon us, staring, taken aback by my tick-tack and listening to Frances who, in compensation for the lopsidedness of the exchange, is talking too loudly for the type of thing she's saying. I press a finger to my lips and look towards the Americans, who dive back into their food. 'Sorry. I just wish I could explain. I wish you could understand what it was like, why I couldn't stay.'

'*I know. You've told me. I understand,*' I gesture.

'You understand?'

I nod.

'Can't you give me a chance, then? If you're leaving Easport, come and live closer to us. Alan has gone to Australia. He's got a sabbatical and Lydia's going off to university. Please.'

'*No. I have my own life.*'

'There's nothing to stop you. You don't have responsibilities, you can . . .'

'*I do! I do have responsibilities!*'

I stand, dabbing at my mouth with the napkin and pulling money from the top pocket of my suit jacket, toying with the idea of sitting back down but distracted by the glimpse sighting of sauce slipping from the American woman's suspended lamb, disabled as she is by the lock of a gawp she has frozen in our direction.

'What are you saying? Please sit down. Stay.'

'*I'm sorry. This is moving too fast. You have your own family.*'

'Don't go. There's something I must talk to you about.'

I walk away, and as I open the door to leave I hear Frances call.

'It's important. I must talk to you, Jimmy. You are my son. You can't change that.'

I walk past the window, see her watching me, pinning me with eyes that don't lie. Carl is standing by her, waiting to be told to take my plate away. Her eyes burn me, make me wish I had the humility to go back, walk past the Americans and resume my dinner as though nothing untoward had occurred.

I see my car parked in the forecourt of the hotel on the other side of the minster gardens and realize that I can be packed in ten minutes, home in an hour. My home.

WITH MY BACK AGAINST THE WALL

I received Angela back into the fold last night, after we had red-herringed Denny Lane, sent false word to him that she was squatting in Leeds and watched his red tail lights fade to black before we stole her in, under cover of darkness. He will come back more vengeant than ever, but not before we have fled to far-flung and foreign captivity, for which our preparations are complete in all but one respect. In the most important detail of our plottings I am most definitely not ready.

Tonight, for the first time in my life, I must kill a man.

In the weeks that have passed since I collected Angela from the Whalebone, I have collated versions of a single truth. As far as I can see, there is only one way in which we can survive: together.

I don't know how I will undertake the snuffing out of the life of an imperfect stranger. For the moment, all I can do is watch the unmoving and naked outline of the woman I have learned to love. She is standing on the balcony of our room in a home we have made with others. Others who do not love her, do

24

not see what I can in her every minute movement.

She is in shadow. I cannot see the complex truths of her, the curves and lumps and detail hair of her, the moles and tiny scars of her, and the other ravages that map her body. I know each one, every story behind each change that has been visited upon her, which you or any other stranger might see and draw conclusions from. I know her completely, I think.

She turns. I can feel her smile on me, and she draws her arms W-shaped across her breasts. The prints of my fingers will be on her hips, a still-burning touch as she looks at me, as pure as snow and like-coloured. She has made unmarked improvements from when I sped to save her from emergency services. You could have watched my progress from here, speeding as I did on the dyke roads that meander across the marshes between us and the sea to the city of Easport.

I swing my legs from between the sheets and feel the chill of early morning. I stand and walk to her, hold her cold skin against mine and try to say that everything will be fine, just like we have it here and now. Right here and right now, but without the thunder-cloud doom of what might go wrong.

'I love you, Jimmy Mack.'

'*I love you, too,*' I motion, with a changing expression on my face. I say it not casually, but with some doubt. Love and doubt go hand in hand, don't you think? They surely must if

25

you have allowed yourself to become sufficiently vulnerable.

'I'm sorry for what has happened. I will get better, Jimmy. I won't let you down,' she says.

I take her face into the hollow of my neck and shoulder. I do it to hide the expanse of doubt that I can feel spreading through the soundscape of the shapes my face will make.

There is an early breeze coming across the flats. It will be warm later, but for now it brings only the smell of salt and a thousand tiny pimples, like minuscule mineral on her neck and back. Her muscles are tight. Something is frightened and trapped in the fabric of her and, as we stand there, each waiting for the other to unseal our skin from skin, I hear the clipped formations of a South African on a station platform in damp England.

'You English, you know, you're so complacent. It drives me bliddy crazy,' he had scolded, to nobody in particular. The train, it had been announced, would be an hour late, and I shuffled, uncomplaining, into the buffet with the rest of the would-be passengers.

'But when your backs are against the wall, fuck me! There's no-one bitter,' he had continued as we shared a table in the crowded bar. I could see the frontiersman in him; I could see it reflecting me-shaped in the mad and tiny pupil glaze of him. We journeyed together, which he was happy to do, even after I messaged him that the conversation would be one-way traffic. He bought me dinner and told me how rich and successful he was. He told me he had shot a man once, watched him die and, although I believed him at the time, now, with my back against the wall and recalling the casual way in which he told his tale, I choose to disbelieve him. I choose to disbelieve that anyone can not be torn apart by the execution of what I must do today.

Angela is the first to pull away. My chest feels a lick of wind as I watch her pad inside, don the silk gown I gave to her on the occasion of her first going away. Not so much 'away' as 'inside', as they say. The gown was intended to make her feel special, but I should have known that it would bring her more harm than good. It was coveted, you see, distinguishing Angela from the others with its illusory statement that she perhaps felt herself to be a cut above the rest. She fought to keep it. It bruised her, my well-meant kindness. But she wears it every day. She has forced herself to give precedence to my good and naive motive over the memories of the pain it delivered.

I didn't expect her to ever come back to me, but she did, returning with a childhood look that was there all along, underneath the deadness she had prescribed for herself up and down the years. And now I can see the child in her again, like a returning stain.

When she went away, I made preparations for the gap that would remain in my life when she didn't make it back. So I bought my dogs. Angela dislikes dogs, says they carry germs and are dirty – if you can believe that of someone who scars her own skin and taints her own blood, who chemicals up her head and mood. And even though I acquired them to replace her, she suffers me my animals because she knows how much I love them. A surrogate kind of love, but enough to measure the lengths I will go to for the advancement of her cause. Because today I will bid my dogs farewell; I may never hear them bark again, the way they are now, waking earlier than is usual. Perhaps they can sense that something is in the offing.

'You'd better go to them,' she says.

I lean on the rail and through the warm mist make a silent call to my dogs. They don't have names. That would be a nonsense. But they respond to me, and I can distinguish them, my twin terriers who you would think are ugly: with their genemangled distort faces and their awesome quarters, bred for bad purpose. They are pit bull and gentle as kittens. They are identical, save for one being bitch and one dog.

They are quiet now, resuming their romp-and-roll play-snarling fight on the grass, like children. They can detect the impending goodbye, sniff it on the breeze.

WE ARE FA-MI-LY

I have tended to the dogs and view the future from our bedroom balustrade. It will be a fine day, long and water-shedding us to winter through haze that comes at us from the east, where their sun will now be cool and low in the sky. You can feel the heat, latent, and if you get yourself into that one-sense hearing zone, picking up waves that shock the very perimeter of your powers, you can hear the stop-start white-noise hum of traffic already making its way to our beaches. And if, like me, you have honed your senses, one by one, so individually they are far greater than the division of their collective powers, you could hear the wash of tide far across the delta plains of marsh and rape and dykes. It could be a beautiful day if it wasn't also to be an end of something most precious.

Like a noise from another dimension there is a knock at the door. Angela calls, 'Come in,' and Wingnut enters with his abstract entourage of multitude tasks for today.

'Ange,' says Wingnut.

'Wingnut.'

And there, in the staccato exchange, more curt

than polite, you can hear the iceberg library of grudge that discolours every dynamic of the coming together of my lover and my voice.

Wingnut is weakest and also most alone amongst the tight bonded allness of us. Us: me and Angela; Jessie and Roy, Wingnut. Us who share a kind of island life on reclaimed saltwater land outside the slow-death seaside town of Warnsea, which from here is an opposite pole to Easport in our hemisphere visions. You can see it clinging against sea with its one road going in and its one road going out. Bungalows, houses, shops, more houses, more bungalows, then nothing. It's a small world which constitutes almost everything that all of us must leave behind.

Wingnut is alien, imported in the first instance for his grasp of language, his reading of my signals, but the rest of us are indigenous, fated into each other and with little choice but to live the life we have created together. Wingnut is as dispensable to me as he is elsewhere employable – not at all, for the avoidance of doubt. He dances to my hand jive, gives me voice. And Wingnut is Wingnut on account of his Jodrell jugs, which are but one of many factors that have dictated the state of his virgin quo.

There is little loss of love between Angela and Wingnut and much cruelty in the juvenile jostle that defines the way they live in close confine, an example of which is the way she is nakedly lounging on the bed in the careless silk flanks of her gown, smoking her cigarette without modesty or shame despite his presence and the fact that she is not proud of her body. I know she dislikes the bone-jut berth of her hips, the way her shoulders taper too sloping. But she flaunts her outer self as if she is setting down scent, intentions and territory. If she had set broken glass on the floor and forced Wingnut to make a bleeding, grimace passage to the balcony, she could not have discomforted him more. And in his reply, he shows a lip-curl disgust at Angela's harlot pose, stands over-looking the lawn with his hands deep in the pockets of his unwashed, low-crotch jeans, shifting his scrawny weight from trainer to trainer.

I have overheard his views on Angela from my listening promontory, but I forgive him whatever malice he harbours because he arrived too late on this particular scene to understand the entirety of her appeal; too long after the seeds of our unfêted love were sown in the prepercussions of my First Act of Vengeance.

'Everything's set, Jimmy,' he says. 'They're coming for the dogs at midday. Then the van comes at two.'

There is a down-tone cadence in the unnecessary deference of his voice. We are friends and family, or at least as proximate to that as either of us will probably ever get. He fidgets more message and says coyly in nervous hands, '*Are you all right, about tonight?*'

He deserves better than a straightforward lie to

31

a question I cannot answer, so I avoid the issue. '*Ask Angela to get dressed,*' I signal him in a polite tone, with a could-you-possibly singing lilt of a flat palm and a quizzical brow.

But he misrepresents me. He misshapes my message.

'Get dressed, Ange. Jimmy says so.'

I forgive him, because I can see how he might blame her for bringing us to the brink of a venture that is neither our style nor provenly in our league. I forgive him even though I know it is not undilutedly the fault of Angela that she has been woven into the fabric of my mind and soul to the extent that I am left with no choice but to risk everything in the some say spurious hope of saving her from herself and others.

In any event, there is nothing for the collective us to fear. We must simply follow a plan that breaks down into strategies that separate into a hundred everyday acts. The acts are easily performed, save one: the very last, which is itself made easier by the absence of choice. So what you might consider dangerous, when we reconstruct the hundred constituent acts into their whole, becomes effortless for me. It is, if you will, what we would all do with our backs against the wall.

Except, I have never murdered a man, nor ever knowingly killed a man. But I have caused the death of the only person I can be absolutely certain that I have ever loved.

★　　★　　★

32

Jessie and Roy are bickering their way through the making of breakfast, like bad brothers whose only means of coexistence are footed in the thin-soil grounds of the pretence of hate. We have been together since we passed from teens into our different stages of manhood, since we were all released into the community on our varied terms and conditions. Not that we had done anything to deserve our isolation from the million humdrum things that happen every day to reinforce your notion that you have a place at a table, a role to play. What we have done with this life we have made for ourselves is to simply change the notion of normality.

Before Roy was a friend to any of us, he led a grinning, solitary life in a place called Newholme with me, Angela and Jessie, until he was temporarily ruined by his love – and incapacity for the reconstruction – of jigsaws. He would eat alone, smiling and looking around, eating too quickly and swallowing whole. He would rush from the table at the first sound of the bell and run to the games room where his jigsaws were waiting for him. But Roy had no talent for the solution of puzzles. His frustration would build and build until the perennial smile faded from his face. Dribble would come seeping from his open, disbelieving mouth and he would take the half-made image in his hands and crumple it into a broken mess. This would happen every night, until one evening Roy came downstairs with a placid intent on his happy

33

face, a bag of tricks gripped proudly in his hand. He sat at the table with calm haloing around him, commanding all our attentions and imploring us to watch as he built a picture piece by piece and beyond all normal thresholds.

The image grew slowly, steadily towards completion. But as Roy turned his attention to the sky and foliage that bridged his completed edges to the fully formed castle at the puzzle's centre, a familiar frustration came shrouding down upon him. We waited for the drool, for the violent crumple. But it didn't happen. Roy sat back, breathed out theatrically, and his smile transformed itself, quite mad.

He delved into his bag, pulled out a pair of scissors and a tube of glue, like a confident and unassisted magician. He took the remaining pieces one by one, clipping off the male extrusions and forcing a dozen fits until he was left with one pile of green and one of blue, which he glued into two shapes that matched the expanses of red Formica which splodged like blood above and to the side of his castle. And when he had finished, he stood over his imperfectly completed and mad cubist jigsaw picture, and he said, 'There,' the way you would when you have finished an ice cream too big and rich for you.

He was taken out of Newholme when he tried to stab Miss Dempsey, who attempted to stand between him and the madcap cuttings and pastings of the following evening's puzzle. And when he came out of what we all called the loony bin, he had changed. He still smiled his constant smile, but he had been made hard.

I had occasion to use him during the dubious formative stages of my insubstantial empire of concerns. One evening, driving away from the docks with a vanful of tulip bulbs, he told me about the jigsaws. 'Jimmy,' he said, 'you remember the jigsaws . . .' and even though the interpretation as to why a misfit would be drawn to such puzzles is no reinvention of the wheel, the point is, he told me about it. He shared with me an acknowledgement of the weakest link in his chain. So, even though he can be a liability, we are together now, a part of each other's lives, because we should all hang on to what doesn't necessarily suit us any more. Can you imagine what life would be like if we didn't?

What Roy did in our home with his puzzle is what I have done here, really, with this home and the businesses we attend to, the recreations we pursue. We have cut off what doesn't fit us, left it mutant outside.

As Jessie carries our plates in from the kitchen, Roy shouts after him, 'No! You tosser, you've forgotten the mushrooms,' appearing at the door with a platter of steaming mushrooms and smiling his constant smile, dancing from foot to foot as if he wants the toilet. Jessie takes the platter and screams, 'Fuck! Fuck!' The platter crashes to the floor, spilling the mushrooms, and Roy bursts into a child's laugh, tucked double. We join in, unable to help ourselves as we watch Jessie rush to put his hands under water, foul-mouthing retribution that steams in clouds above the sink. Roy is dancing delight in the doorway, goading Jessie, who is a foot taller, several stones heavier, but not nearly so insane or fear-free of pain as Roy.

'See that? See that? Fuckin 'ell, I got him. See it, Jimmy? See it, Ange? He forgot me hands are tough as fuck. Hey, Jessie, you tosser. Me hands are tough as fuck.'

Jessie's threats are lost in the sound of water.

Roy is leaning against the door with his stubble head creased in manic pleasure, and the way the sun is catching him, he looks suede. His head is number two'd, his eyebrows are number two'd and his face, right up to the top of his cheekbones is number two'd. He is primeval, in spite of the pretty face that looks like the cutest bad lad in every class you have ever been in.

Jessie comes back to the table and Roy dances round him, sparring with his hands held up in fight stance, but Jessie merely hitches his trousers so they won't bag at the knee, bends down and picks up the mushrooms – the ones that Roy hasn't trampled on – putting them on a plate and taking them back into the kitchen. He rinses them and pops them back in the pan, like any good, frugal mother, calling through, 'It'll be three or four minutes now, thanks to the moron,' in a make-do and mend, turncheek castigation.

Roy pulls his face and lights up an Embassy Regal, and we sit round trying to keep our laughter to ourselves until Jessie brings the mushrooms in.

'Sorry about that,' he says, looking daggers at the still-smoking Roy.

'Thanks, Jess,' says Angela. He is her favourite. He has that effect on women. We tuck in and Jessie tells us how Anne-Marie has agreed to receive him back into still-warm loins – not his words – which is an insignificant event that happens once, sometimes twice each month. But to hear the measure of his gravetone conviction, to see the seriousness of his furrow face, you might believe he is actually going to be faithful this time.

'I tell you, Ange, I think it's really going to work out. I've told her she can come over, when we've settled.'

'*What!*'

'She doesn't know anything, Jimmy. Just told her we were going away for a bit.'

'You tosser,' says Roy.

'Jesus, Jessie,' says Wingnut on his own behalf, then, looking across at me. 'Where did you say we were going?'

'I didn't.'

'When did you say we were leaving?'

'I didn't, I . . .'

'When!'

'Tomorrow. I said I'd see her tomorrow. Last time for a while, I said. But that's all. I didn't say anything else.'

'Ange,' Wingnut behalfs me, 'call Anne-Marie. Tell her we're not going anywhere. Tell her if she says anything to anyone I'll have that scumbag brother of hers fingered as the lousy fucking grass he is.'

'Don't say that, Ange,' says Jessie, 'she'll be upset. We were going to have a kid. Start trying,' says Jessie.

'You!' shouts Roy, 'I bet you can't even have kids. I bet you're a jaffa. All them birds you've had. Never a scare.'

'Not like you, eh, Roy,' says Jessie.

'I've had plenty of birds.'

'One.'

And even though Roy is in the wrong, Jessie receives a collective look of reprimand for going below the belt. Roy has fathered a child called Ollie in his indisputable image, but whose mother deems that visitation is right only when she wants to go to a nightclub or on holiday. His access is restricted to the fornicating and doubtlessly twice-shy protected timetable of someone he has known only once and very briefly. As for the legalities, Roy is uncertified, a non-parent. There is no record of their union. She has taught Ollie to call him uncle, but in spite of this the child is loved by all of us, and not least because he is the spit from the mouth of Roy.

Separations are pending: Roy from Ollie, Jessie from Anne-Marie and, looking down at stains the egg and sauce have made on my plate, trying to interpret an everyday shape you might say the name of to a therapist, I feel as if I have patented blame, because there is little justice in the quorum that will be us when we convene in Spain. There is no kind of merit governing the terms of our departure, its arbitrary divorces.

I first met Angela after I had ceased to have the family Foster that was never my own anyway. At school, my teacher said, 'I'm fed up of telling you, Hunt,' and she pressed my nose to a chalk spot on the blackboard, from where I was unable to join the peer chorus of 'Your name is Hunt'. But I wouldn't want you to think I was more unloved than loved throughout the years that followed my mother's desertion of me.

Mrs Hunt would be waiting for me each afternoon, clenching my hand tight as I watched the other children skip freely away, unattended. At weekends she would take me to the park, monitoring my heights and angles of adventure, restricting the risks I put myself at. She would sit me on her knee for the hour or so before Mr Hunt came home from work. Mr Hunt, who wore dark suits and brilliant-white shirts, and ties that Mrs Hunt said were 'swish'. Mr Hunt, whose briefcase made man smells when it opened – leather and newsprint. Mr Hunt, who, once the plates were cleared from the lacecloth table, became quite silent in his occupation of different parts of the house, and with whom I experienced only limited contact: in the hall, on the landing.

Occasionally, I would hear the print of my name buried deep in arguments that would climb slowly through the floor of my bedroom like frightening jungle plants. Whenever this happened, a shaft of light would come out of the falling silence, lighting up my bed, then shadowing me dark as Mrs Hunt tiptoed towards me as if she were floating on a gangplank. Then she would peel back the sheets and slide in next to me, holding me tight against her waxy skin, her soapy smell making it difficult for me to breathe. But I always fell swiftly into sleep, lulled as I was by the steady beat of the rise and fall of her sobs.

Until one day I woke to the sound of Mr Hunt's angry voice, with his face big and warped in my waking vision and his spit light-raining on my face. I can't remember what he said; I was half asleep. But Mrs Hunt was sat upright, in bed beside me. She said, 'You're the one with the problem, Lance,' which made his face freeze and his eyes and mouth return to normal, except he looked different, as if something might have been drained from him, as if his dead seed had finally stained him. He left the room, turned his broad back on the two of us, left us to listen to the distant hum of his voice disappearing into telephone lines.

I didn't go to school that day, and when Mrs Hunt had stopped wailing, beating Mr Hunt's chest with her fists and leaping up to try to scratch his face, she took me on a bus into Easport, in and out of tears all the way. She left me in an office and I never saw her again.

★   ★   ★

The house is quite empty, save the boxes in the hallway. It feels like a dead place, waiting to have new life breathed into the magic mortar of its walls – part windmill, part house. My room is at the top of the tower, and in the evenings, when Angela is sprawled on our bed with the reading light on, you can look up from the terrace and swear blind it is a lighthouse. We have been more happy than sad here, the five of us, but even in the molten core of the very best of times – the barbecues, the parties, the weekends when Roy and Jess and Wingnut left me and Angela here alone, like house-sitting teenagers – it has always felt to me as if we are delicate things in flight around a candle that flicks and which you know will either go out or burn you.

I can hear my dog and bitch echoing each other's barks through the French windows, so I throw the doors open and call my silent call. I lay down and, with the disappearing dew cold on my back, I wait for them to roll me over and lick me and tell me they love me and to hear me say it back. In this respect, they are the only ones.

IF I CAN SAVE JUST ONE SOUL

This is the first – absolutely the first, and without doubt the last – time I allow drugs to pass into and out of my hands for any purpose other than the enhancement of my own mood and sensibility, from which temptation I have, in any event, been largely celibate for many years.

This is for money, which shames me, but I do it not for profit but because the residue deposited by the swift passage of these substances through my hands is of greater value than money. It will allow me to invest in a better future. This is a one-off, and you should not judge me by this single decision, nor for some of the other and petty crimes I have committed. I simply did what other people would have done if I hadn't got there first on account of my back being pressed most painfully to the wall.

Some might say that Angela has asked for everything she has got, apart from the very first hand she was dealt. But I cannot help myself from wanting to help her out of the state she is in, because the essence of Angela, as far as I am concerned, is that she shared the same space for almost the same time in the womb of Lisa's mother.

Lisa is the girl I loved with all my heart: when my heart was so big and warm and pounding that it made me want to cry; when I saw her from my window in the Newholme gables, going through the yard with her skirts always cleaner and prettier than the other girls; when I'd brush up on any one of the dozens of points of contact I would invent for us each day. And in return, Lisa didn't hate me. I think she might even have loved me, the way you would a brother. But I loved Lisa, every way you could and to the hilt.

Lisa isn't here any more, and the way it's left me feeling, with a brooding Manic Street Preaching sky which is never far from my horizons, is that if I could save only one soul . . .

It's a Christian thing. A door-knocking in the middle of something important. So fuck off, right now, until I've got time for God or whatever it is you're selling. That kind of thing. The sort of Christian thing where their whole life is worth it if they save just one sad and sorry unbelieving soul.

But that doesn't mean I don't have difficulty reconciling myself to the chosen method of saving her. I do. All the time. All the fucking time. There is a dark crescendo coming in off the North Sea where an unknown life will sail towards me tonight. I can hear the rain-cloud orchestra tempesting up the estuary. I can feel myself untether in Angela's defence, hear a rant forming itself into chords that augment.

It's like – drunk driving is bad, and banning drinking and driving is bad too because it undermines the fabric of our society. What's wrong with a bloke quaffing a skinful with his arse roasting in front of a fire and making steady automotive progress home? What's wrong with that? I'll tell you.

Save one young innocent life and all the funstrangling legislation is worth it. All the fat-cat pinstripe legal fees are paid for in God rupees or whatever. And another.

Apartheid. Forget all the nuance. If one black guy – innocent and joyous, walking in the sun for no reason other than he enjoys it – doesn't get shot for doing the most normal thing in all the natural states of all empires, then all the legislation the world can offer on its gravy-stain salver is worth it. WORTH IT!

That's what I think. And that is why I will do what I have to do. I believe in the saving of individual souls because that is probably as big an impact as we can ever hope to make. Angela is worthy of these efforts. She is the living half of the complete good and bad yin-yang whole of a person whose better half did not survive my meddlings with her fate, even though I loved her from the first time I saw her until she died. When she and I were both fifteen.

So the least I can do is save Angela the only way I know I can. It has to be expensive. It has to be horses and sun, because as anybody who is acquainted with the forensics of habit will tell you, there is nothing better than a good habit. Nothing. That is the natural justice of the price you have to pay, which is why good habits cannot be allowed to last, why they divinely and irrepressibly morph into bad habits. Without the equal and opposite of the physics of checks and balances, everybody would be overdrawing. This is the simple economic of why the price has to be so high. Which is why we need the rental for the hacienda in Almeria, a new club nested big enough to support us all through the many second summers of love.

As for the true price which I pay for these new, good and real habits? My belief is that these drugs, beginning westward passage now, would have got into the wrong hands anyway. They are on voyage to where they were always going to go, regardless of me and my intervention. I know that's no excuse. But, please, hear me out.

Say I did put the beautiful booty into the North Sea sewage wastes. What good would come of such flushing and squeezing of supply on the streets? It would merely escalate price, raise the stakes for everybody's favourite day job. Habit crime soars, and because of what I have done to try and save some scallies who will somehow get their stuff even if it kills them, which it will, old ladies who cannot afford insurance will lose their television sets, kiddies who have been good all year will wake up with their presents gone from under the tree. At

45

least now, with so much stuff coming over so often, the users can feed themselves on a tight budget. In Easport, they don't smoke grass on the streets any more. The heroin is cheaper.

If you ask me, they should go the next step beyond and prescribe the evil stuff. It's tuppence a hit to manufacture. So do it. The crime is the only thing which suffers risk of loss. And the profit. Aha, that would mean no escape for me and Angela, but so what? And in any event there would be nothing from which we would need to take flight. But there is little to be gained from arguing the fors and contras of problems that don't exist. My problem is specific and immediate. I have to break the circle.

TOMMY CURL AND THE BREAKAGE OF CIRCLE: THE BIG ONE-OFF

The circle: the million billion tiny dots of my life that make it the shape it has become. I can see it all from the balcony that runs the perimeter of this tower I call home. It is a home which has been crafted from a derelict windmill on abandoned land that was once sea, has been reclaimed and which turns saltier in its marsh with the passing of each day – save the irrigated garden we lovingly tend. But its passing is inevitable.

Easport is to my south, where Flint and the controllers govern lives in the tower blocks and on the estates. If you scanned north, past the refineries that line the estuary and the marshes that cover the sunk island; if you continued north to Warnsea, you will have covered half the circle. In the other half, somewhere out there and probably watching, is the harm that will come to us if we don't pay back, if we don't leave. It's not just Denny Lane or other mad and dangerous enemies Angela might have made for herself; it is something else, big enough to be faceless –

47

our past histories – that we have to distance ourselves from.

That is the circle.

And last week, after we came back from Spain, Tommy Curl, my closest approximation to a father – who paid my first fine and helped me to somehow turn the bad things I once did into some sort of less bad career – called on us to finalize a scheme for the breakage of circle.

I reiterated to Tommy how grave was our need for a big one-off, and whilst Jessie served up his tapas, carving perfect tissues of the Serrano ham he'd brought back from Spain, Tommy fed me reminders of the relationship that reward has with risk. He tried to dissuade me, said there were times everyone thought they needed an out-shot, when everyone was desperate enough to delude themselves that it was possible to get away with it.

'Jimmy,' he had said, 'there's always a price. You get what you pay for, and it works the other way, too. But some things you can't buy. Whatever you do, wherever you take her, she'll be the same.' And he looked up at me, prepared to say something he might regret. But he swallowed his words, because Tommy owes me, even though I owe him. This is the formal arrangement of need and favour that has governed our behaviour towards each other. So he helped me, even though he knew, for sure in his estimation, that it would do me harm.

You see, I was there to help him pick up the pieces when he got his come-uppance.

Tommy flexed his fingers on the tracks of York, Market Rasen and Beverley a couple of times a month. He robbed winners. He had honour, and under his beerstale, nicotine-breath skin he had a charm that harked back to a past I wish I'd known: old timbered streets and scurvy, laden barges from the continent and beyond; when I would have joined a horde to look for riches in London town.

Tommy was good. But one day he lapsed, became lazy, slapdash on a single and ruinous trip to the Whalebone. He'd left home without his wallet and was late for a card school in the back room. So Tommy did what came naturally. He answered a call, a whispering call on the breeze of what he might have called his work ethic, and he went to work, turned right instead of left on Canalbank and did one job.

Outside Wallis, Tommy saw what he described as a 'tarty piece', in her leopardskin arse 'nice and tight' and with a patent handbag loose on her shoulder. So Tommy bundled into her, said he was sorry and he stroked her jacket smooth, copped a little feel as he did it. He makes us laugh the way he tells it, with his Steptoe gums and his no-chance leer.

He can laugh about it now, even though it was Chancey's new girl he had turned over for a hundred miserable quid. Chancey; Eric Chance. Flint's man, who ran Dockroad. And the girl, when she noticed her money had gone, remembered

49

Tommy's Steptoe features. She told Chancey, who put a name to the face straight away, and Tommy paid the price for doing one on his doorstep; right on his doorstep, where he's a face that fits. He broke that first rule.

Chancey broke Tommy's fingers and thumbs. One by one he snapped them back. Once at each joint. Twenty-eight slow cracks. And I was the one he came to. I drove him to hospital, with his screams blistering the roof of my car.

And that's the story of Tommy Curl, who thinks he's in my debt because I gave him a job when no-one else would touch him, clearing glasses at Max. Which was poor as ideas go because he's always dropping them. His fingers can't grip, you see. He's all fingers and thumbs that curl the wrong way. But Tommy is so grateful that he came to me with the information, despite himself.

Tommy's still in the inner circle, in the star-chambered back room of the Whalebone. So he put his ear to the ground and heard that heroin was coming across from Amsterdam by boat and, get this, windsurf. The last five miles they will be using a windsurfer because these clever Dutch had sent in a small shoal of cannabis – Leb and the colour of red herrings – to the south side of the estuary, ensuring the leakage of misinformation to English police, who would be patrolling bogus waters while the windsurfer man rides into Easport on a wing and a prayer along unmonitored horizons.

According to Tommy, the stuff will be coming

over on its route to Manchester to be collected by a new outfit. Users turned pushers turned dealers turned buyers. Fucked up on their own juice is how I choose to see it. Tommy told me when and where, and he named the lighthouseman who, for fifteen of the dwindling thousands from my safe, will delay the signal of the windsurfer's arrival by fifteen minutes. A grand a minute for letting me slide in and out, take the booty and leave false tracks. Easy as that. Easier than it ought to be for a lighthouseman to do one on Flint's doorstep. But that, my friends, is the power of debt. That represents the strength of the chemical forcefields of brown, and even though he is forty-five and the fourth in his line to have cast light on the waters, even though he has a teenage daughter off to university, our lighthouseman is far from immune to the charms of the needle.

Fifteen grand, let me tell you, is a lot of money to me. It's what you might call a shitload of money. But half a million, that's many shitloads of money. That's money To Die For.

And half a million busts a hole in a circle. It builds you another one somewhere else. Thick-skinned. A perfect circle.

TAKING CARE OF BUSINESS

Telescoping the apron of delta from my balcony, I have felt all day that eyes are upon us, but have failed in my searches for confirmation. My skin prickles as I roam the garden, dogless and on the edge of a frightening future. I want to lie back and smell the mown lawn, feel the warm cake of loam on my shoulders and close my eyes with the big, big, high sky shadowing orange and yellow on my lids and the weakening sun still glowing hot in the skin of my face. I want to be able to sleep, to wake seconds later, but feeling like hours, with fur in my mouth and with lurking dreams flexing time, and for our entire predicament to have been the invention of an unknown dimension.

But all there is now is the regurge of the hundred ways I can come to grief, the beginning of the practical steps into tomorrow. And tomorrow. We must go into Warnsea soon to collect money for the lighthouseman, to pay my sterling, unspoken and possibly last respects to the officers of the small empire I have created.

We climb into the car, drive slowly off with gravel

grinding and the Saturday afternoon scorelines from other fields of battle coming at us from the ether. Angela closes the gates behind us and says she'll see us later, about eight. I look back, for a second, which is all I can bear. It is all it takes for me to see the constellations of ways in which she might come to grief with or without us.

Jessie drills us along the dyke roads on a high-speed meander between fields of rape and fields of nothing, and I am expecting someone I might or might not know to come into my sights, like a savage on a Tucson ridgetop, to fire in the air and swoop down to take us for torture. I'm romancing again, on celluloid because I know my end will be more bitter than that. Looking at the nothingness around I fear for us all.

The house is soon out of our vision. The windmill tower is sinking into reeds and dyke banks. It is an illusion, though, the place we made home. It has been done with mirrors. Warnsea is our stretch of coast, where I have tried to make changes for the better. It is what Flint – who for years now and without document or compromise has divided and ruled this estuary – has been prepared to lease to us.

We are riding high, only a mile from Warnsea on this final afternoon, but it's quiet in the car. There's no serious skulduggery passing among us, simply a four-paper skunk that no-one seems to be hogging, and even Jessie is giving us a break from his doe-eyed droolings over how he hopes that this girl and that girl will understand that he has got it back together with Anne-Marie, how he doesn't want to hurt them with his changes of heart, which we all know to be tortured, genuine, soft.

The dunes disappear to our right and fields are giving way to bungalows, which stand aside for tired, splintering Victorian terraces, which in turn peter into the high street that was best before 1970, but which today is acting as if someone has put electric-shock pads on its heart. There are queues at the chippies and the pubs are emptying.

I try to commit it to a memory that I know time will fade, the way it has the shops. There's Ladies and Lassies, with outfits you would recognize from old family photos; Charis Gift Shop, lacking all kinds of matic; Little India restaurant with its white waiters; The Golden Haddock; Elegance Clothes; Booze Brothers; Kandy Kitchen; The Army Cadet Force.

We slow down, and Wingnut and Roy hang out of the car, feeling their feet on safe ground, among familiar faces that go animal in friendly foul-mouth jibe. This is the best part of the week, and it's down to us that everyone here has the time and the place for it, for once, bang on and synched up to a squeaking fuck-of-your-life perfect tight fit.

Max is where we conduct our business, but it should be called Min, because less is more. Thanks to us, on Saturdays here in Warnsea, in and out of season, you can wake up in your clothes with the smell of cheap perfume, fags and booze on your best cloth and someone else's lustre dry-filmed in your nethers. You can have fried food that's mum-delivered with racing pages and footie fixtures, then a quick bath and into the pub by twelve for the best session of the week, still feeling drunk and topping up, wedged between Friday's goodtime and Saturday's bettertime promise of more where that came from.

And there's no reason to stop, so at quarter to five we're going into Max, seeing Steve Ryder say goodbye on the multiscreen. There are sweet lotions of cheap balm drifting in on the seagull breeze, and even though it's still light outside, the fun is on the inside. It's naughty; it's decadent; it's TOO MUCH. And the cage is coming down with the music phasing in from nowhere and the place is half full of girls who get in free before five.

By eight o'clock and for the first time in weeks, I can feel myself becoming calm, like something before a storm.

Jessie is with a girl we've not seen before, giving her a familiar spiel. She looks around as he whispers in her ear, wondering why we're all laughing. He really believes that she is 'the one', better than all the rest. She's been here for an hour, my guess, because he's telling her he loves her. You can tell because she's looking back at him as if he's a barking mad dog. And it looks as though she's saying, under the music, 'You can piss off if you think I'm going to fall for that.' Roy and

Wingnut are laughing. But underneath, Roy looks like someone who has had his food taken away before he has finished, like he wants to stand up and deck Jessie and scream from a rooftop, 'Why can't I, just for once, have a bit of the action?'

Jessie is latin-looking, latin-libido'd, and he is Jessie because of his affliction of the heart. 'You're a wuss. You're a fucking jessie, Jessie.' He falls in love too easily too often, but he can't help himself, and he's not in it for the action. His heart drags him feet first into bus queues and flower shops; it has him loitering outside their offices and on the corners of their streets. He tells them he loves them and he means it. He courts them with meals and scent and they love it – for a while, until he freaks them out. They find out about Anne-Marie and they go berserk, failing to understand that he is not a bastard, that his declarations and intentions are unequivocally legitimate.

Jessie is whispering new things into her ear, remodelling the shape of her face into a slow-spring good-news smile of someone being given a free ticket to somewhere they have always, unwittingly, yearned to go. Wingnut and Roy adjust in their seats, click fingers for drinks and start looking around for something new, because Jessie has done it again and it's not fun any more.

Angela arrives and comes across to join us, looking sad. I face-quiz her on *what's wrong* and she tells me, 'Oh, nothing.'

'*Come on, tell me.*'

'I'm worried, Jimmy. About tonight. I have a bad feeling. All day, I've felt . . . I don't know, like someone's been watching me. Maybe I shouldn't have come back.'

I look around, put my finger to my lips and pull her towards me with my hand on her neck, feeling her hair in my hands, smelling her in the air I breathe. I feel her brittle jaw with my thumbs and the pale marble flesh of her cheeks in my fingers. I look into her eyes that sparkle with fresh stuff, and I say, *Trust me, I'll be all right.* I take my hand from her face and put my thumb and finger together but not quite touching. *This close. We're this close.* With a tilt of my head and my hand going back onto her face, I try to press into her that I will look after her, do whatever is necessary to replace bad with good in every corner of her life. I can see her eyes filming over. She comes closer, right into my face, with her open mouth on mine, but she doesn't kiss me, just breathes my air, and me hers, trying to be closer than the mere contact of flesh and flesh.

The end game is a familiar sequence that starts with the blood-tingle Motown intro strains of Martha and her Vandellas taking us into 'Jimmy Mack'. The crowdswell noise is building and building until there's a velvet throb in the lounge. I stand up and go to the dancefloor, where they are making big circles, hands around each other, antheming out verse one.

And there, standing on the stage the way he hasn't done for years, is Wingnut. He takes the mike off the DJ as Martha fades slowly to silence. The crowd has got the rhythm in its backbeat grip and Wingnut smoothes an a cappella swoon with his angel voice: 'My arms are missing you, my lips feel the same way, too.' I look back at Angela, into her scared smile that mouths the words, as if she's talking to me, 'Hey, Jimmy, Jimmy, oh Jimmy Mack, you'd better hurry back.'

By the second chorus, everyone in the place is booting out the song, as if they're on stage and I am the only audience. It makes me feel as if I might belong in a place where once I was cast out; makes me feel, fleetingly, like a chill lick in a hot place – bulletproof.

WHERE SEA MEETS SHORE
WITH A FLATLINE

The time has come.

I love the slap of sea on dock in the dark, it reminds me . . . it reminds me we are mortal, that we cannot be all-knowing, all-seeing, blind as we are to the secret swell and wash of oceans tugging on the moon. If you are weak or stupid or show it no respect, this sea will take you without blinking and not even notice. And don't make the mistake of thinking you will be missed for long. Tides come and go, and nothing stays on a beach.

With my back against a wall I am stood on the jetty that juts from land. It is, as far as I am concerned, foreign turf. According to all the non-statute laws that govern life on the estuary I should not be here, because this is Flintland. But, for the moment, this is the bed I have chosen to lie in.

I am picking up signals from the elements, reminding myself there are no innocent victims coming into my sights. There is clearly more bad than good in the air where land meets sea, where aggressive forces pound and the weak surrender on the cusp of invisible change.

'Two wrongs don't make a right.' These are the words of a fuckwit.

Sap rises within me and my eyes lid down. Through the wind and wash I am receiving. I can hear his board skimming across the top of shallow water. Sea winds make his sail crack like a gun, loud and sharp in my honed eardrum. I can hear him riding, raw-powered and magical with the depths beneath him diminishing, earth plates rising from beneath the sea.

I open my eyes and he comes into distant view. He will be seeing the shore rise into his sights, seeing what he could rightly consider to be the end of his journey. It is a shame that such genius travel must suffer such denouement.

I wish it would last, this moment of peace. I wish it would stretch and linger, but blood is dumping down through my veins and arteries. I wish I could allow narcotic formulas to come within my compass, to restrain the restless parts of my brain and psyche and limbs and will. But you shouldn't always indulge what your body craves.

I regroup my various selves, show each of me the possibilities available. A beautiful inversion is within my scope and I will not be denied by anything other than good and worthy bullets. I am ready. I can face death, eyeball whatever dares confront me.

His shape moves across moon mottles on the sea,

as if the tiny shifting light pools are plotting him to me. He is small on the infinity of my vision, but I can hear his heavy breaths that sign his struggle of sail against wind. There is a good wind tonight. Not an ill wind. I can hear the sail cracking again, like more gunshot, can feel a chill in the very walnut centre of my addled and too oftbroken heart, and in the low heat of calm and balm between night and day, my pulse retreats, slows to an almost standstill, and I know that I am ready as he comes to me, bigger in the moon, into the safer sea of shore.

He wades now onto the beach and I put my curses to one side, gather only positive thoughts as I loop round and down from the dock towards the beach, checking my back. Time ticks, tocks, up from the unsignalling lighthouse into the ozone. I have ten minutes. He is hauling the board, mast and sail onto the mud-slime shelf, and the North Sea stings my nose with its diesel and driftwaste.

In viewing his face I see the same features that his wife or mother would have seen this morning across a breakfast table, standing on a doorstep, or from between curtains in a room with a television in its corner. I can see a real life within the flickers of horizontals not held. Children will be orphaned; a widow will emerge bloodshot in black from the carnage tears and dead petals of a funeral, and then life will go on, with an altered picture.

I steel myself.

I put on my smile, a big and 'welcome-to-my-country' smile. He returns it, pleased to be at journey's end, within a stretching grasp of his filthy lucre. He opens his mouth, but I can see in the wet glitter of his eyes that he is preparing meaningless introductions. That would be too much to bear.

Lacking the luxury of safe numbers, unable also to afford any armistice of my weaponry of surprise, I skip away from myself. I leave the good and real heartbeating me shoeless on the sand, and with a spin and an expert thrust I whip him with a single blow to the ground.

His fall is soundless, just the dull thud of lead on flesh, of pipe on skull, appearing to resound in the splash and wake, splash and wake of the sea. His dying sound reverberates. Fossil waiting to happen, vertebrate written in stone. Blood trickles from his mouth and he twitches. Once. The red of life on the sand of dead stone looks like black on silver in the moonlight, as if it has not achieved its potential in the hands of an unworthy artist.

He twitches again and his eyes open. His smile is stuck, so I take it in my hands; I take his head and I wrench him onto his belly and push his face into the water, because this is what I have to do. I hold him there, feeling a life slipping like dry sand through my fingers. I rise.

It is done. This horrendous task is accomplished without even a ripple of applause or condemnation, simply the soundless pounding of time, silent in the night and beating a countdown drum from deep within the unilluminated house of light. I have six minutes in which to get him to the car, to secrete

62

the board, and to remove all signs of me and him from this scene-of.

But I don't. I can feel somebody else stepping into the perfect fit of my shoes, grabbing him under the shoulders and hauling him above the high tide line in a backward walking stoop.

His lips are salty and there is grit in his mouth. I spit out the dirty sea, the saliva we have exchanged. I go back onto him, emptying my lungs into his. I lean on his heart with my hands, pressing on, going back onto his mouth, tasting the sea in him agian. There is movement within, a rising bubble of life that could be that last gust of something about to die. His eyes open. They are big in my vision, the way you would only see a lover. I kiss him once more, and this time there is bile, which taste of life makes me want to be sick.

Time is money, and what I have bought is about to snuff out on me. Soon, light will be cast and I still have a sailboard to dispose of. A sailboard on this stretch of coast would not go unnoticed – you would have to be on drugs to use this beach for leisure, where sea meets shore but with a flatline. You can almost hear the beep beep beeep of life on its way out. There is only the expectorating steel tubes of plant away to my right in Easport to say that there is some kind of life here. If life was this kind of beach you would top yourself.

Like something token feeding a meter, light comes beaming across the beach, spreading into a pool flood all around me. Then it is gone, to return, to cut me off. My time is up, and with a fast-beating heart I drag the board to the bottom of the dock wall, cover it quickly with broken pallets and boulders to be retrieved later and destroyed when coasts have recleared.

The surfboard man is smiling up at me. I got into him so quick that I knocked his smile into a dazed posterity. And having brought him back, it is as if he has stuck. He has good teeth and kind eyes. I want to dwell on what kind of desperate situation he must have got himself into to be carrying such bad booty to me across waves on a sailboard in the North Sea dead of night. But I check myself, shake sentiment free and drag him by his feet to the steps. Now I have to carry him, get him on my clothes – not his blood which is expert minimal, but his DNA, invisible flakes of his skin. I really didn't want to burn this suit, but I will have to. It's what it takes, and in the scheme of things this is a minor and pathetic irritation which casts me in a poor light, I know. It would be insane to mourn the cremation of a suit. It would be wrong.

The beam from the lighthouse swoops towards us with gulls trapped in its beam, then escaping, others taken in. It travels slow across the sea, then accelerates across the beach towards us. It blinds me, and by the time I blink my vision back, two engines come into field, in different keys but getting infinitesimally louder and louder, rising and falling in the contours of the diminishing gap between where they are and where I am.

There is no time to erase traces of myself from the beach, so I pile surfman into the boot. I am both happy and sad to have not killed him; neither happy nor sad that the hardness I have constructed into my life failed me. I move us slowly off, on the only road out – one and the same as the only road in – towards people moving fast in time delay, coming to collect in response to the morse and tardy signal of a lighthouseman, not knowing they are late, that time is tradeable.

I draw on a cigarette as they whoosh past in a manoeuvre of unwitting joust. I drive into the vacuum and rear-view the nightlines of speeding red lights from Manchester, which curve and glow and fade, then stop on another blind line between sea and sky. I slow down, and through the downglide of window I listen to the open-slam open-slam, open-slam open-slam of distant doors.

With bad cargo I drive to a safe alternative, putting on a tape to soothe my mood. I slide up the volume, breathe deep and, in my head . . . in my head, I sing along:

Somewhere . . .

. . . bey-ond the sea . . .

A FIZZ OF TONIC IN
THE LAPWASH LULL

I drive now, with scant and normal traffic on the roads, to where Angela is waiting with the boys. The new sun streaks weak blood in the thin-cloud sky. I can see the chimney of our prefab hideaway from here, even though it's many miles away. You wouldn't be able to find it unless you knew the roads that cut travelled furrows through the marshes, alongside waterlines and territory edges. You would lose your bearings in the rising falling swoop of rape.

Rape is everywhere: at its best in the early morning when first light burns its yellow bright, stark contrasting out of the night and making the big sky bigger. But it is out of place, too vibrant, a thousand miles too north. From far away you might think it was sunflower, and from above – and I have ballooned above, looking down with the hot fizz of burning gas and flying birds beneath – it is an out-of-body Mondrian to the numbers of Van Gogh. Oh yes, I know my art.

This adrenalin-sinking glow echoes a different era of my life: days when we scrambled around on the edge of crimes that were petty and tantamount to victimless, and after which we would convene with our booty. We would get out the cards and whisky, party in a hideseek wilderness like Indians who've taken over a safe house on a prairie. The parties would last through days and nights. We would lay ourselves waste until long after it was safe to retreat into our real world. Angela would bring girlfriends and, well, you can imagine. Like rattlesnakes! But that was a previous life, in olden days. Before we climbed into bed, got monogamous, with the law. This feels like the closing of a circle.

I found the prefab years ago, snaffled it away up my sleeve and kept it secret all the time my cuffs have been getting finer, more silken and quality crafted. It used to be a caravan park, but the people stopped coming and went to Magaluf instead, where everything was cheaper. And just as soon as the tattoo tans were drinking their English beer and digging into export Yorkshires overlooking the Med, they wheeled the caravans away – took them somewhere with less wind, more to look at and probably something to do apart from carry out.

The prefab is stood on its lonesome in twenty acres of crumbling hardcores, standing in the middle of marshes that run straight into the sea. No beach, just flaking low cliffs and enormous concrete blocks that they lift in by air to stop sea having its way with land.

★　　★　　★

Wingnut is first to come running to the car. His arms and hands have gone dervish, like a '78 technofreak on acid. He's talking so quickly that his wrists snap, crackle and pop, so I tell him to slow down. I take one step towards him and, with a flat-palm spread of my hands, I silence my translator. The noise in my head subsides.

Roy and Jessie have come out, too, with their mouths going crazy and their bodies gibbing and jiving in bad language, like footballers – Italian and pleading with stigmata hands in upturned prayer, crowding the ref when they know one of them is surely dismissed, trying to influence his all-seeing wield of truth and consequence.

'What happened? What happened!'

'Calm down, lads, calm down,' says Wingnut, taking the words right out of my mouth. I signal him. 'Come on, you three. Inside,' he says. And it kills me, the way he says 'three' when he is one of that number. Sometimes he is so bloody good at his job.

They leave me and Angela on the steps, with the dawn promise of a beautiful day stretching European across the hardstandings to sea.

'Did it go all right, Jimmy?'

'*Yes.*' There's a familiar, slow tread in the movements of the expression on her face, in the slowslur of her speech.

'I was worried. I . . . I took . . . just a bit of something to keep me up, till we get away. I don't want to let you down. Just a bit of blow, Jimmy. I'm fine . . . do you mind?'

I shake my head. I put my arm around her frail body, lift the rucksack swag over my shoulder and we climb the steps to the prefab.

I sign Wingnut, toss him the car keys and tell him, *'Take Jessie, bring the Surfman in. He's in the boot. Put him in the back room, and be careful; he's a bit worse for wear.'*

'Jesus, Jimmy. Course he'll be worse for wear. He's fucking dead, man.'

'No, he's not.'

'What?'

'Just bring him in.'

'What'll we do with him?'

'I don't know,' I sign weakly, in obscure shapes that betray the ridiculous shame of what I have not done.

Wingnut sits at the table, playing with cards that fan from hand to hand, and Jessie carries bacon sandwiches from the kitchenette. Roy has got a bottle of Scotch, as if these were the old days, when we would have been laughing and joking and with the promise of a better life ahead of us; when we would have been occupying a lull between now and a return to the life we led. But this is different. This is an end, not the middle of something so ace you simply have to get pissed and laid in case it all turns out to be a dream. I look at the rucksack.

We have to lay low on our combat bellies until

Tommy Curl calls us to signal that coasts have cleared, which they won't, but all we need is a glimpse of sky between clouds and we can head south, like birds who can't wait for the end of summer.

South because Angela has heard of someone on the M4 corridor who will take our stolen substances from us, who can passport us to our new home. She heard of him through Denny Lane, which is ironic. He's a friend of Lane, who is an enemy. But when I say 'friend', well, friendship can be fickle enough, even without half a million sterling of heroin distracting loyalties. Angela has got his co-ordinates and I am satisfied that these are big enough sums for the air to be too thin for Lane.

I signal Wingnut, who verbals me to Jessie.

'I had to leave something behind. Someone's got to go back for it. Will you do it?'

'Sure,' says Jessie, not as confident as he tries to appear.

'There's a sailboard, under some pallets down by the jetty. Keep your eyes peeled. If you see anyone – anyone – carry on into Easport and call us on the mobile.'

'All right.'

'There's a can of petrol in the boot. Take the board down to the sea and fire it.'

I wouldn't want you to think for a moment that I'm taking this lightly, this business of virtual murder and actual bodily harm, theft and narcotics. Oh no. I can see clearly the pissed-off faces of bad men from Holland who will not receive payment, and the choke-eyed frenzy of the Manchester poachers who won't make it to the game.

I put an arm around Angela, feel the slow flutter of pulse thid-der-thud-der in her breast. She smells of no sleep and too many cigarettes. I try to think of a new future where I will lift Angela into a bath, tip warm water over her body in a hot, red Bonnard summer. Where I will lift her pale and too-thin body and lay her down on fresh white sheets and spoon vichyssoise into her blood lips from fine china. I will pat her mouth dry with starch linen, dress her in a single silk garment and take her to a lovers' seat in an ancient garden with Cézanne patterned on the afternoon air. I want to watch the sun kiss her and make her better, usher a child's smile that would hark to a pleasant past she never had, but which you would have seen etched on the fairytale and almost identical but completely different face of her sister.

'What are you thinking?' she asks.

I want to make you brand new. I want to actually get on with my biggest task of forgiving us our pasts.

I shrug.

'Tell me,' she says. And she drums on my thigh and jigs up and down on her chair. 'Come on, Jimmy Mack, tell me.'

'*We're almost there.*' But before I can elaborate, Roy comes in from the tiny bathroom.

'Where's the stuff, then?' he says. He has changed

71

into a thirty-nine-ninety-five suit, with cheap wool-mix trousers that he has tried and failed to get a crease in. It is what he would doubtlessly call his best gear. He looks as if he is dressed to wait under a Sunday evening clock tower for a date to not show up.

I stand up, get the rucksack, and clear a space on the floor where I set it down, looking around to see that I've got everyone's attention. Wingnut says, 'This is for looking at. No-one takes any. NOT ANY!' I whip my instructions in karate tones and pull the cord to open up the sack.

It grows. It gets bigger. It hisses.

'What?'

'WHAT!'

'WHAT THE FUCK!'

The rucksack makes an apeshit, inflating transition from bag to boat, making itself twelve feet long, orange and blue.

The room falls silent, just the sound of whisky spilling from an upturned bottle and the ratatat clink of glasses on the toppling table. And into this Jesus-weeping silence, comes a dazed and confused ailing voice.

'Aah, good. My boat. But where is my board? My board has all that good schitt inside it.' And we all turn, peering over the inflated dinghy, looking at the Surfman, blood-smattered and dazed, living and breathing, head-nursing, not-dead Dutch.

TRIPPING TO THE SEASIDE, DOUBLE-QUICK

I have made Surfman secure, tethered him to the stove. His daze is on the wane and I can see fear gather, a recollection of what he has failed to do dawning through a Turner mist. There is no time to waste. A dreamstart bounty of good schitt is sealed within a board custom-built for the carriage of fine gear and about to turn to ash from Jessie's petrol touch.

Wingnut and Roy are shoehorning themselves into Angela's soft-top mini which she thinks is ever so cool. I have grabbed a rug to help me in my fight against fire, but it is clear that we are not prepared. I thought we could do this, but we have no facilities, no resources. I grind the soft-top up through the gears and, with all our wills combined, we hit sixty-five – against all the odds and under top weight.

On our zigzag marshland way, on backroad dykes that seem to take us away from our destination, I am at least bestowed with time to see that I was surely right to bring Surfman back from the brink. Murder is serious business. It is, in my experience of viewing from a distance, like the boozer's first swig, when dominoes take effect. One is too many and a thousand is not enough, and I feel that maybe the Fates might recognize this, give me a break.

But this is no time for complacency. No. We are here – driving too fast on a single track with deep ditches flanking us, taking corners blind and kicking grit into the rape fields – because I have been lax. I can feel a pinprick rekindle of fury; it bristles and twitches. I have ventured us toofar toofast into this new world with its thin air and margin-free error zones.

I must take more effective charge. Not because I want to, I get no kicks from the winnings of power games, but because someone has to assume command. We need to know our position in the universe. And just as I need to know that Flint is above me in whatever chain governs life on the estuary, so Roy and Jessie and even Wingnut need to have orders to obey. The most powerful man in the world would be lost when, returning from a nuclear face-off, he didn't feel the firm and uncompromising squeeze of real power from the wifely touch upon his balls, or the impeach venom of a spit-and-tell mistress.

We are close. I can smell strains of oil and gas and fish through the vents. I right-angle onto the coast road two-wheeled and the lighthouse fizzes into vision: squat and ridiculous, mid-terraced between the pub and the post office on reclaimed land. I pull her back into third, boot her up to sixty and the outreach bungalows go to blur. The gearbox screams blue murder, but we're getting there, and the newspaper kid stops, turns on his BMX. He fades to a speck in the mirror until we are once again on our own, bearing down on the jetty, with the brown sea and its yellow froth whipping up in the wind, misting the wind-screen.

I handbrake us to a jolt. There is no time to be circumspect. Looking out on seas that Captain Cook sailed at the start of his voyage, this is a time for swift endeavour.

'OUT!' screams Wingnut.

The jetty is falling apart, losing a battle against wind and water, and we take the wooden steps three at a time, striding out across rocks onto the sand, as heavy-footed as a bad-dream chase. Jessie is waving at us from the edge of sea, but the wind is against us. I forget the lessons of an almost lifetime and contort my lungs, throat and mouth into a silent scream. I grab Roy and signal to him in a foreign language.

'Yeah, Jimmy. Looks like we made it in time. I can see the board. Jessie's . . . Oh no. Oh fuck. That's the petrol. Shit.'

But the wind whips up again, wet sand scratching our faces and fighting off Roy's scream of 'No!' And when we look back, blinking through gritted crying lenses, Jessie is uncrouching himself and cowering away from the first quick-spreading flames. He runs towards us, smiling, his mission accomplished.

As if in celebration of a goal, he is spreading his arms wide and far to receive his plaudits. The board cracks, glass fibre burns furious, pungent in the air. The flames distort, different coloured and noxious, like a sherbet candle flashing Romanesque. Black dust goes mental in the wind.

I stop running and slump to the beach. It has taken four hours in a round trip to come full circle to where I started, to short-circuit sweet destiny, but at least Jessie is happy. He tramps up towards us with a winning smile, as if he has completed a fine and worthy errand with Boy Scout perfection, Brownie points in the bag.

'Did what you said, Jimmy. Took like a dream, must be that fibreglass stuff they make it with.'

'*You stupid STUPID fucker!*'

I turn round, searching for my voice, but find only the weak and bambi-leg traipse through sand of Wingnut limiting my reactions.

'Put the petrol on like you said. Spilt some on me keks, just here. Look, Jimmy. Don't even need to get rid of the ashes now, do we? The wind took 'em. Hey, I think I'll get buried at sea. Romantic, innit? Are we going to party now, Jimmy? Can I call Anne-Marie?'

Shut the fuck up, Jessie, I mute, misrepresenting myself, but in no doubt at all as to whether I should laugh or I should cry now.

SILVER IN BLUE

I look out to horizons beyond the dock cranes and oil and gas plants that seem to be at sea, but which I know to be terra firma'd on curling spits of marsh. There are false horizons everywhere you look, where river turns to sea, where land turns to beach.

Just a few miles down the coast a sailboard has turned to sand, its contents now gusting with the gulls, half a million notes flapping like migrants in the ether. The early morning sun is pale from the fjords. South of that lush arctic greenscape, a few degrees to my right, are nether lands that you could have skated to before the ice ground mountains and valleys, whose dialects still make waves in certain of these parts. This is where our outcomes will be determined, where don't-fuck crims will be twitching from the non-return of my captive Surfman, the non-return on their investment.

I don't know how long I have been sat here, looking at my future and not knowing what I see. We should be moving on, covering tracks and plotting the next point on a new graph, but I have to find some strength from somewhere, rediscover my will.

Turning inland, away from the source of my fresh troubles, I see that the boys are standing straight-backed by the car. When I blink through the sand swirl I can see that Silverpiece is with them, his spine bent like a branch in a strong wind. He registers me, walks away from the car and Wingnut follows, patting his hair down. If he had a tie he would straighten it, out of respect not for Silverpiece – for he is, after all, police – but in deference to our fondness for the benefit of his favours.

'*Jimmy Mack.*'

'*Silverpiece.*'

We exchange signs. Silverpiece can communicate some basic pleasantries which I taught him years ago, when our relationship was zenithing after I sorted out his Biggest Ever Problem, with my Second Act of Vengeance.

In past times he would haul me in when I'd been slapdash or desperate. He would instruct the duty sergeant to bring us tea, then he would deliver tips: where to not go, what to not do. He would introduce me to codes, procedures, techniques, names – important things that grant you kinds of immunity. And I would sign him the shapes of my name, and 'hello', other simple things.

So he signs, '*How are you?*'

And I reply, '*Fine, how are you? How's Sarah?*'

'*Fine.*' 'You're not, though. Are you?' he says

with a father's smile, but with sad eyes that say, in this crooked exchange of ideas, that something bad has happened, that ruinous things are upon us, and he cannot help me as much as he might like. I am about to be cut adrift. Something in me goes heavy and starts to sink.

'I'm sorry about Lane dosing Angela like that. There was nothing I could do.'

I take his arm and turn him round to face me, so I can see his reactions when he hears Wingnut say, 'You can't touch him? You were warned off him?'

Silverpiece nods.

'Oh fuck!'

'You're going to leave it, aren't you?' says Silverpiece.

'You think that's why you were warned off him?' says Wingnut on my behalf. 'So I'd go after him, do someone else's dirty work. You think someone's set me up, used Angela so I'll go and do Denny Lane. Some bastard nearly killed her for that?'

'No, it's not that. Look, I can't have this conversation. Just take care of yourself, Jimmy. If you don't . . . Jesus, you're not making life easy for yourself.' He starts walking again. I follow him, with Wingnut in train. His hands are in his pockets and an unadministered cigarette in his mouth goes ember ash ember ash as he talks in thin smoke trails and plumes. 'This is serious, Jimmy. It's not a bad thing you're trying to do, I know that, but . . . I don't know . . . I hope you know what you've got into here. We got a tip-off, Jimmy. There's a smell about this whole thing. And this Manchester lot, they're serious. They came here tooled up and with a boot full of cash. They got a big-swinging Manck barrister over here within a two hours of me hauling them in. But they're not really the ones to worry about.'

'The Dutch?' says Wingnut.

'The Dutch? I don't know about them; they fucked off out to sea when we sent a launch out.'

What's the bad bit then?

'You're not going to like this, but the Mancks, and probably these Dutch, too, when they find out, if I'm reading right what you've been up to . . . Well, they assume it was Flint that stepped in and took their stuff.'

'Flint!' says Wingnut, unprompted. 'Oh fuck!'

Flint. Flint! OH FUCK!

'We had to let the Mancks go. We followed them as far as the motorway. But Flint's been on to me already, sent some serious lads to put these Mancks straight. But when they find out . . . when Flint sees what you've done, on their patch . . . there's nothing I can do.'

Nothing?

'Sorry, son.'

Time is squeezing hot breath down on us and we have to retrench, return to our skeleton home as quickly as we can. There's no point hiding from Flint. We may as well be somewhere comfortable, somewhere we might be able to hold what little we have.

Silverpiece motions for Wingnut to leave, which he does, with me replying in slow and exaggerated mouth moves. I don't like talking this way, there is no tone to my voice, no pitch from my movements, but when privacy is paramount, it's my only way, and Silverpiece can at least read me better than most.

'I see Angela is back.'

'She has done nothing wrong.'

'Is that why you hid her away? I heard Lane's off in Leeds, looking for her. He'll suss that you've made him look a dickhead. He won't be happy.'

'That won't be a problem.'

'You doing a runner, then?'

I shrug.

'You'd better square things before you go.'

'I think Flint can find me, don't you?'

He nods, tries to smile. 'I'm not talking about Flint this time.' He throws his cigarette to the ground, takes another from the packet and lights it in a stoop. He leans on the sea wall and looks out to sea, not at me. 'I knew your mother, Jimmy, knew her before . . . well, anyway, a long time ago.' He laughs, petering into his coat, coy. 'Had a bit of a thing for her before I met Sarah's mother. She didn't feel the same, though. When she moved out we lost touch. I thought she'd left completely, so did most of us. I suppose that was the idea.' I can't ask him where this is going or why he is choosing to fuck me up here and now of all places and times. He has fixed his gaze on a point out at sea. 'Funny, all the things I've seen you do, the things you've done for me, and I never knew you were hers. You shouldn't think she was a bad person, Jimmy; she wasn't. It was unfortunate what happened to you. Might've been all right now, I suppose, but then, she took too much on. Do you know what I'm talking about?'

He turns and I nod.

'She called me a few months ago. We met up. She called me again last night. If you're going away, Jimmy, if you're in this much trouble, I . . . I just think you might regret it, if things don't work out. It would be worse if you hadn't made things right, at least given her a chance to make things right.'

He has turned away from me, not wanting to receive a reply, or for his embarrassment to be recognized, made official. He walks away, leaning into the wind, and I am unreservedly mute.

HOME FROM HOME

Back at the windmill, Jessie is tending to our supper at the end of a long and empty day that has brimmed with the phoniness of uncommenced war. He has filled the whole house with fantastic smells of fish, oil and garlic. He had never heard of garlic when I first took him in, but now he uses it all the time. Our reacquaintance was founded on the basis of what some might say are more masculine qualities, but a part of him has got what it takes to be useful around the house. He can multitask, which by all accounts is a female trait, not that I hold with such theories. Angela does, and she considers there to be something odd about Jessie: the way he listens to you, hanging on every word; the way he chatters about nothing, enjoys a good gossip. He remembers birthdays, too. And even though she likes him, Angela has told me that sometimes he gives her the creeps.

Jessie has always been around. He spent some time at Newholme, but his stay was shorter than most because, for all the faults of the Newholme personnel, they could at least see that Jessie was no bad apple – not through and through to the core, like some of them – nor did he malfunction or disturb others in the ways that most of us were deemed to have done. Despite his name and his achy-breaky heart, he has other skills that have served me well over the years. He is good with knives, can use them for purposes other than the concoction of the Mediterranean diet he swears by and which, so he says, has done wonders for his libido.

It is quiet around the table. Confidence is ebbing low, and in the echo peace you can almost hear the molecular structures of heads breaking down in contemplation of a coming together with Flint. It's like a mess gathering of rookie soldiers: hard lads who are well trained and who joined the army to go to war – not to learn a trade or get off the dole, but because they like fighting – but who one day will have orders bestowed by an officer from impossible social heights who, spitting plumstones, will say, 'This is it boys. We're off.' And suddenly they can see the sense in slogans of peace not war. Suddenly they are thinking, Fuck! This might be the end, and realizing that they have never told their dads they love them.

I signal Wingnut, '*Go upstairs, get Surfman. He may as well join us. I think we're going to need him.*'

Jessie puts his knife and fork down, takes Wingnut's plate and puts it in the oven to keep warm. He sighs as he does it, as if his toils are being ruined. Like a person whose work is never done.

★   ★   ★

84

'*Ask him about Holland, where he comes from,*' I say to Wingnut, which elicits startled looks from Surfman, at me and my quicksilver fingers, the throw of my voice. '*And explain to him about me.*'

Surfman is reticent, too afraid to be silent, but anxious not to divulge anything, so he appeals to our better natures, tells us he has a wife and a child, that they live in the north, near the sea. He tells us that his child is three, but withholds names, whereabouts and everything else that we might wish to glean for the infliction of a serious threat. He simply shakes his head when we press him, and I can see that he feels strong, resilient. I let him eat, grant him brief and delusory respite, and sanction the sanctity of worthless, unnecessary secrets.

Although I cannot believe I nearly killed this human, I know he will spill the beans when the time comes for us to exert the fullness of our powers of persuasion. For now, we eat in relative silence among Roy's fidgeting and occasional nonsense talk, within which I contemplate our real adversary: Flint.

Let me tell you about Flint.

Flint is untouchable, feared and envied by everyone on the estuary and by many further afield. The proof of my never having crossed Flint, nor ever having put myself into those fields of influence and control, is that I am here talking to you now. Flint does not deal in second chances or kindnesses of the heart. Five years ago, the blood of those who doubted this flowed for a night and a day down Dockroad and onto the sandbanks that mark the eastern limits of what you could call Flintland.

Hitherto, there has been little to be gained by Flint in undermining my parish of negligible influence. Indeed, while I have been here, running my small corner of a small corner, I have kept away others who might have wanted to flex their muscles, stretch a little, put their arms up high into fast blades.

You could argue, as I have been doing with myself all day, that technically our devalued and current situation has nothing to do with Flint. It was an opportunity which arose from the meeting of two other spheres, different worlds: one west along the M62; the other east, a lying-low land across sea. But where they came together – starcrossed and hoodlum in the dead of night, with me and the sailboard at the jetty – is slap bang in the forcefield Venn centre of Flint's diagram. The ensuing battle, if all had gone well, with me taking flight and the Dutch and the Mancks diving at thin air for my ghosting coat-tails, would have taken place on safe pastures in sunnier southern climes. But all has not gone well, and the godlike formulation of what is planned for our future will be calculated where land and sea meet – in Flintland.

So as I occupy myself with ruses for escape, I am stalled by the words and pictures of Flint, Magimixed in a bowl of whirring, cutting things:

stage left, stage right, flame-throwing up from the orchestra pit. The curtain goes up and I turn to mush.

The phone rings as Jessie and Angela are taking the dishes away. Roy is quizzing Surfman, asking him if he supports Ajax – pronouncing it like the scouring agent – how often he goes to Amsterdam, how much skunk is these days and whether all the prossies are dying of Aids.

'Jimmy!' shouts Angela from the kitchen.

My heart skips and supper rotates slowly at the top of my stomach as she appears at the door, tilting her head, imploring me with the outheld handset.

'Want to do it on the speaker?' says Wingnut.

Angela shakes her head, making it obvious to me that this is not the call we were all expecting. I know who it is, know that Silverpiece, who had earlier pricked what I still consider to be fallacious conscience, had furnished her with my number. At least this way I can use the full power of passivity. I can listen until I wish to listen no more, and I can cut her down with silence, having said nothing that could be considered malignant.

'Jimmy, are you there?' says my mother and I beep the fingerpad once. 'The other night, it was nice to see you. There was so much I wanted to say and I spoiled it. I . . . I've never said how proud I am of you, the way you've come through everything. I just want to say that I'm here, if you can ever forgive me. I . . . Don't hang up, don't be angry, but I spoke to Denis yesterday. Denis

Silverpiece. We knew each other, when we were young. He's the only person I could think of. I just need to know you're all right. He didn't say anything, but I got the impression . . . I, I don't know. *Are* you all right? Let me know if you need anything. Please. You will, won't you? We should meet, meet properly; there's something I have to tell you. Please, Jimmy, if you're going away, please come and see me first. It's important. I love you. I do.'

DON'T TAKE LIFTS
FROM STRANGE MEN

By the time the inevitable visitation happens it is almost midnight. Adrenaline flows are peaking like waves, and I breathe deep as I watch Chancey coming out of the headlights like something from war, getting closer in the split-screen panes of the hall. He advances and I go out into the night, meet him halfway with an underfoot gravel grind, henches following in his wake. I look into his eyes, stare into him and stiffen all my resolve. I weld myself, and what I find, what I see in the unblinking knot of our opening exchange, is that somewhere deep in the innards of his soul lurks surrender. I can see, with his face coming right up to mine, in his eyes that are so pale they seem all white, that the power of my motive is greater than his.

I gesture towards the house, invite him in.

'No,' he says. 'You're coming with me. Flint wants to see you.'

'   '

'I said, let's go, you dumb fucker.'

I gesture to Wingnut, who is coming down the

stairs. He stops cold, freezes. I turn back, stare deep into Chancey and try to get the will of my message unspoken into him.

'Ha! I forgot. You can't speak for yourself. I forgot you're a sad fucking mute bastard.'

Jessie and Roy come through from the kitchen. I can feel them flex, can almost hear the silent surge they repress, knowing they must control themselves.

Chancey's van is bull-barred, with big American curves and doors that electro glide; inside it is all suede and bassbooming. It looks the part, but it sounds all wrong, with Stiff Little Fingers belting out an anthem from a different age: Saturday nights at the Whalebone. Tin Soldiers.

We are spun away from home, me and Wingnut, leaving our world behind and going round in circles along roads on inverse contours that break Ordnance rules, below sea level.

Chancey's boys think they have got the measure of us. The jibes gather momentum, build under their own weight. They think there is something amusing in the fact that I lack the power of speech and that Wingnut has no knee-jerk mechanisms of pride or loyalty that might induce him to talk my corner.

I'm a dumb fuck. I'm a mute cunt. The cat's got me tongue. I'm speechless. I'm lost for words. I can't speak up for myself. I'm not so tough now, I'm scared. I'm soft.

I am trapped inside me. There is no voice to my

scream and I rant soundless echoes in my head. But what can I say? It is nothing I have not already heard, and I have learned enough about the art of war to know that you do not rile an enemy who outnumbers and is better positioned than you are. I know to bide my time, but it becomes apparent that they know I am aware of this, that I do not rise to their bait, so they start flicking at Wingnut's ears, mocking his Jodrells. They get a pen, start pushing it into his ears, and I can see him start to fall apart, with his trousers going damp in the nethers, tears welling in his eyes and a tremble to his lips. He looks at me, ashamed of himself, and I know the worst thing I can do is what I am doing; I know that Wingnut should learn the scarbruise hard way to fight his own battles. But I do what I know to be both right and wrong, regardless.

I reconstitute my rantings, make chords from chromatic mess. In my head I compose a big and blasting widescreen soundtrack to my bloodsurge anger. I let it build and build, tight coiling. I breathe deep until it implodes on itself, and I watch my hands whip away like cleavers into the throats of the two men taunting Wingnut. It is my sole means of expressing what I think of them.

I take the head of one of them into my lap, as if he might be sick, as if I might be tending his disease, except I have his pen in my hand, not a scalpel. I have half his shitscared glare between my finger and thumb, with the tip of the pen actually resting on the lens of his eye. I could prick a hole in its tearskin thinness. I could go into him, make his lungs scream an acid scream that would make the suede peel from the walls of the van. I could make him whisper a whisper that would shrivel his manhood. I could sample any sound from his churchmouse hush.

Chancey turns round. His wide-eyed shock speaks volumes and he bawls at his boys, 'You fucking losers! What's going on?'

I put the pen between the prising finger and thumb that hold his eye wide open and, with a partial freedom of speech, I single-handedly flick a message to Wingnut, who says, 'Don't think I won't defend myself, Chance. There is nothing I won't do.'

'What the fuck are you . . . ?'

'DO YOU UNDERSTAND ME, YOU BAS-TARD?' I mute, directly. And with a skinrip stretch of the sight in my grip, I get a clear view of his understanding of me.

But I know that I have not won here. I know that I have been drawn into a conflict I should have avoided. There may be a time when Chance will outweapon me or take me unawares, catch me in shadows or with the assistance of numbers I cannot overcome. He will have his day, or he will be there when Flint does. He allows himself a taster of his last laugh, now; gives me a thin smirk that says, Wait till Flint hears about this.

I hold the look. I try to say to him, *But what will Flint think of a hard man who has been overcome by a dumb fuck*. But I don't think he gets it because, between you and me, I have my doubts about his intelligence. No doubt at all, actually.

Wingnut is shaking. I can see his shirt flutter and his fingers are busy in beadless worry knots as his feet tap tripletime. He won't look at me, scared as he is of any kind of contact in this violent confine, as if even an exchange with an ally could harm him.

We are circling into Easport, looping round the curvature of land and sea-joining, charted by the lights from the refinery. It is isthmus, spangled in the night. You can get a hook on where you are, establish your relationship with something as fixed in the night sky as the stars that sailors can rely on. But the refinery lights grow dim as we enter the neon glow of the city, losing their magic, and as we get up close, you can see them for what they are – just a thousand bulbs that someone will spend all his working life replacing.

It seems to me that we have taken a wrong turn. Flint's place is out of town, west and South Fork vulgar. I have seen it from afar, seen its low-slung, redbrick ponderosa sprawl, with its white fences; its electric and semi-automatic hinders. Chancey is on the fidget. His agitation tells me we will be stopping soon, even though we are in the middle of Easport, in the lazy froth of Sunday night, with its interpub gaggles that splinter in the summer chill.

The van takes us hard left, rumbling over cobbles and into the old fish docks, but as we slow to a halt and the doors slide open there is no smell of fish, just the barest hint of oil and gas on the breeze. And whereas bygone days would have singed the hairs in your nostrils, what you can smell now is perfume, food cooking and good times.

We are in the marina, which is new. And in a city that has more shops shut than open, more offices skeletoned than furnished, it is a raging success, commercially and aesthetically, with the rent rolling and the deeds sealed for the benefit of Flint.

We are led away from the bars and restaurants into the chime rattle of masts. The smell of salt is in the air, on the lap of sea. A different world has been created here, lagooned without laws or enemies – no prospect of rescue, and I know what is happening to us when I see Flint drawing a cigarette glow on the bridge of a yacht.

JUNKIES AHOY!

The boat is not what you might expect. Among the high-rent, big-wash, sun-seeking bragboats, Flint's craft could almost go unnoticed. But if you knew what you were talking about, this is what you would covet, this forty foot of Nicholson. Blue water class.

'So, Jimmy Mack, we meet. I've been waiting, for years; thought you'd chance your arm before now.'

She smiles and I shrug, trying to seem cool, trying to exude that there is no point in her trying to hurt me on the basis that I don't mind pain. Wingnut is in freefall though, looking round at Flint's henches: tall and wide like mountains. Flint is looking at me through quizzing, no-make-up eyes the colour of the Med, with a realizing dawn that brings crow's feet to a pale and studious face more suited to archives than highlife.

'Ah,' she says with a lopsided smile, advancing towards me. 'How do we deal with this? I'm sure we can get some words out of you. Or are you simple? Just need some education. Maybe that's it.'

She is wearing a suit, like Chairman Mao or '64

Beatles. She looks like a teacher, a stern one with fantastic secrets behind her closed door, beneath her clothes – something to detonate a hair-trigger and uniform fantasy. She comes up close, nose to nose, presenting no kind of threat, taking a long draw on her cigarette, red in the night.

Aargh!

My head screams at itself, soundless. I am on the floor, doubled up like a baby in a womb, spitting and coughing and snorting like a bull. I claw at my nose, rake inside my nostrils with fingers that burn on still-hot ash. I crawl through the vapours of my own silent screams across the deck to a table, empty an ice bucket onto my upturned face and wait for the pain to go with a Schweppes sound that won't come.

I get to my feet, still snorting, and through crying eyes that feel as if they're bleeding I see that Flint is laughing. She's looking right into me, saying, 'Yeah, maybe you really are mute', laughing the mocking bad laugh of playgrounds. I take a step forward, take my arm back – my right arm to lull her while my left cocks for a short-arm throat jab. It's cocked, ready to go, but she just looks into me, unflinching, not blinking. I want to let the left go but she doesn't take her eyes off me. The badness has gone from her; she looks like a mother now, with her stiff hair that she must roller and set. It wouldn't move in force six. You might cut your hands on it. It would be solid, no matter what you did with her.

My left makes itself pacific. And right on the edge of her solemn poise, Flint sprinkles a broken hint of a smile. Because I am known. I cannot hit a woman. She knew it from the first time she saw me. She knew me better than I know myself.

She nods at the saloon doors that lead down below decks and says to Chancey, 'Stay here while me and Jimmy Mack see what we can do about this mess he's got us all into.'

We walk down four steps into a glistening brass mahogany saloon. The sound of chinking masts goes dull, disappears and comes at us again as she takes the lead up four steps to the stern of the boat. Her suit is perfectly tailored. She has good buttocks: high, round and solid-looking. Tea-planter chairs are set out around a bar on a poop deck, and by the rails a huge telescope is set up on a podium.

'Get the drinks, eh, Jimmy.'

'*What do you want?*' I quiz with a gesture towards the bar.

'Scotch. As it comes.'

I pour the drinks and she turns her back on me, which gives me a second chance that she knows full well I will not take.

'I know all about you, you know.'

But she can't hear my reply. Her back is turned, by design.

'That girl you've got. Bad news, Jimmy. But I understand. We've all got our histories. That's why I'm here, living this life. I don't always want to, but we have to be strong,' she spins round and leans back against the rail with her feet apart, legs stretching her skirt, 'don't we.'

I nod.

'You know about my Richard, don't you?'

I have heard stories that don't tally. There is a version of the two of them, received as truth, which I consider to be more probably legend.

'Richard wasn't a bad man. Forget what you hear. He was an accountant, you know, looking after the taxman for Chancey. Everyone tries to make out he was harder than he was . . . It just suits Chancey to pretend that Richard was like that.' She looks past me, towards the bow of the boat and probably Chancey. 'He lost his bottle, you see, Chancey. When they came to take us, Chancey was there. He was there when they did what they did to Richard. And he'd have been next if he hadn't given it all away.' She looks at me, considers me as if I am canvas in a gallery, nods as if she has decided something. 'Only me and him know that. And he doesn't know I know. Chancey was there, by my side, when I reclaimed Richard's turf, his life's work. And more. But he wasn't really by my side. I don't rely on him, you see. He's there for my convenience. He'll be my gift, when I owe someone enough. A token.'

She informs me of these things as if she is brandishing a weapon. A bequeathal of a secret is no good thing, more like a suspension of a terrible sentence, the implication that you are not going to survive for long enough to betray a confidence.

'Can I trust you, Jimmy Mack?'

'   '

'I think you know I can,' she says with a smile. She hands me her glass; holds on to it as I reach out to take it from her. 'I know I can. You see, I know you, Jimmy Mack. I know all about you – how you feel, the way you think. We're both alone, you see; we're very similar.' She takes the recharged drink, swirls the whisky and watches legs form in the glass. 'I'll tell you a story – about me. Do you have a cigarette?' I hand her one and light it for her.

'When Richard . . . just before Richard died, we decided to have a child. I'd have liked to have been younger, but me and Richard, we found each other late in life. I was pretty scared, actually, but we went ahead. I was four months gone when he died. He was so excited. He was going to get us out, just like you, Jimmy. Somewhere in the sun.' She's got me in her sights, twists me as she unleashes her all-knowingness of parts of me, my past and present. God knows how.

'I lost the child the night Richard died. As if I couldn't carry it on my own, like it wasn't meant to be less than perfect, not meant to grow up without a father. Something inside me chose to reject it. You understand that, don't you, Jimmy? But it doesn't mean we want to be lonely. Does it?'

I shake my head.

'But what worries me . . . what concerns me

about you, Jimmy, is I didn't have you down for dealing in drugs.'

I don't.

'I don't know how you came to be on my patch with half a million of heroin and dropping me in it with some Dutchmen I've never met. Some lowlife Mancks who are out of their league.' She pauses, looks out to sea. 'You can always make something positive out of the bad things that happen. Can't you? You've done that, Jimmy.'

I know exactly what she means. And I wonder how she will denominate repayment.

'You're wondering what it is you can do for me. Aren't you?'

I shrug.

'You don't know that I know the Dutchman's still alive.'

I don't, didn't. And I can feel cold hands upon me, the way I did yesterday, as if I was being watched.

'Come here, Jimmy. Look at this.'

She smells good, expensive. Like citron leather. Like First Class flight.

'Look at that.' She directs my vision along telescope lines, west above the factories and offices and shops to the gravestone blocks of Wesport. 'That's where it ends up. That's the effect you're going to have. I know you've not dealt in this before. I don't like it, either, but I'm a realist.' Her breath is malty warm on my cheek.

I can see the tops of the flats, painted pink to

make them look newer and more habitable than they are. From the outside. But it's still no place to live, unless you have no choice, and even then it's still no place to live, garrisoned by its own bad laws, modes of behaviour. There are two boys on the roof, edging to the brink and unable to take any more. My guess is that they are no more than sixteen, which is no time at all to reach a tether's end.

'Some of them think they can fly, think there's some sort of freedom to be had,' she says, tapping me on the shoulder so she can set her sights on them. 'But not these ones. They've just had it, think they can't take any more. They're thinking twice, though. They're not going to do it.'

She steps back, lets me resume vision. And I can see that she is right as the boys retreat and go back inside, which is not a question of having no stomach for it, because you might have to be stronger to endure. I am on the fence as far as the courage/suicide debate goes, but I can see one thing. Flint knows her Ports, east and west, knows its people. This is Flint's world. We just live in it.

'This is the reality behind what we're doing, Jimmy. But you mustn't be distracted. All you have to do is follow some simple instructions. That's not a high price. Is it?'

'   '

'You see, even if we don't do this, the bad stuff will still come. The price will keep falling. It's going to be like the NHS used to be: available to everyone for less than the price of a bloody prescription. That's the way it is, the world we live in, the rules we play by. But that's not your concern, Jimmy.

'I know how these people will react. The Dutch. I know their sort. These druggies, they act like mug punters. Lose one, double the stakes. They'll come back for more. They'll have another deal, a bigger one. And they'll come over here thinking they can enter someone else's world, take what they think is theirs. You know what's coming?'

I can guess, but I shrug. I don't want to hear it.

'You and your surfer are going to go into the lion's den for me. And we're going to have these Dutch bastards' drugs and their money. And then we'll see who can walk into my world. What do you say?'

I point at Wingnut, ask if he can come up, join us and voice me.

'No,' she says. 'Here. Write it down.' She comes across, leaning into me, hearing me as I write. I can feel the rise and fall of her even breath, hear the 'hmm aha', the dynamics of her part in dialogue.

'I will do what you want, anything, if you get whoever is supplying Angela, get them to back off,' I write.

I turn round. Her face is up close. She has a mole in the crook of her nostril which disappears when she smiles.

'You know it's Denny Lane who's been supplying her.'

102

'*Yes, but can you do it?*'

'I can do better than that, if that's what you want, Jimmy. But you do yourself no favours. You could do a lot better than someone like her.'

And her mole goes into hiding.

SPLIT PERSONALITIES

As we had walked away down the gangplank, Flint embered in the night from her bridge, across the moat of dock that separates us in myriad ways. And even though the pirate riches of her empire are beyond us, we have nonetheless been woven into a part of her world. For as long as she stands to gain from us, I will be part of the fabric of her bad society. I have been instructed as to her requirements and my options. The latter equal to or less than the former.

I unravel my position to Wingnut in the cab home. I sign him the cut of my cloth. And when I am through, he says, with a tremor to his voice,

'What's she going to do to us?'

'*Nothing. She won't do anything to you. This is my problem.*'

He shakes his head. 'Let's just get home, eh, Jimmy,' he says.

Home.

And that is the point. The people who occupy this house of ours, and even someone as king-of-castle in Brainland as Wingnut, think they can use a normal word to describe our not-so-safe haven.

They think we have created something real, out on the sunk island of land on land, think we have a home, that we are a family and that I am a . . . I don't know. A big brother? A father? I know the absurdity of it, but Roy and Jessie, even Wingnut, are unaware that if they could, by some amazing dereliction of meaning, be right in the terms which they apply, then they are suffering the worst betrayal. Because I have set us on a bad course. Sextoned to ruin, we are sinking out of our leagues now – in so deep that I can't imagine how any of us will survive.

Wingnut smiles and turns towards me. I could swear that he has tears in his eyes as he rests on my shoulder. His head is light and I can feel the tension in his neck and shoulders. He hasn't let himself go, just wishes to feel that there is something beneath a part of him.

In the dark motion of the cab he talks moist words. 'I feel as if I've had no starting point, as if I've had to pick up from the middle of something. That's why I took to languages the way I did. I was good at it. It showed I wasn't just crap at everything. And there was always somewhere to go, another dialect, and when you'd got as far as you wanted to, there was another language, somewhere new to move on to. Like when we started out, everything was new, we were going somewhere.' I can feel the reverb of his soliloquy in my shoulder. 'But I'm scared now, Jimmy. Not scared of what will happen. Well, I am. I'm scared of the pain, but not *really* scared of that, because it will pass. What I'm really scared of is, if it works out and we get to Spain, it will be for keeps; there'll be nowhere else to go. You and Angela will work things out, but what will happen to me? I'll be on my own in one place. I don't know what I'll do. I'm scared of that. That's when you need someone, when you stop moving, and I've got no-one, Jimmy.'

Time feels rationed. As I go into the house I try to savour the sights and sounds of our construction, as if they are about to end, just ghosts of goodtime to take with us. The night stretches featureless in front of me. I won't sleep, don't want to explain to Angela and the boys, unready as I am to face facts.

But I am resolved to what I must do, for all our benefits. The time has come to cut myself adrift for good, and I can feel myself on the brink of loss, about to be cast out to sea, alone again. I have been getting away with too much for too long, getting away from the loneliness that Wingnut talked about and which I know was intended for me from the start. I am not indulging myself with self-pity. It is the truth. Why else would my birth and breeding and everything that followed happen the way they happened?

Angela is at the top of the stairs, descending slowly along the stairwell curve, like a dressed-down Scarlett from civil war. She is heavy in my hug, barely breathing and pulling away to look up at me. And up close . . . up close she is the spit from her sister's mouth. Which is no surprise.

After my well-intentioned but barren fostering, Mrs Hunt had taken me into Easport and left me in that office. When I was eight, I was placed in my first home. They sent me from one room to another all day. Everywhere I went, men and women would come in ones and twos with their quizzical peers, talking about me as if I were something on glass under a lens. They would go away, leaving words I didn't understand and – I would later work out by processes of elimination – declining responsibility for me. It was finally determined, after I had been shown pictures and patterns and given buttons to press when lights were shone at me; after I'd had tubes in my throat and shining metal instruments put into my mouth and ears, that I had elected to be the way I am.

'He can understand,' they said.

'He's not simple.'

'He's just simple.'

'He can't understand.'

'He's mute.'

'He's not.'

And all the time it was said, in words on official paper, that I was nothing but trouble.

I tried to do as I was told. I made myself strong, not playing up or being ignorant or obtuse or any of the things that adults seemed to relish accusing me of. And at the end of the day, when their white coats went gaberdine, I was left alone. I couldn't keep myself at bay any more. I allowed myself to cry and, like taking a finger from a dyke, my head noises got louder and louder, bumping into each other until I wailed a soundless wail and threw myself to the floor, making the only sounds I could with my hands and feet and head until they came running with bindings to contain me. They put me in another room with a nurse, gave me syrup and led me into the cold outside, lay me down in a van. I closed my eyes in the dead of night. I made myself blind and urged a sleep embrace to take me. When I woke into a disinfected aftermath of dreams, I was in white brushed cotton, as if I had slept in blanket bandage.

I climbed down from the steel-framed bed, higher than I was accustomed to, and wandered into the corridor echo of tunes towards a girl who held a radio to her ear. She smiled at me, the smile of an angel, as if I hadn't woken. She had the softest, tiny purr voice which said to me, 'What's your name?'

'   '

'Are you shy?'

I pointed at my throat.

'Are you deaf and dumb?'

I shook my head. Deafandumb. Def'n'dum. As if it was one word, one condition, one possible state of affliction.

Listening to the radio, she beamed a satellite smile and said, 'I like this song.'

It is still my favourite song – all eight of the desert-island discs they'll never ask me.

'I'll call you Jimmy Mack. Do you mind?'

I shook my head and let her lead me with her hand, still warm from the radio. She took me down some stairs, sat me down and served me cereal in the quiet expanse of the kitchen's summer morning steel.

That was Lisa, and I have loved her from her naming of me until now, and for all points of my future.

I saw Lisa later that day. She was swinging in the Newholme yard with her friends. I stood there watching, waiting for her to be my friend again. She looked the other way, as if she didn't know me. So I went up close to her, felt the warm waft of breeze as she cut arcs in the air around me. I put my hand out, so she could lead me to whatever was next on her agenda of tasks. She jumped off the swing and said, 'You're the dumb one, aren't you.'

I nodded and smiled, and she spat in my face and ran away shouting, 'Dumbo dum-bo dum-bo.'

And I didn't realize until supper, that was Angela. They were exactly alike and as different as can be.

Now I can hear blood's lazy flow through Angela's body. It pulses slow in my ear, which is pressed against her head. I can smell the clean oils in her hair. I pull away, see the scalp of her parting darn stitch big, and I feel as though I could never again know anyone this well. The pain would be too much to bear – as much joy as pain in the discoveries, but the bad of one sometimes greater than the good of the other.

'I know what you're thinking Jimmy Mack.'

'You don't.'

'Oh, I do. And I hear what people say. You *would* be better off without me.'

No!

Roy and Jessie are coming into the hallway. Even Roy's movements have slowed, as if he is treading warily into something he doesn't want to meet more than halfway. He's smiling the way he always does, but you can see it's more shield than window, part of his defences.

They shuffle away when I say, '*Two minutes, boys,*' and I follow Angela upstairs, onto our balcony, where the wind is up and the chimes chink and clang, as if we are in harbour.

'Jimmy . . .' She's turned away from me. Ferries potter redlit along a horizon of black meeting black. 'Jimmy, I know you're in trouble. I know that you think you have to do what you're doing for me, but sometimes . . . you should maybe think about how it makes me feel when you do these things. It's as though you're driven, I don't know . . . possessed.

'She was my sister. It was my fault, too. Sometimes I'd wish for her to be dead. Everybody saw the good in her. We weren't that different, not really. How could we be? It didn't matter what the

110

truth was, though. She was everyone's favourite, so what else could I do? I had to make myself different.

'I miss her. I do. We were never close. Can you believe it? Since the day we came out of the same belly . . . She didn't like me, I could tell. But she tried so hard to be nice to me, to love me.'

I am holding Angela's head against my face, feeling the sound of her words humming in her skull bones, hearing the mucus tack of her sad sounds. When she has finished, I will kiss her. Her mouth will be warm salt and her saliva will be thick, strings.

'I liked you, you know. All the time you went around following her, doing what she wanted. But I didn't show it. That's the way I am and I hate myself for it. All I'm trying to say, Jimmy, is you should look out for yourself. We all have to do that. We're not responsible for each other; we're all on our own. I'd be all right. I'd survive.'

I pull away, try to signal to her my under-standing. But she says, 'You'd better go. See the boys. Don't tell me what Flint wants until you're certain about what you're going to do. Go, Jimmy. Please.'

TWO CARROTS AND A STICK

We are out on the night-balm deck, with the lawn stretching away like black water into the sea and sky. Roy has lit the torches in the garden and he's staring into the flames, losing himself in the music of their ballet. From here we can see way across the marshes, towards foreign fields. Proving ground. But for now, and above the torch flame flicker, we are marooned from the stray neon of people living in close city confine, and we get the full benefit of pinprick sailor night. It could be a perfect time, an empty span to morning that you could fill with anything, stolen time when there's nothing to get hung about.

Except there is. Jessie is lounging in a chair, and Wingnut is leaning on the rail, taking nervous sips from a highball of Scotch and rocks. But most scared is Surfman, sitting chained to the rail, facing us with his frightened-rabbit look.

'Things have gone badly,' I say via Wingnut, which makes Surfman double take again, unacclimatized as he is to our ways, 'and I'm to blame. For years we've worked Warnsea and Flint has

112

left us alone. But I broke the rules and now I've got to pay a price. You might look around and see money coming in, a good life. But what we've made, we've spent. Everything we've got is on some kind of lease.

'What I'm trying to tell you is we've reached the end of the road. I've done a deal with Flint. I can do it on my own. Just me and Surfman.' Surfman looks at Wingnut, startled, then at my sentencing hands. 'It's best if we go our separate ways. I'm doing what I have to do for my own reasons, and it's not right that I should involve you. I'm sorry it's come to this. It's my fault.' I have to stop because the rhythm of my signals is coming through in Wingnut's voice. I can hear myself falter; lump shapes forming in my unvibrating throat.

Jessie is standing up, looking around, uneasy, as if he is on a high and precarious edge of something. 'What are you saying, Jimmy? You're going on your own; you don't *need* us?'

'It's not fair on you boys. I did the deal with Flint.'

'But what . . .' starts Roy, the permacrease smile gone from his face, his bushy eyes crinkling in a search for serious words '. . . what are we going to do now? What *can* we do?'

'You'll be all right.'

'We won't,' says Jessie. 'This is all I can do. There's nothing down for us here.'

'You can always move on.' Wingnut quizzes me with his eyes as he represents me.

'Move?'

'Move!'

'Where?'

'We can't do that.'

'We don't know anywhere else.'

'We don't know anyone else.'

Jesus, boys. Give me a break.

'We'll do anything, Jimmy,' they say with combinations of words and gesture-pleadings.

They want to put their lives on the line for me out of the total lack of alternative for themselves. We cannot be family. For all the blood we have spilled on each other's behalfs, we lack lineage. What we are breaks natural laws, cannot last.

'I have nothing to lose. I can afford to take chances you wouldn't want to take.'

'Actually, Jimmy,' Wingnut hasn't done this before, in all the years my words and views have been sluicing through his vocal cords, he has never censored me. But now he is silencing my signs, putting his own sounds to my shapes, and I am out of kilter with him, 'I don't think you understand what we're saying. You can't expect us to let go. I don't think it's fair to make decisions for us. We should stand together. Christ, Jimmy, I'm not hard like the rest of you, but I know what's right. Who's to say we can't cut some sort of deal with Flint if things work out. We've got the place in Spain. Why don't we do what Flint says, together.'

I am trying to butt in, but he won't voice me and I can see a glimpse of hope for them, because

114

they have attacked the weakest link in my chain of command, showing that maybe they can act on their own.

'*Listen to me, please. Wingnut, tell them—*'

'No, *Jimmy*,' he signs me. '*We've talked about it, me and Jess and Roy. We want to stick together.*'

'*You're fucking idiots*,' I say, laughing inside as Wingnut phases me back in, waves me on. You've got to laugh or you'd cry. 'Jesus Christ. I can't compromise my actions, the risks I'll have to take. And I can't afford any weakness. No slip-ups. This is Flint we're dealing with.'

'Don't forget the Dutch.' We turn as one and look at Surfman – an outsider at the heart of our collective task, our family business. 'They are evil.'

And you can see the fear come up close, see them practically shiver.

'Right,' Wingnut relays me to Roy and Jessie, 'here's the score.' I look at Surfman and hit him with changing face tones that transmit in clear signals the inescapable depths of his union with our plight. 'We have to get our shit together. We're going on a voyage. Flint calls it the lion's den. We're working for her now. There's a man called Burg, in Holland. She wants us to deliver a package to him.'

'That's all?' says Roy.

'A package?' says Jessie.

And Surfman says nothing, other than to betray in the pig hollow of his shit-scared eyes that there is nothing simple in the task we have been set.

I have listened to Surfman babble his US TV vocab in his US TV dialect about how he could not possibly comply with my requirements of his near future; heard how the Dutch would kill him, and how he wasn't a criminal anyway, not really, just a surfer who got too deep into the easiest hole of all, and this job was supposed to be a one-off.

'Aha, your big one-off,' I said to him in Wingnut's voice.

'Yes, that's right. One big deal.' He saw our wavelengths merge to make identical sounds from a like frequency, which was when I gave him his carrot and carried him on the incoming crest. 'That deal went bad, for us all. But there *is* such a thing as the big one-off: it is what we have to do for each other. We are going to put our heads in the lion's mouth. You're going to tell me where his den is, and we are going to make him weak, then before he gets strong again, we're going to take all the gold from his teeth.' He listened to me like a baby, as if I were telling him a fairy tale, and for a while we surfed on one board, until the fear came, until our lengths unwaved and he fell from my spell.

'No,' he said. 'I can't,' and he repeated himself about how we didn't understand what these people were like.

'No! You . . . you! YOU! are the one who doesn't understand,' I raged at him, with my arms gone

116

violent orient to Wingnut's words. 'You don't understand what WE are like.' I motioned Roy and Jessie to take him outside, show him the stick.

We have fire to fight fire. We really do. But Roy and Jessie plumped for an ordeal by water, which I liked. For a surfer, don't you think?

They took him down into the black night to the black water, and they undressed him. They put sweet paste on his balls. They stood him naked, with the water lapping in dead echo, and they waited for a bite from the first baited leech. And the sensitive soul, he said yes. He said he would like to go back inside because the water looked far from fine.

He eventually told us that, yes, he had heard of Burg but had never met him. And after further persuasions he added that he knew a man who did know Burg, who was as close as you could get to him.

And with that we arrived at the unromantic, bludgeon ending to the tale of the carrot and stick of how Surfman came to join us, agreed to host us in his homeland, hostaging his own fortune. He is part of a fraternity and, in a tight-weave mesh of self-interest, we are brothers.

We are on our way.

MY SECOND ACT OF VENGEANCE

The telephone wakes me, rings loud in my drums, and when I open my eyes I am blinded by eastern sun.

'Jimmy,' says Silverpiece, 'hang up now if you're not secure. Give me the sign.'

I press our beep-rhythm hash code that selects *continue* from an invisible menu.

'I heard you saw Flint. I don't know what you agreed with her, but someone dumped Denny Lane on our steps this morning. Wasted, he was. But not a scratch on him. His pockets were full of crack – enough to send him down. He's a shit and he's got it coming, but this has got Flint all over it. He was one of hers, you know that. This is what she does to her own, so think long and hard about what she'd do to someone on the other side. I can't help you any more, Jimmy. These Dutch, I don't know what Flint's said, but I've asked around. They're bad, Jimmy. If I was you, I'd leg it now. Go anywhere.'

Let me tell you about Silverpiece.

Silverpiece is what you would probably expect of a pathetic, crooked detective inspector. He is various parts rat and mouse, but I know the whyfores of the way he is, such knowledge being part of the education that has shown me good always lurks in bad – as much as vice versa.

When Silverpiece was thirty, and Sarah, his daughter, was three, his wife ran off with a small-time criminal who supplied her with benefits she would never receive from a small-time copper. Until then Silverpiece had been on a by-the-book plod to pension, but he had the rules changed on him. He caught up with old news, what his wife had been doing in his absences, and he re-educated himself as to how he viewed his daughter – without an accusing quiz in his eyes. He taught himself to love Sarah regardless of what might have been. Whether or not. He taught himself to forget much of what he had learned.

And when he was strong enough, he began to reap his own vengeance on the world: taking a wrongful place on an invisible payroll. Nothing spectacular, but Sarah was moved to a nice school: all girls and all paid for. A simple matter of a man doing his best to provide for one he loves, putting some spine back in his life.

Until one evening when he lost his faith in the power of law completely, at the same time as I was finding strength, stepping out of a weaker me. Under the same dark sky, looking down on different people's different habits in different parts of this delta, both our lives changed, quantum.

I first met him when I was taken into a new

and more severe custody after my First Act of Vengeance. I didn't know then that it would lead directly to my Second. Silverpiece said he could introduce me to a man who would give me an alibi, and then he tasked me to do something for him. To be honest, I hope I would have done it anyway, without pro quo or quids.

As it was, I shifted up a league the day after I delivered to Silverpiece a harmless-looking package, a small carton which I wrapped in brown paper. The parcel was light. I remember carrying it to his house. As I waited for him to answer, with the sound of sobbing coming young, ceaseless and unhealing from a bedroom window, I was appalled at how light that box was. Its mass bore no relation to the significance of what it contained, the weight of burdens it wrought on Silverpiece's life. Because in that box was the wonton scrotum of the man who had raped the daughter of a faithless single parent and policeman.

Sarah was sixteen and three weeks away from her O levels the night she hobbled home with her clothes-torn shame, bleeding and with the vicious grunt coming of a middle-aged man seeping down her thighs, on the night I happened to be hauled in on separate twine.

I told Silverpiece 'no' many times; communicated that I would have no part in his pact. Then he took me in his car, and we waited together outside a house, waited for a man to leave, and Silverpiece gained entry to one of the flats with one of dozens of keys he had on a ring the size of a saucer. Silverpiece showed me the magazines. I saw the pile of tissues by the bed for myself. He showed me a photograph of a young girl, like a holiday snap gone wrong. No smiles. 'In care,' he said, and I understood, agreed to comply there and then on a good and unwavering impulse. He gave me the spray and a knife, and he left me alone in the room, saying as he left that I would be taken care of, that someone would come in when I had finished. Silverpiece didn't want him dead, you see. He wanted him stitched up good and proper, this scum.

He didn't trust the law to reap grim vengeance, but he trusted me, and I repaid that trust by handing him the parcel, delivering his order, like pizza. And I watched his joyless unveiling of accomplished mission, like somebody who had lost his appetite being served a substantial meal. He blamed himself, believed that Sarah had paid the price set by some unloving God in retribution for the misapplication of lay laws. That is a theory I choose to reject, because an omniscient dictator could have foreheard the repercussing clatter of crime to follow.

As I made my way down Silverpiece's path that night, I heard the latch fall and the sobbing continue, fading in the dark as I passed from one side of the law to another. Nothing changed for Silverpiece or for Sarah. But something good came out of the bad, for me.

CHERRY PICKING

Angela looks brand new. She has blown her hair, auburn in the flooding sun and tumbling onto her shoulders. 'You can trust me, Jimmy, not to let you down. That's what you think, isn't it?'

I nod and she looks away into the mirror and puffs her hair up, drags her fringe down with her fingers, busy against some truth she might see in a look I might let slip. 'Oh, Jimmy, I'm scared,' she says into the mirror. 'You're going to be all right, aren't you?'

I slide my legs from between warm sheets and walk towards her. When she is like this, it makes you wonder how she can be the other way she sometimes is. I hold her and she is solid under the shifting silk of her robe which ripples in the warm breeze, like half the marble melt of sculpted piety.

She shrugs free and dresses, gives confirmation, in her everyday hallmark mannerisms, of why I am able to love her. I can hear Roy and Jessie through the chimes down on the deck. They are talking quietly under the breeze. It sounds like an ordinary conversation, as if they've managed to distract themselves from the bad reality of what is waiting for us. But it isn't.

'I don't know when I'll see Ollie again. He'll be left with her and fuck knows what she'll do when she wants to go out. I won't be here. She won't stay in, you know. She doesn't give a toss about him. She'll leave him; she'll fuckin' leave him in the flat on his own.'

'He'll be all right, Roy,' says Jessie. 'You could ask Jimmy to have a word with Silverpiece, or Tommy Curl. Keep an eye on her, put your mind at rest.'

'I don't want him going into care. Fucking nutters in care.'

'He should be with his mum. You're right.'

'Maybe I could get him. Maybe I could come back for him when we're settled.'

'You've got to do what's right for the kid.'

'Kids love it in Spain. That's why it's a fuckin' holiday place. He'd be on holiday all the time.'

'What about school? He wouldn't speak the language.'

'I could teach him.'

'We're all leaving something behind. Me and Anne-Marie were just getting it back together.'

'What about Jimmy, though?' says Roy. 'Angela's coming, isn't she.'

'That's different.'

'Fuckin' isn't.'

Angela's voice comes at me from inside.

'I don't want you to do it, Jimmy. We could go away, the two of us. Let the dust settle. Now Lane's being put away.'

I rub finger and thumb together. '*No cash.*'

'We wouldn't need much to get by.'

I take hold of her, sitting on the edge of the bed. Her pale arms are cold – too thin and not as violated as they have been, but with more than sufficient lingering signs for concern.

'I'm coming off it. Honestly I am.'

I splay my arms, rotate my hands in a tumble shape, and she understands that I will believe that when I see it. I point outside, make a big circle with my arms and clasp my shoulders with crossed arms.

'The boys would be all right on their own.'

I shake my head.

'Maybe it's you who couldn't cope without them.' She smiles, not starting an argument. 'You and your bloody mates. Just be careful. You haven't dealt with Flint before.'

'*And you have?*'

'I've come across some of her so-called friends.'

I make a soundless whistle shape with my mouth and smile.

'Not like that!' She slaps me playfully and I fall back on the bed in mock fear. She continues the game, leaning across me and beating on my chest with her fists. She lifts her leg and straddles me, as if we are playing a children's game. Like two boys wrestling on summer lawns, with cut grass in the air and the sun strong and high.

Except young boys can't show you, in the arc of a leg with a skirt riding up and the downy dark shadow of groin disappearing into brilliant white cotton; they can't show you what it would be like to . . . I don't know; it's just that moment, that ante-room of time in the moment before, when anything is possible and you cannot believe that you could ever tire of the hotcold drywet motion of mouth on mouth; hands on silk and cotton and flesh, and the sounds of zips and clothes and breathing. Then a moan and a gasp and the whole thing turning serious as she looks down at you, with her face remoulded into a new distorted shape, hair pouring down like frozen peat water. She is studious now, with her hands on your chest and getting herself right on the point. Right on it, with her mouth going pucker, as if she has lost something precious. But still she grinds it out, the way she likes, and suddenly she is taking you to the end of it all, and even though it's great, it's the best fucking moment ever . . . it's not. Because you know it is about to reach its own conclusion.

Aftermath. We lie on our backs and drift into near sleep, until the breeze comes in and makes our sweat chill on each other's skin.

I first slept with Angela when I was just sixteen and she wasn't. It was a crime – I didn't know then – and a week before Lisa died. Lisa who said that Angela had done what she had done with me in order to hurt her, which hurt me, being the only thing she had ever said that harmed me. It led to our first argument, our last conversation.

I didn't go out with Angela until five years after that. But what happened when she was fifteen was that Angela made a man of me. She removed the reasons to hide behind my weaknesses, and in a liberating and allegedly selfish, hurtful act, she made me stronger. You could say that she advanced my cause more than all the kindnesses proffered by her sister. But regardless of her motives, what she did changed both our lives for the worse, because what I felt empowered to do was fight, for Lisa.

'What are you thinking?'

'   '

'You cut me out of so much . . .' I know the conversation we are about to have. '. . . You drift away; you're in a different space to me. I can be touching you and you've gone. I can see you, taste you in my mouth, but you're not here any more. Not with me, anyway.'

'*Don't spoil it, Angela.*'

'How do you think it makes me feel? It's not my fault, you know. If it's anybody's fault . . .'

'*Yeah? Yeah! Come on then. Come on! Let's have it!*'

'I miss her, too, you know. But it's twelve years ago. She wouldn't have ended up the way you think. It's not fair, I've had to put up with things and you know what? You know what, Jimmy? You know what you do? You stop me from grieving for

126

her. You get in the way, because . . . because you still have these thoughts about her. Don't you? How can I make peace when you're like that.' I can see her strength falling away, like coal-mountain slack, and she's going into her handbag. She is broken. 'Lisa dreamed her way through life. She always did, and look what good it did her. At least I'm still here, even if you think I'm a bitch and a smackhead.'

'*I don't. I don't. I don't.*'

But it's too late for that. I watch her dress for a second time. I watch her being sad for the things she has said, and she leaves with a pleasureless smile spreading empty on her pretty face, goes without even a kiss or a kind word, and I try to envisage whether things would have been better or worse, just now, if I had been able to fully articulate why I am the way I am; why I crave the things, for her, that I crave.

GOT IT TAPED

The boys have been milling around the house since dawn, and even though it is still only mid-morning, it has already been a long day. They are tense, sniping at each other in the garden, wanting and not wanting to get into the day, to cross the water and see for themselves what these Dutch are like, how they match up to the word pictures we teased out of Surfman. The longer it takes for these Orangemen to make themselves known, the bigger and more fearsome they will become in the collective imagination; the bigger and harder will be the rock and the place we have to put our bollocks between.

There is nothing more we can do by way of preparation, so I press '>' and listen to Surfman's frightened voice rupture the silence. I listen to the information – mis, dis, spot-on, or otherwise – we leeched from him regarding the associate who stands between him and Burg. The boys had got him taped. They had recorded him in the confessional and Surfman, who is beside me now on the lawn, flinches in his deckchair at the sounds of his deep and perfect English canary singing.

128

'I . . . I brought the shipment for a man, an important man in Amsterdam. I don't know him, though.'

'Burg?' says Jessie.

'No.'

'Cut the shit. Who is he?' said Roy's voice.

'I don't know. I am telling you the truth. Aaarrgh. Hugghh.' Surfman grimaces next to me in reflective pain at his own tape sounds and puts a soft cupping hand to his nethers. 'All I know is the man who took me to him. They met me in Amsterdam. I am not in that world. I am married and I have a son. My wife, Monique, she has followed me with my boarding – all around the world. She has sacrificed so much . . . this was a chance. I was so close to being . . . to making it, you see.' His voice was cracking.

'I've got a son, too,' says Roy. 'I'm not allowed to see him, not regular. If I was like you, if I had a wife, I'd get a decent fucking job, look after them. I'd be a proper dad.'

'It's not like that,' pleaded Surfman.

'Who the fuck are they, these people?' said Roy, past time.

'Please. Please, I don't know.'

There is a silence on the tape, sounds of Jessie coming back into earshot and Surfman's breathing going out of control. 'No. No! I know the house, the one in Amsterdam. It is on Herengracht. The man I met, he is called Stapp.'

I feel as if I want to grant Surfman a pardon.

I have to dismiss the notion of a grieving, loyal wife and a vulnerable baby son. Perhaps he resents them for halting his beach-bum life. Perhaps he is here to receive his come-uppance for being that kind of bastard, which is something for me to take purchase on.

'And what did the guy say about Burg?'

'Nothing. Everyone I came across in this whole thing, they fear him. No-one speaks or smiles. People stop breathing when he is mentioned.'

There are crows in the far field, squawking white noise, into which quasi-silence our contemplations fall. The boys slurp their tea and crunch their biscuits, and Roy mooches around the lawn kicking a football, treading gingerly on the plants when he loses control and has to retrieve it, making sure Angela isn't watching from the balcony. The pictures that Surfman's words have conjured get worse with the passing of time. Perhaps we need to reconsider our options, in the undertow drag of attack and counter, action and consequence.

Perhaps Angela had been right: we should break for another border; build a new life somewhere, right now. Maybe I should try trusting her to survive in adversity. We could go to the south coast, cross unnoticed onto a continent where land is unsevered from steppes and Himalayas; midnight suns and Yellow Seas; savannah and Zulu tribesmen. Why make life difficult for ourselves?

There is a gravel grind of visitation. One, two, three, four car doors are slamming in series and

130

Jessie goes to the fence, looks across to the driveway.

'Oh, fuck,' he says.

'Right, Jessie,' says the lead man, full of himself.

I jump up out of my chair, see Surfman looking scared because what he must be able to see is my reaction, confirming we have more to fear than mere Dutchmen.

'What's going on, Jimmy?' Angela shouts down from the balcony.

'*Nothing. Stay inside. Get inside!*'

'Jimmy,' says the first henchman, three more in tow.

'*What do you want?*'

'Cup of tea'd be nice.'

'Fuck off,' says Roy, up to the fence like a dog in a cage, knowing he can have any of this lot, not necessarily knowing that is not the point.

'Where's Chancey?' says Wingnut on my behalf.

'Not here,' he says. 'Flint wants you to have this.' He passes a package through the fence. 'Says you give it to Burg, give it to him personally. You have to be there when he opens it. Says you don't open it, though, just deliver. She'll know if you open it, you'll regret it if you do.'

I take the package and hand it behind me to Wingnut, who receives it with a shaking hand, as if it might harm him.

'Thanks. Now you can fuck off,' says Wingnut,

his heart not in it, like a child reading aloud without meaning from a book in a classroom.

'No, not yet,' he says, a smile on his face, job satisfaction waiting to happen. 'We've come to collect something. Kind of a swap. For safe-keeping, collateral. You know what I mean, Jimmy. We've come for your tart.'

There is no fear in his eyes. He knows I will do nothing to threaten him. That would be idiotic. He knows I am not an idiot. Flint will have told him.

'*No way.*'

I beckon Wingnut, who says, 'No fuckin' way. If Flint can't trust me, the deal's off.'

'That's what you want me to tell her, is it?' He's smiling. I know it's the answer he wants, and if it is the answer he wants to hear, then it's the answer I should deny myself, in recognition of the elementary law of equal and opposite reaction.

Jessie and Roy are broadside. Roy is bouncing from foot to foot, psyched up to bursting with a smile that's splitting into something gone berserk. He backs off, seeing indications of what we are probably capable of, crazier than he thought.

'Don't be stupid, Jimmy. Think about what Flint will do.'

'Flint will do nothing.' It's a female voice, coming round from the front door, making tiny noise on the gravel on the other side of the fence.

Angela has an overnight bag. She is wearing a white cotton shimmer of a dress and a hat. She looks so beautiful you would want to whisk her

132

home and show her to your parents before she spoils. And in this moment I love her. I know she is worth it, know all my dilemmas have gone smokeless into the ether. My options have turned into something quite, quite imperative.

LIPS TOGETHER, EYES CLOSED

As we drive through the gates and onto the Outreach road, my mother's words repeat in my head like fast food at an ulcer. 'There is something important we have to talk about.' Important, perhaps, to her. I do not consider myself to be harsh in my dismissal, am not wilfully cruel. In this case I am simply unable to see what good might come of reopening a healed wound, looking for an organ that has been removed.

Usually, when we are on a job or taking a trip, the car is like a fairground ride for whose guaranteed fun you would pay good money. It normally sings with rollercoaster laughing, and there is spliff going front to back, back to front. There are juvenile jokes and the laying down of plans for later. But today all is quiet.

We turn off the Outreach road away from Warnsea, off limits. This is Flintland, and after the subsidence of the birdman fun, not one of us is getting even remotely excited about the boat ride or the duty frees; the blackjack table, the disco or larking about with the bunk beds. It is as though we are going to work, Monday morning.

Waiting for the ferry to come into port, we are parked up opposite King Billy, equestrian and regilded when I was a young boy – as if to say that here on the eastern extremity and far from that other troubled north, there is still something relevant about conquering Dutchmen. And beyond King Billy I can see the top of the department store Fischers.

Fischers is a tiered cake of a store, where I would wander as a child on Saturdays, watching bogey-nosed kids plot petty theft and well-to-do children holding parents' hands, parents who held a kind of court in big-coat, rich-hair gaggles, with silent nods of recognition to others of their own kind. The rich kids would look miserable, wishing maybe that they weren't rich, that they could just for once run amok. The way those children looked at me then, you could almost see a desire on their part for a worse future, different parents. Perhaps no parents at all.

It was outside Fischers where the changes that accelerated me to here and now began, the week after Angela had made a man of me. It was where Lisa's fate was set in motion at the end of a week of change.

Lisa would come to my room when all the other boys had gone on adrenalin travel: footballing or fire-starting; taking without owners' consent or mindless vandalizing. From my window in the Newholme eaves you could track them along the red-brick road. I watched the motivelessness of the loll of their actions; the ways in which they found purpose where there was none. What can you do when someone's plight can't get any worse? When they have seen your disincentives and raised themselves to say, 'Fuck you. Surprise me. Go on. See. Fuck you!'

Lisa had always come to where she was not strictly allowed, to sit with me on my boys' windowledge and watch the others. She would look out, across Skullcoats towards the prison, and she would talk about what she was going to do when she got out. When she was sixteen, she would do something with her life. She had plans.

One day, she came across to the bed, sat next to me. She would put her arms around me, but I knew that really it was because *she* wanted to be held, so I held her and felt myself tremble inside; felt myself get hard; felt like I would burst, got myself all knotted up but not moving because I didn't want it to end. I even tried to stop breathing, in case that prolonged it.

But then I heard the heavy throb of a familiar car and Lisa craned her neck, pushed her face to the pane. I watched every detail of her movements as she waved down to him, watched her smile, watched her go coy. And as she waved him an extravagant farewell, as his horn sounded in the dead of afternoon, I watched something she disliked in herself rise to the surface. She came across to the bed, sat next to me and held me.

'Can I see it?' she said.

She looked down at it, sticking up in my trousers like a mad thing. I was dumb and now she had seen my stupidity. I was pathetic. I couldn't control anything about myself. I could feel myself crying inside and she could see it, too.

'I'm sorry,' she said, smiling in the way that a bird with clipped wings might try to fly. She tilted her head to one side and made her nostrils flare. 'Look.' She unbuttoned the top few buttons of her dress. I had seen bras before, ladies getting undressed at the beach inside towels. It was no good when you saw them in a swimsuit. But the sight of a bra . . . Jesus. Lisa took my hand. She was looking away now, out of the window, and she closed her eyes. She put my hand on her breast and closed her eyes, said, 'I can do it . . . I can . . .'

She had her hand on me, making me flinch, making me fold in on myself and go to mush. 'I know how to. I'm not a virgin, you know.' But she was; I had heard the ridicule it visited on her. But I felt as if I wasn't any more, as if I had lost something. I sat there, with my face gone cold in her shadow, wanting her to take her hand off me before she noticed. But she didn't; she didn't mind. I took my hand off her breast, but she kept hers on me, feeling me go small, my pants going wet. And all the time she was learning more about what she had come here to discover. But she didn't just go. We sat there until the voices came back into the yard to the bottom of the steps, and she stood up and said, 'See you, Jimmy Mack.'

She kissed me, on the mouth with her lips together, eyes closed.

PART 2

PART 2

FRIENDS AND FOES

Midnight's strike leaves us with six slowly reducing hours until we arrive on new shores. The disco throttles up and our table is fat with the heavy glass and pot stoppers of Grolsch. Roy is below decks, changing into something he would like to think might impress, and meantime Wingnut has been amusing us with his demonstrations for new and sexual encounters, trying also to persuade himself that tonight could be the night, with his left-right-left observations, the childish task-setting, the 'I dare you' chat.

On the other hand, Jessie had gone straight to the floor, talking into a girl's ear – a sixth-former is my guess, because an older man, mid-forties, goes across, takes hold of the girl's arm and is dispatched with a quick lash of Jessie's other kind of persuasion. A couple of words sentence him to a scurry below decks without so much as a backward glance, leaves Jessie and his hands to fuse with other enticements. He takes her into a fit-where-it-touches bodysuit of a smooch, even though the DJ is playing a fast-riff Indie song.

'Right boys.' Roy appears. 'What do you think?'

he says, addressing his own strut stance, with inward-splaying palms.

I just smile, '*You're all right.*' But he's not. He might have been all right to the sounds of Spandau and Teardrops exploding. In a disco for the blind. '*Go get 'em.*' I nod at the floor and watch him looking daggers at Jessie with his girl. Roy, you might say, is dressed like shit. But you can see from his peacock gait – a bandy-legged peacock on amphetamines – that he thinks he looks a million dollars in his cheap-cloth tunic jacket, pinstriped and tapering into his waist, where silver-flecked bag trousers are multipleated. He has tried to gel his hair back, but there isn't enough of it. Even so, he bristles with goodfun in prospect. He is primeval innocent, and if boys played with dolls, and if they wanted their dolls to stand a chance with Barbie, Roy, right now, is how they would dress them to stand a chance at this type of disco. And they might get Ken to jig doubletime out of synch to impress the dolls, like Roy is now, looking around himself as he does.

I motion for Wingnut to scoot round, so I can make myself heard, jiving my message out of time with the music, in my lap, as if we might be overseen.

'*Someone's watching us, I'm sure, Flint is one step ahead of us. She knew about Surfman. She knew I hadn't killed him. No-one knew that, only us.*'

'*The boys? No way, Jimmy.*'

'*It's not right, Flint letting us come on our own.*'

142

'*Angela's her insurance. Maybe that's it*,' and he hesitates, measures me. '*She was quick to go with Chancey.*'

'*No! No way. She's not perfect, but she wouldn't betray us.*'

But I can't fend off recollections of recent conversations up in our room, what might have been the sound of conscience seeping from Angela's lips. '*You should look out for yourself, Jimmy. We all have to do that. We're not responsible for each other; we're all on our own. I'll be all right. I'll survive.*' It could sound like something it wasn't, if you heard it through different ears, saw it in a different light.

'*You trust me?*' Wingnut motions.

I hesitate, not because I am unsure, but to shout a Chinese whisper that will keep Jessie and Roy on their toes. Eventually I make shapes that say, '*Yes. Yes, I trust you.*'

'*What's the plan? What do we do when we get there?*'

Plan? I shrug, watch him panic.

'*There is no plan. All we have is Surfman and what he told us. We go to Stapp, take it from there*,' I sign.

'*And that's it?*'

I nod.

'*So the lion's den, the lion's mouth – that's for real?*'

And from my unmoving hush I can see his realization of the overestimations he has credited me with. There is nothing up my sleeve.

I try to smile. I sign him, limp, that *'we'll be all right'*.

But the damage is done. He drains his beer, too much too fast. It spills on his chin and shirt. He plumbs his depths for a smile of his own and says, above the music so he can hear it for himself, 'Still, we've got Spain. God, that place is great. No-one'd ever find us there. I can't wait. All of us together in the sun. The girls are so pretty out there.'

I nod and try to smile, but a giggle comes from nowhere, it bubblebursts and I say, pointing at the dancefloor, *'Come on.'* He looks nervous, not drunk enough to dance yet, but I stand and he follows me, weaving through to where Roy is thrashing a space for himself, thinking that the faster he moves the better he is dancing. He smiles, holds his arms out and the three of us pogo up and down with arms around each other's shoulders to the sound of the Clash, wondering, in a sweat-metal searing thrash, whether to stay or should we go now. We do it at sea, on no-man's water and well beyond the point of any possibility of return.

Jessie is sweet-talking into the uneducated ear of his new love. Her eyes are closed and her teeth are gritting pleasure from pain. They have spread a coat across their laps and I can see her feet, estranged and sticking out from the coat, twitching in a kinky-boot coming. I tap Jessie on the shoulder and flick my thumb back to say, *'We're going.'*

'You're not going?' she says in a high-pitch

moan. She is pretty, and it is easy to see that in a year or three she will be many distances away from whatever it is that enables Jessie to do this sort of thing. 'You're *not* going. You *can't* go.'

'*Come on, Jessie, I'm serious.*'

And he stands up, good as gold.

'Sorry about this.' He stoops down, gives her one last kiss and says something under the music that gets her smiling.

'Me, too,' she says.

And we're off.

'Christ, Jimmy. She was the business, no shit. You could have left us. I mean, I really liked her. She liked me, too, I could tell. We had so much in common, I'm not kidding. She's from Durham, you see, and . . .'

'*Jessie?*'

'Jimmy?'

'*Shut the fuck up.*'

THE NIGHT WATCH

When we returned to the cabin, Surfman – alone and bound to stay where he was – waited with an impossible gift. In a vase on the table was a sweet-smelling bunch of tulips which, according to Surfman, had been brought by a man without uniform. He had left the flowers, then left the cabin, not saying anything, simply placing a single flowering head into the tape that silenced our comrade.

I was unsurprised to hear Wingnut's findings: that one of the stewards had told him there was nowhere on board that sold flowers.

And so it is, with the perfume of an unwanted gift bursting around me, that the night watch has filled my head with bad thoughts on this sea route towards a famous figment of another Night Watch. It is many years since I have seen Mr Rembrandt's dark and unfulfilling representation of forebodance. If he was here, now, he would have Goya'd his audience up to recreate the overpowering stench of trepidation I suffer now. He would shout out his light and shade until you felt the invisible hand on your shoulder; until loose shifting fibre mined the fear in your stomach tracts; until you saw landmarks slipping in the bob and weave of bad future.

I think I know what we must do.

I have sketched, in outline, the bigger picture. All I lack is some detail, a little colour, some borrowed light.

Bob.

Weave.

All night long.

It is silvery dark in the cabin, just a moonsheen Bacon warp of four companions, dark lumps in the bunks from my seat by the porthole. Within the motion of the boat I can hear two distinct sound types: one of two sleeping bodies, and the quieter sound of two wakened bodies making a taut silence.

'Surfman? Surfman, you awake?' whispers Roy.

'Yes.'

'Jimmy?'

'   '

'Jimmy, you awake?'

'   '

Roy and Surfman are on the top bunks. One tied to the frame of the bed, the other not. Roy leans up on one elbow. I can see him in the watery mirror of the porthole.

'Your kid?' Roy whispers.

'Yes,' says Surfman.

'Does he play football?'

'No.'

'Mine does. He's going to be something when he grows up. You can tell. Parents can tell, can't they.'

'Yes, I suppose so.'

'I'm going to have him living with me when this is over. Your wife. Is she all right?'

'Yes. Yes, she is all right . . .'

'What's up?'

'I have done something terrible,' says Surfman to himself.

'You awake, Jimmy?' says Roy.

'   '

The cabin goes quiet. I can smell the tulips, feel Roy finding sleep – making a kind of peace in a corner of the cabin that is filling, saline in a sinking ship, with the guilty considerations of what I am denying its occupants. I backstroke through recent history, consider the possibilities of betrayal. In a locked cell that passes through sea like a radar dot, I look at the flowers and remember from within a grey recess that Angela cannot abide tulips, and I use this to reconstruct untainted faith in her, but as I do this good thing, I shiver in an unilluminated glare.

INSIDE OUT

The morning is coming pale across the sea. The others are still sleeping and I use the silence and light to reconstruct the ways in which I found strength to overcome enemies.

I achieved it from an indifference to life and death. When you have been in the position of lying awake, not with the moon-pull bow and stern, port and starboard roll of sea, but to the soundtrack of grunts and thumps and cries and pleas, waiting for it to be your turn; when you've lived like that for eight years, you, too, would be able to take purchase on the devalued currency of living and breathing. You, too, could use that to springboard beyond the furthest place your worst enemy can go, because nothing could be worse than to continue like this.

But my life is now much improved. I feel as if I might be on the brink of something too good to risk. How can I be sure that this will not make me a weaker man, that this stake of good future will not perversely prohibit its own fruition?

After Lisa had kissed me that day, on the brink

of my cusp of change, she left my room and me in it. I took myself and my matting shame to the bathroom and washed myself clean. I knew, then, what it was like to feel a high-board flex, but not what lay beyond the edge. I was about to take steps towards the unknown.

The Newholme boys had come back up to the room to get clean before tea, but Angela had followed them, straying off limits to tell them to go downstairs, which they did in deference to the sex of her improbable powers. She went to the window, looked outside and said in her sister's voice, kind and soft so you would think you were with the wrong half, 'I've told cook you're sick. You don't have to go to tea,' and she said, 'I really *have* done it. I can show you properly.'

She sat beside me on the bed and without any ado, she had my face in her hands, pushing my mouth open with her tongue and circling her face over mine. She put her hand in my trousers. Inside! What kind of day was this that somebody above had ringed in red without so much as a whisper of forewarning? I grew like a playbox jack and tried to say no, but I couldn't, of course. She brought her mouth off mine, still with one hand on the back of my neck as she smiled at me, smiled really big and wide, as if she was the one getting all the pleasure. And as I came into a dizzy falling void, she said, 'Now we can do it properly. Just wait a bit. It's best when you've just spunked up. Feel me. Here. No. That's right.' She said it as if she had been telling me how to find an extra life on a secret level of a computer game. She said it in a way that made me believe her, trust her. And she stayed and we did it. Properly.

She came to me the next day, for us both to enjoy more of the same.

The same, except this time I made her cry. I saw her power leak away and turn to vapour as she told me that she loved me. 'I love you, Jimmy.' So I stroked her face and mouthed, '*I love you*.' And she said, 'You love me more than Lisa, don't you?' But I couldn't answer, and in what I can now see was her only possible riposte, Angela jumped off the bed, screamed, 'I hate you, you bastard.' It was five years before she forgave me.

Throughout that week I burned for Lisa. I wanted to display my method, express myself, prove myself. But when I sat in my room, watching the others play, all I got was a grandstand view of the purring car that slowed to a kerbside halt for no longer than the instant it took for Lisa to climb in. She returned within the hour. I could just about see the cloth sheen of his suit between the visor and the steering wheel. Lads flocked out of the yard to pay homage to the sharp lines of the MR2. I saw Lisa's pretty face pan across and kiss him in the windscreen. Then she got out of the car, flashing her thighs as she climbed up from the low-slung seat. She turned round, halfway to the gate, with a rehearsed hand on her jutting hip, far too casual. And he roared off, tooting his horn. Once, twice. Her, so proud.

Within that hour, between the going of the car and the coming back, Lisa had changed. Less coy, she had made an irreversible transformation.

But I was changing, too. And so much did I surrender to the forces of my whirlpool hormones, that by the end of that week in which my innocence died, I was ripe for a fearless launch into a new and dangerous life.

I was alive and kicking, Saturday at Fischers. You couldn't sit back and expect things to come to you. I couldn't afford a sports car, then or in the foreseeable, but so what? There had to be other ways and means, methods of adjustment available to me. The longest journey starts with a single short step, or in my case, a short series of lengthening copulations that allowed me to receive visions of first-draft sketches of more positive options. I had seen blinding images of an inversion of myself.

Inside out.

Wear the badness on the outside, start feeling good about yourself. Show them something to respect, something they can be scared of. And the inside had been made harder than my surface anyway. Scar tissue had formed all around my heart and soul – what made me live and breathe. As they said, I was just a dumb fuck anyway. Hide that. Turn it in on itself.

Lisa was in a doorway at the back of Fischers, where deliveries were made, where empty boxes were stacked and no-one came in trading hours. All of which made it as quiet a place as you could find in which to get up to no good. It was no accident, me being there. I had sat next to her at dinner each night of that week, committing each detail of her every conversation and listening to her whispering confidences of being in love. All the time, swallowing the truth: that me and her were meant to be. I knew it to be true.

She was with him and his gelled-back hair, fifty-quid shirt. He was bigger than me, but he wasn't worthy. There was nothing beyond the moment, beneath his surface. I approached them, unseen and feeling my new outside prickle with sweat.

My new inside churned as he stepped towards her. She took a step back against the wall and looked around anxiously. 'No,' I heard her say. He was busy in his trousers, then tugging at himself with one hand, bending his knees and reaching up into her skirt with the other. He went right up against her now, pulling one of her legs up, as if they were performing a lunatic tango. He reached up again and pulled at her pants. 'No!' she said. He raised his hand and she flinched, let out a tiny yelp that she strangled for herself. He laughed and I was now close enough for her sobbing to come into my fields. 'No, no, please,' she said in a clammy groan. 'I'm sorry, I'm sorry.'

I caught Lisa's eye, and her mine as she turned away from him. She shook her head, but I didn't go away, simply checked left and right to make sure we were alone. He raised his hand again. I tried to shout, forgetting my limitations.

I ran up to them and grabbed his shoulder, knowing the inevitable would visit me in punches, kicks and maybe worse, with nothing gained. I tugged at him so he came round to face me, off-balance and fucking and blinding at me. He swung at me and I dived under the curve of his fist, drove my head into his belly. I clutched him tight to limit the swinging of his punches and kicks, but he threw me to the floor, twisted me round with superior strength and know-how. He sat on my chest and put his knees on my arms. The air gushed from my lungs and he spat in my face.

'Who's your friend then, eh?' he said to Lisa, with hate in his voice.

'Let him go. Please, Steve. He's no harm.'

'He fancy you? Is that why you don't want it? You getting it from him? This little shit? Is she?' he said, looking back down at me. 'Is she?'

'He can't speak. He's mute.'

'He can, look,' he grabbed my face in his smelly hand: traces of burger and worse, a smell I didn't know. I know it now, a smell her sister has, too.

He forced my mouth open with salt, grit fingers. He grabbed my tongue with his nails, scratching the soft underside you never use and making me want to scream an impossible scream. 'Look, here's his tongue.'

'Leave him, Steve. Please.'

'Does he use this tongue on you? Eh? You slag.'

154

He had turned away from me and I gathered air in through my mouth, gagging on the taste of his hand in my mouth. I gnashed down; I gnashed down as fucking hard as fucking fuck on his hand. He tried to pull it away. But it was too late, I had him in a five-knuckle bite, bone jarring on my teeth.

I opened my mouth and his fingers dropped away, trailing behind his body which slumped off my chest. I started choking, choking on a taste I knew. Everyone's blood must taste the same. Funny that, how fingers don't, but maybe we are all the same on the inside. He was groaning, with Lisa kneeling next to him, not caring about me, or him. I can see in the perfect vision of reflection that she was tending to her own safety. I roared inside at him and at her and at myself, and I kicked him and kicked him and kicked him, until Lisa had tired of pleading. Until he had stopped groaning.

I became myself again.

Except I was never myself again after that. And since then, I have been disabled by the conviction that I can do anything to anybody. Because I had offered myself up and been rejected by come-uppance, I have had that card to play until the decks turn against me.

But now we are in a different and less fierce phoney field of conflict, where enemies lurk invisible, soundless. They can come and go unseen in day or night, taking information and harming us with tokens of kindness. I drop the tulips in the bin and

155

a tannoy message blares like a slap across the face. Its sting calls us up on deck.

We are approaching dock at the end of this long and retrospective night, during which I have begun to think, No. Maybe, No, I don't want to offer up my life – the possibility of losing it – as my strongest card, because now, stretching from a sleepless night, I can feel a faraway shadow of the Spanish sun blinding me through an opening shutter, the brilliance of day shattering a dark and wafer chill, a thousand miles from people who threaten me. I can feel the sanctuary of the company of brothers and a sister who might be there to catch me if I fall.

But this is no time for weakness. So I cover it up and smelt my soft self and signalshout '*Come on!*' waking them up, forging us forward into the day and giving them no basis for suspicion that my heart might not be in it. Leaving no clues that earth plates might have shifted on drifting continental passage, I steel myself. With the chimneys and refineries and sprawling plants of distant Rotterdam glistening in morning sun, I make myself ore. On the surface, I am pig.

HOME FROM HOME. NOT

The ferry port is pristine with the metal shine of recent refurbishment gleaming on the polished floors, and with all smells absent there can be no doubt that this is not Easport, that this could not possibly be Engeland.

Coming out of the arrivals lounge, with coffee and cakes strange tasting in our bellies, we are brought to earth by the sounds that Roy is sending through the car park as he drives the car round to meet us in the company of some no-style boy band he is singing along to with the windows down.

Jessie is looking left-right-left in his horny, casual fashion, checking on the whereabouts of his sixth-form love. But she will be long gone, straight off the boat and on her chaperoned way to sample soils, or to praise paintings, or whatever it is that's on the agenda that doesn't feature Jessie. He looks around, breathes in a lungful of the early morning sun-chill air. He lets a smile seep. As if he can read me he says, 'She was gorgeous. Still' – fingering a piece of paper – 'got her number.'

'Jesus, Jess. What about Anne-Marie?' says Wingnut.

Which makes the smile disappear from his face, as if he had actually managed to completely dismiss from his mind and libido the fact that he is engaged to be married to his on-off childhood sweetheart.

You might think that you had not travelled any distance, that you had just spent the night circling offshore in roll-your-own disco blackjack heaven, just cut afloat for a night.

Like home, even the travel lines that lead us meandering towards our base are taking us everywhere and nowhere. We could be back on our own delta, across the pond. No seafood or Gauloises or toilets that have burst their banks. No gibberish tongues or alien glyphics. We are on the wrong side of the road, that's all, and with windmills. But the windmills aren't postcard clogged with Gouda women in rainbow clothes. They are modern farms on which land has been manufactured from sea and where they have poached other elements for their convenience, drawing power from wind to beam in TV dialects from Stuyvesant land.

In Easport, we have surrendered to the sea. It barriers us from oil and gas, still bears us some fish, but it has its own way up and down the coast, scything chunks at a time, exposing strata and ruining lives. We submit to its will in the same way as we stoop into the north wind. It seems, with the benefit of distance, that in Engeland we are simply hanging on, worlds apart from what is passing itself off in the name of trade here – at the world's biggest harbour where resources come in constant transit to be naturalized – like the heroin that is to be processed and depurified by these scrubbed-clean Dutch who would dirty their palms on whatever stuff might pass through their hands, taking more than the angel's share. In truth, we have entered a grander scale of things. We are on the world map now, in a bigger league.

And if Surfman is telling the truth, if what he believes to be the truth is fact, what the boys don't know is that we are within a few miles of the home of Burg. We are driving past the signs for the chain ferry that will bridge us to him and his haven, which is between here and home. Where, not many hundreds of years ago, we would all have been swimming with the fishes.

'How far to Schev, Jimmy?' says Jessie.

'Are we nearly there?' says Roy.

Schev: Scheveningen, is, as the boys say, the bollocks. It is the last place that anyone might search for people charged with such objectives as ours. Unless they know where to look.

We have taken a wide and hire-car berth around Den Haag, with the sea on our left and a constant backward glance in the mirror. Even in the absence of evidence I feel as though eyes are upon us, from near and far. I look in the mirror and the image of a distant car clots with the unknown bringer of flowers.

The boys are pressing up against the windows

now, crouching, making a gawp mist on the glass as they sense that we are nearing the first of our destinations. I am the only one who sees the need to look backwards in order to safely direct us to what lies ahead, registering, as I do, the closer attentions of a gun-metal grey Audi that has been sucking on our fumes ever since we swung off the motorway. We are within a mile of the familiar stead which will be our home; space on a beach that we have shared before and which is also a place where Angela and I have holidayed alone. But before we decamp, I take what I hope will prove to be superfluous, paranoid precaution. I . . .

'What the . . .'

'Fuckin'ell . . .'

'Jimmy! What . . .'

The street turns inside out in a shopfront blur. Hotels swap entrances and the sea crosses over to the other side of prom. I disengage the handbrake and we sit in the burned rubber of our own tyres for the nanomoment of stillness which comes before the throttle-clutch pump of pistons that take us first-second-third up to sixty in six, maybe seven seconds, and gunning us at the beach house with heads turning, the gun-metal grey of a dot getting smaller.

We stop at the end of fast, furious and many-chicaned, broken red progress into the backstreets between the promenade and the Den Haag road. We are in the spotless hinterland of window-box suburbs, and I have explained to Wingnut and

160

Jessie, Roy and Surfman what, precisely, the fuck has been going on. We are tootling now, as good as gold, like a Darby and harem of Joans, towards the perfect civility of the welcome which we know full well Mrs Van der Land will extend to us as we turn onto the barely perceptible track in the sand that leads down to the Van der Lands' house by the sea.

It is midday and I said we would be there at eleven. But sure enough, there she is, headscarf in the breeze and her tabard perfectly starched; a gleaming smile spilling on the downtrodden features of her face, which is lined with hints of lovely youth. Our millionaire hostess could loose-change us to salvation, but she takes our money, counts out the notes one . . . by . . . one, before handing me a receipt and the keys. She makes us sign an inventory and she shows us inside, takes an imprint of my credit card – the damage deposit, she tells us with a sad face. These are the undisclosed terms upon which Mr Van der Land allows her to eke contact and worth from her life. Measurable in guilders, Euros, no doubt.

And as she shakes us by the hand, each in turn, she asks me, 'And how is Angela?' I reply with a nod and a smile that make her happy face uncrease. She can see the lies that lurk in the recess of the way in which I reply.

On the stilted deck, with a midshade horizon underlining the common, big blue astrodomed sky these shores share with ours, I am equidistant from the giant dams of Amster and Rotter, twin poles that mark the extremities of the circular path back to Flint. Angela and I have stood here on this ocean front; we have exchanged all manner of love and promises and woken to the sound of surf; taking our coffee and fresh juice on this deck, feeling the snowmelt of clearing heads, seeing the sunlit uplands of our shared future.

But now, and importantly for our immediate purpose, this is also an isolated place which the uninvited would consider twice before visiting, where they would be easily seen. In the all-or-nothingness of what we are gambling in pursuit of perfection, it is, *au contraire*, a place where help is far from at hand.

I hear Jessie, through the open French windows, see his good mood spread like a picnic cloth in a sudden, almost chemical unravelment. He is as excited as a new bride nesting.

'It's great, Jimmy. I'd forgotten these views. It's perfect!' Which worries me, because what I hear is someone whose consciousness has suffered a dislocation from the reality of why we are really here. And it seems appropriate, though it gives me no pleasure, to tether him to a reunderstanding of the glaring mortality of our coil. I instruct him to bind and gag Surfman, who has just suffered a non-mechanical breakdown along telephone lines as he tried and failed to convince a wife of the goodness of his motives.

BRITS ABROAD

We have walked along the beach – trousers rolled to our knees and splashing in the shallow children depths; Victoriana – and are now approaching the prom, where bars and hotels have replaced dunes.

I motion to Wingnut, who advises Roy and Jessie of the score.

'We'll have a few beers, then back to the house, chill out, maybe go see a film or something.'

'What about the casino?' says Jessie.

'No. Tomorrow we're going to Amsterdam to check out this Stapp character.'

'Can we go to the coffee shops?' says Roy.

'Maybe. But this is serious.'

Which is enough for them all to whiff the reality of our situation. This is why staying in Scheveningen is perfect, because a slow falling dread is descending like a colour wash through all of their faces, and even though Amsterdam is our main source of business, I have to walk us along a bloodrush tightrope. We could not possibly spend too long in the emporium of all pleasures, softlanding in its drugnets, cushioning us from harsh realities.

'Beers?' says Roy, nodding up the beach to the first of many splendid dozens of bars on the sandside of prom.

'Just a couple.'

Roy tramps away from the sea, not bothering to unfurl his cloth and practising a pimproll, which goes wrong because he is bogged down by the infinity minus one of shifting grains beneath him.

We can blend with other Brits here, force a fit with an almost common annexe culture of casino, beaches, clubs, bars, golden sand and plenty guilders for your lsd. And even though Schev is our kind of place, that doesn't prevent it from being an ace resort, more Côte than Skeg, with its beach-bars and sand-decked parasol tables. The pier is way off to our left with its hi-tech steel coil, a million miles from Brid or Yarmouth. Tonight there will be reggae and funk blasting out to sea. Beautiful people will lounge on cane, huddling bare-chested round the fires that roar flaming from the middle of low-slung tables you sit round on cushions. They will drift in from the casino, chill before they go back across the prom to discoland.

Not that it has always been like this. When we first started coming . . .

'Hey, Jimmy. Can I have a couple a quid? Please,' says Jessie.

'What for?'

164

He hides behind a barrier of schoolboy coyness, behind a secret he doesn't want to tell, and I peel off a ten guilder.

'Ten? Cheers, Jimmy.'

He doesn't realize what he has been given, hasn't a clue. It looks bigger than it is.

... When we first started coming here the place was like our own eastern resorts. A little less wind and not so many turds on the beach, no smell of fried batter hanging in the heatwave air. But it was tacky. Kitsch, they would call it now. 'Kitsch' – a word reserved for people who are describing something from safe Club Med immunity. But don't get me started on that.

Since then, evolutionary processes have been at work, and while we have been dumbing ourselves down into Murdoch-land, with rolled-up *Suns* in our chipbarm arsecheek pockets, these Dutch have Darwined themselves up so that now they can look west to SkyLottery Britain and piss themselves through the electric fall of their German car'd, Victorian-familied back-to-bourgeois . . .

'Jimmy. Look! Look, Jimmy. Got change, too.'

'*Jesus, Jessie.*'

But I can't resist the outbreak of a big beaming *I love you boys* smile.

'Come and have a kickabout, Jimmy. Come on. Come on, Wingnut. Where's Roy? Three an' in, eh?'

Jessie is ripping the plastic netting from the ball

like Christmas morning. He pays it a gameshow-car homage, then boots it with all his might towards the sea, but the wind takes it and blows it back over all our heads onto the roof of the bar. It is only a toy ball, too light for a proper game. But they don't care. Roy is coming back with the drinks, putting them down on the table with a waitress scowling behind him, talking to the owner, saying something like, 'The English. No manners.' But Roy's concentration is spanning five, ten seconds in the other direction now, saying, 'Fuckin'-ell lads. Come on, Jimmy, three an' in, eh?'

What can you do?

Jessie used to work in France during our early winters together, when our work was seasonal. He fitted carpets in three-star hotels and, returning from one visit, he helped me fathom how England has been left so far behind in whatever race it is which we have been slowly losing.

'I tell you, Jimmy. We're the Pakkies of Europe,' Jessie had said, cracking me up, not knowing about correctness, political; hierarchy, economic.

We are having our idea of a good time and doing no harm, playing footie in our suits and spilling beer. But with Euro families and well-groomed locals watching us from behind their coffee cups, you can see the stark contrasted truth in the gist, if not the words, of what Jessie had said.

And you might wonder, as I do, looking around at these natives, that there could be no way we are among invisible tyrants who make their money

166

by distilling badness for blended export, who would use their fiscal-chain advantage to further worsen our conditions. And if life wasn't already bad enough, we are here to extend Flint's arms across the ocean, for purposes never agenda'd in Westminster or Brussels.

You might think, Jesus, where are we going to find people like *that* in a place like *this*?

Roy lashes the ball as hard as he can into the wind; it buffets on a breeze that takes it onto the roof of the bar again, but over the other side this time. As he disappears in chase around one side of the bar, the ball makes a reappearance on a flat trajectory. It sticks into the sand without bouncing, deflated and dead with the six-inch blade of a wooden-handled knife skewering the broken plastic to the sand. Through the blue coloured air of the lament of good fun ending, I am sure that I can see the diminishing dot of an Audi, gun-metalled grey.

THE SHAPE OF THINGS TO COME

The train is pulling us through bulb-field pennants of viburnum and tulpen, all pistachio and acid pink, hues in between and either side. Jessie is moaning, turning the morning mist a hue of blue in respect of a bag he accuses Roy of hiding.

'What's in it that's so important?' says Roy, innocent but enjoying every inch of Jessie's spreading sulk.

'Nothing,' says Jessie, lying. 'Never mind.'

We leave morning and the colour of corn behind us, break into the midrise promise of the capital, with its greyskin usher of fumes and life. Somebody, somewhere is slowly turning something on.

Pulling into Amsterdam on the train as if we are schooltripping, we might have been granted spending money and an hour on our own, but with questions to answer when we return for examination. And even though we are not far from home, separated as we are from our small-turf Blighty by less than twenty miles of reclaimed land and then sea, you cannot help feeling that we are suddenly further away than that.

Yank voices are grating in the sound and vision of South American poncho'd pipers and yellow-haired Scandies, all lounging on the steps of the station with maps and guide books, bread rolls and sweating cheese, slices of pizza that flop. The sun is on their frontiersman backs. They sit in wait for real life to start, these comrade travellers, nestling between commuters and the long-term hedons who never made it back from Woodstock. There is a smell of weed in the air. It puts a spring in our steps, this confirmation that we have indeed travelled further than we could measure in miles.

Surfman is our rucksack, packed heavy and high for long travel, dragging us down. I am in possession of the co-ordinates of his adopted cabin in Harlingen, on the other side of the Waddenzee, where he has sent his wife and child to the safe arms of his cousin Arnold. We obtained the number from redial when he called home to arrest any inclinations a wife might have to further burden us with police presences. I wanted to instruct Wingnut to assure Surfman's wife, Monique, that I would do everything I could to safeguard her child from becoming half-parented. But I resisted; I schooled myself to do what I knew was in all our interests. I censored myself.

When he had finished, I told Surfman as earnestly as I could that when our tasks are accomplished, he can go back; that if all proceeds well then he will receive fair share. But if, through fault of his, matters do not progress satisfactorily, or if he tries to make any kind of escape, then we will go to cousin Arnold's place, we will track down his wife and . . . well, we secured his company with that.

Between you and me, the prospect of innocent victims appals me. It's the football-violence argument that posits there can be no harm if all parties are up for it. The Krays had a point. What we cannot countenance is children wearing replica shirts and harbouring dreams of one day holding silver aloft teeming crimson in a blade shower.

We have walked down Damrak, into and out of the hippie sprawl of Dam Square, and are now on Spui *en route* to the Leidsestraat, with the trams brushing our sleeves and cyclists making like high corn that sways round javelin wind. It is a working day in the city, if you can disregard all the thousand spaced-out smiles at twenty past midday.

KasbahKoffee is in a side street off the Leidseplein. We make our entrance past the shuttered Byzantium of a goody kiosk on the left, past the expert thin-cone rolling of weed by a seven-foot crackhead at the end of the bar. The Dead are piping out music to loll to, and there are six or seven groups of threes or fours sat on the floor around tables in the back room. We annexe a small corner of their Californian Europe and I give Wingnut fifty guilders, tell him, '*Stick to the weed. No Temple Balls. Take it gentle. I'm going to take a look at Stapp's place.*'

'*You want me to come?*' he signs.

170

'Right,' says Roy, 'I'm having a Temple Ball. Go on Wingnut, you got the money.'

'*No, I think you'd better stay here,*' I signal to Wingnut.

'No Temple Balls,' says Wingnut. 'We're not here to get bombed. And stick to coffee, no booze.'

I leave, safe in the knowledge that Wingnut is thriving on his responsibility, winding up Roy with what he can and can't have and savouring every guilder of the power that comes with being banker. I walk out of the psychedelic weave of music and hedoncense, and as I re-embark upon the light of day, I double-take the angel vision of a girl coming in from the street. She smiles as if her pale, pale eyes recognize me, but I don't look back; I choose instead to focus on the manifold of my task.

I am searching out Stapp, the middle man who stands between us and Burg. Burg, that real mover, the shaker who in turn stands between Flint and the richer endowments of a broader church. Stapp could look down on me now from on high, overseeing the Herengracht canal we passed earlier, when Surfman's head twitched left as we went over the bridge. If you've never been here, then rest assured that Herengracht is the finest fulfilment of your best imagining of what Amsterdam might be like. Tall and thin, seamless, terraced, stucco gable houses lining the curl of canal. Hubbub bridges, chatting cafés and, somewhere in the ether, the sound of *fin de siècle* sitars, out of place and in perfect keeping. On days like this, with the sun on your back, you actually want to stop people and say, 'Fuck, man! Isn't this just the coolest. Let's go smoke, get to know each other. Waste the day.'

Herengracht has always been a good address for the city's merchants. This is where Peter the Great was the first to gentrify what was always pretty smart anyway, where four hundred years ago they dug the canals to turn bogs into upmarket housing, where the locks held captive Amsterdam's turds at high tide and sluiced them away when the moontug was right.

I sit outside with my coffee and a ready-rolled, not really knowing what it is I am looking for, hoping that something will announce itself with unmissable fangs.

I sit and I sit and watch nothing happen; nothing out of the relative ordinariness of the mental whizz of heirloom bikes on spaghetti routes. Some pulling dogs, some laden with shopping, some old-ladied and some microskirted and showing it all; and all of them circling on the cusp of control. I draw on the joint, and time speeds by – re . . . al . . . slow.

I have had a kind of fill and, despite all my disinclinations, am reconciled to returning to Kasbah with nothing more than the benefits of a fourth-D feel for the place and its impenetrabilities. Until, over the bridge, four ordinary-looking men approach, dark-suited for usury. They somehow announce themselves to me from out of the crowd, looking left and right, ominous and too much in the synch of a common, grave purpose. One of them knocks on Stapp's door – once, then a pause; twice, then a pause; three times, then . . . then the door opens and the suits step to one side. A youth with a sports bag comes from nowhere, from beyond the field of my focus, wearing a shell suit – Adidas. He goes inside, leaving the suits outside, milling around and looking at their shoes in casual sentry.

For five . . .

Ten . . .

Fifteen minutes until the youth comes out, taps his breast and the four of them file away. One in front, one on each flank, one behind.

I have the shell suit ultrafocused in my sights. I can see the nerve-twitch of his jowl as he stops at the corner of the street, nodding towards, but not at, me – at the café two doors down from here. I can see his lips move in word shapes that only someone of my particular specification would or could remember, the way you might recall the sound of something somebody said to you. Nothing remarkable. I commit the shape and movement of his message to canvas in crisp, clean shapes. I finish my spliff, throw it into the canal and make my way back to the Kasbah, mouthing the shapes I have seen until I could do it in my sleep, as if I were a schoolboy with a stanza from Shakespeare, the type of lesson I was never taught.

HIGH. MIGHTY?

KasbahKoffee has filled and people are now sitting along the bar, taking something to give them an appetite for late breakfast, as if a door is creaking slowly ajar, glinting first shafts of dawn light in crackland.

The boys are sitting at a carved table, with an empty plastic sachet on the Arabian latticework and skins everywhere. Surfman's mood has been operated upon. He is pissing his sides as he tries and fails to roll a joint. Roy has an arm around him, jibbering mumbo-jumbo into his ear and, get ready for this, looking as though they are two compatible halves of a single best buddy.

'*What is this stuff?*' I ask Wingnut.

'*Soo . . . Po . . .*'

'*What?*'

Wingnut is slurring his signals. He giggles, looks at me glazy-eyed and points at the menu. 'Super Polm, Maroc. 1.0g per 25 guilders.'

'*How much did you buy?*' I ask.

He puts up two fingers in a victory sign. A 'peace mahn' shape.

'*Jesus. Where's the rest?*'

174

Wingnut starts laughing, shaking his head.

'Can we have some broodies, Jimmy,' says Roy.

'Yeah, Jimmy. Can we have some broodies,' says Jessie, not even looking at me and slowly measuring his words with a weak smile in the direction of the next table and its young Latina swarth.

'*Broodjes?*' says Surfman, the Dutch way, the proper way. 'B-road-yuys.'

What can I do? I have to feed them, straighten them with sustenance before they start to think the world is turning against them. I must maintain and modify mood, cocktail this herb skulduggery with food and caffeine and moral support, banish the bogey-man who will want to watch and follow us, inhibiting our every move, inhabiting each crevice of our demeanour.

'*Come on,*' I sign. '*Let's eat. Indonesian?*'

'What's he say?' Roy asks Wingnut.

'I don't know,' says Wingnut. 'I think he says YES!'

And, of course, they all piss their sides, to the amusement of the Latinas and every other spaced-out fuckwit in the place.

Wingnut, who cannot speak, is making spastic signing pleas for my attention and finally resorts to the universal rubbing together of his finger and thumb, a gesticulation at the bar.

'*I'll pay the bill and then we're off.*'

It's the funniest thing I've ever said.

'*I'll speak to you later, Wingnut.*' But he simply

smiles a beaming vacant smile which he might have caught off Roy.

I wait at the bar, willing myself down to their pace, the slowspeed of the place and its service, and – as I slowly put a knife into time, and feel its happy spasm – pale, pale eyes look at me from the far cusp of bar. I look away, count notes from hand to hand.

'Hi,' I hear.

She is smartly dressed and perfectly groomed. Mid-twenties is my guess, and affluent, respectable. She taps out her pipe on the bar, puts the resin back in its pewter tin and looks up at me, makes a connection that is strangely familiar.

'Your friends?' she says.

I look back for Wingnut to come over, but he is lying on the table, chanting a mantra which is chorused by the Latinas.

'They're funny. I am Elvira.' Ridiculous as it seems, given that we have only just met, she shoots a sidelong look that makes me hot and cold. 'I have to go,' she says, leaving twenty guilders on the bar.

I reach out, tap her on the shoulder.

'Don't go. Wait, please.' I message with a napkin scribble. 'I am mute.'

'*Aah*,' she gestures. '*I'm sorry*,' and she leans into me, looking at the paper as I scrawl.

'Can you tell me what this says, in English,' I write, indicating my mouthshape replications. She watches as I redraw the Dutch shape of recent message.

'See . . . you . . . back . . . here . . . at . . . six,' she says, her smile broadening as the lip translation unravels its ambiguity that is clear to me.

I have a plan.

She is saying yes, reaching up on tiptoes and kissing my cheek, leaving vapour wisps of hash. '*See you at six*,' says Elvira, with a tilt of her head, a luscious downlidding of her pale, pale eyes. She has spoken to me in my own silent language, but with lashes and lips and a glistening tongue that would make you sick to the back of your very back teeth because you are most definitely going to be somewhere not here at six, and shortly after six you'll be leaving town with no intention of ever coming back.

She goes on her way, stumbling slo-mo towards the door like a small boat on high seas, taking a whole minute to cover ten yards, negotiating her way through a crowd of three people and finally making it to the wild outside, out of the purple haze and the mystical sound, into the sun. She climbs clumsily onto her bike, sitting up and begging, practically asking to be mown down in crazy traffic streets. But no. No! She's off, straightlined and safe, calculating zigzag paths between trams and cars and pedestrians and, worst of all, other narcocyclomaniacs making collective, like they're wrong-poled magnets, interacting tangleweed.

I HAVE A PLAN!

LET'S DO LUNCH. GO SHOPPING

Mountains of noodles and sweetsauce meats have been swallowed, doubtless unchewed in the ravenous overdose of banquet. The food helps to plane us down, land softly, and by four o'clock we are back on the streets. The boys are receptive to the setting out of the components of the plan. Not the whole thing, you understand. To freak them out at this stage – disarmed as they are, unprotected against the harsher cutting edges of truth – would achieve nothing. No, first the practicalities of our preparation.

'Shopping?' says Roy. 'For clothes? Ace.'

'Jimmy's choosing,' says Wingnut, sucking wind from Roy's sails.

We are in the market for the dark suits of bankers – four, for Roy, Jessie, Surfman and Wingnut. I have prescribed the colour and cut of what is available to them, and then we will go for the trimmings, in a hair parlour off Spui, to cut and paste until we perfectly match the four suited men who will be expected at Stapp's place come six o'clock. Except we will be early.

In the meantime, I leave the boys to try suits for

size, go back onto Leidsestraat to shop for a suit of my own, variety shell, label Adidas.

So when the combination unlocks the door, there will be five of us going in, storming the place and hoping that we can overcome whatever and whoever is inside.

Even though it is summer I feel a chill in my naked nape, skinned as it is. Roy and Surfman are in my mirror sights, with the soft brush doing the rounds of my neck and a mirror reflecting the back of my new shape in the image of another mirror. I nod and the barber slaps lotion on my neck, making smells from a distant decade I can faintly remember.

As Surfman takes my place in the barber's chair, Wingnut enters, double-taking me, then saying, 'It suits you, Jimmy. You look good with short—' until he stops himself dead in his soundtracks in realization of this being neither the place nor the lifetime and certainly not the kind of company in which to say such a thing, with Roy coming into earshot and Jessie already looking as if he has misheard something.

'We've got an hour,' Wingnut says on my behalf. 'Once you've had your heads done we'll get a coffee and run through the plan.'

'*Wingnut, you get the knives?*'

'*Yes, Jimmy.*' If he had been speaking to me his voice would have fear waves breaking it down. As it is, I can see it in his eyes.

★   ★   ★

179

In the coffee shop, enjoying the essences of beans and nothing more, I run through the plan once again, underlining the upper-case constraint of time, the thin slice of clock within which we must gain entry and overpower, exercise upper hand and leave – with Burg's whereabouts – between the hours of six minus twenty and six minus two. They nod, silent. They digest, swallowing big lumps and doubtlessly feeling the same flutter as I do, in my heart and in my belly, in the fast arhythms of my lungs.

I look around at them and, one by one, they reflect back at me the seriousness of our situation. We are now, in the midst of Wingnut's second recapping, deep in the sanctum of doubt, where all you can do is come up with reasons not to go ahead, good reasons to be elsewhere.

Wingnut slow traipses to the washroom. His feet are heavy and his pockets jangle with the touching of steel on steel. He holds court in a locked and tiny chamber, receiving visitors one at a time, and like a bad Santa in a grotto from hell, he gives out presents to the boys – serving suggestioned and best before six.

At twenty-two minutes to the hour we leave the coffee shop. Stapp's house looms big and daunting as we walk along the canal towards the bridge. My stomach is on the move. I want to be sick and I look around at the boys, see they are ghostly white. Roy's clean-cut and newly handsomed face has unsmiled for the first time I can remember;

180

Jessie's hands are on a rummage search through his pockets, twitching up and down to his chest, to the subtle lump of his not-so-subtle blade. Sweat is beading from his head and temples, like corn popping in a slo-mo microwave: 16 rpm.

The house grows in my vision, and with the sky moving too quickly in a trick-of-the-light apparition, it gives off the optical delusion of collapse. The cobbles underfoot have gone soft. My tread is slow, deliberate, feet taking too long to reach out and feel the floor beneath them. The empty sportsbag begins to weigh me down. I feel lost, debilitated; don't know where I am how I got here. I am cold, bloodless inside, can see a large and perfectly painted black door with a single brass knocker, the sounding of which will surely summon some alien gatekeeper to unpearl our futures.

HOUSE ARREST

My hand reaches out in an act of unmeditated lunacy. It raps the knocker, makes a distant noise. As one, we exhale, steeped in the sweet rancid fumes of adrenalin. I rap the door twice, then thrice. We take a unison step back, hands fluttering through cloth onto blades as we wait for morse to decode. The door rattles, then creaks. We flex, hands feeling for weaponry in the jackets of our suits of shell and dark, sombre grey.

A wrinkled old face squints from the jar in the door like something in the page-flip of scary bedtime adventure. The woman's face adjusts to bright, slanting daylight and as I feel the bone handle of knife against my hip, I issue a gushing, manic smile.

'*Ya?*' she says. I make a soundless shape, and Wingnut says something in Dutch, leading us in, but with Jessie standing tall and smart and handsome; Fifties noir, but cardboard cut-out and rooted to the step. I beckon him inside, but he stands rigid until Roy mind-reads me, steps back out, puts his hand into Jessie's pit and jerks him

182

into a slow step. The woman scans us, looking now beyond the thinskin suit surfaces of us and speaking a Netherland passage that has 'Stapp' leaping from it. 'Stapp,' a sound that sticks its head above a parapet.

Wingnut replies in like language and the old woman shrugs and continues onward up the stairs. Wingnut nods for me to follow her, taps his jacket where the blade is. As we walk up the stairs, I file past him and he sings to me. *'He's in there; she's taking us to him. Oh fuck. Fuck.'*

'Tell the others to follow my lead. Do whatever I do.'

The stairs swoop up to a large landing with many doors. The old woman gestures to the nearest door and speaks to Surfman, who replies in the same instant as I put my hand over her mouth, in the same instant as the spring of Roy's blade announces itself with an expert ring, close-cutting and perfect measured onto the skin of the Dutchman's throat, as effective as if it had scalpeled his vocal cords.

The woman's face is cold and hard-skinned, with bones that feel as though they would break if I recalibrated my grip, so with my other hand I show her my blade; I take my hand from her mouth and raise a single finger to my lips. I can smell her musty stains on my finger. She makes no sound, simply points downstairs to the front door and makes a prayer shape with her hands. But I have to deny her. I signal Wingnut to hold her, not hurt her – as if he would or could anyway. He takes her by the arm and says something in a tremor voice that seems to soothe.

With my blade at the ready I mouth the 3–2–1 of countdown, turn the handle and stride quickly through the doorway into a dark, dull silence.

The room is heavy-curtained, small, empty. Soft electric sounds come through another door and I motion the boys forward, with Roy trying to usher Jessie to life.

Jessie and Roy are on my shoulder as I storm out of the ante room and many steps closer to being posttraumatic. As we enter new space, a single stooping figure stands by a large desk in distracted scrutiny of scales – digital – and six, maybe eight, packages. Stapp looks up with a fastbreaking dawn of ruined expectations. I look round for Wingnut to message me, but as I wave my blade it's knocked from my hand. I spin round, looking for an assailant, but see only the blur coat tails of Jessie launching himself at Stapp, knocking him to the floor and, in a flash, Jessie is on his feet again, stamping down as if he's trying to kill fire. The metal sound of a gun falling to the floor comes through the lapwash of groans, and Jessie picks up the weapon and says, 'I fucking hate guns. Fucking hate them, man.' He has an inexpert hold on the firearm, a fresh expression on his face, as if something powerful has taken effect. He examines his insuperable wield, starts playing with the trigger as if it were harmless.

'No!' shouts Stapp, gesturing to the cellophaned powders on the desk. 'Take it. Go on, take it!'

'Stay on the floor and shut the fuck up,' shouts Roy, stepping forward and taking the gun off Jessie, replenishing his smile as he does it, giddy on the real thing is my guess. 'Jesus, Jimmy. What do we do now? This is fucking gear, man.'

Jessie and Roy start laughing and Wingnut, too, gives vent to the manic relief of chuckles.

'We've fucking done it. This is more than we lost.'

'We have. We've fucking done it.'

'No!' shouts Wingnut, talking incredulous to the shapes of my whipping hands. 'No? No, we haven't done it. We have to find Burg.'

'Burg?' says Stapp from the floor. His voice has found another pitch, high and cracking. The sound of a name has made his heart more faint than my blade or *Jessie's stamping or Roy* with a gun could.

'Where is he?' says Wingnut.

'I don't know. Nobody knows. He moves all the time,' says Stapp.

Surfman sounds up from the background, wailing otherlandish apologies and pleading innocence, is my guess.

'*Shut up! Shut the fuck up the lot of you*,' I message with a brandish of my blade. I check the seventeen forty-eight of the spreading hands on the face of my watch, stretching hands that reach towards the vertical of six – a witching hour if ever there was. '*We've got ten minutes to find out where Burg is*.'

'He won't tell you,' says Surfman to Wingnut.

'He fucking will,' says Roy, walking to Stapp, putting a shiny new brogue on his throat, pressing down with all his weight and placing the barrel of a gun into the eye of an already frightened man, making metal accompaniment with a hammer cocking. But it is clear from the meeting-with-maker calm closure of his eyes that Stapp either doesn't know, or is choosing the prospect of this kind of death in favour of another. He shakes his head in a tiny spasm arc and splutters, 'I don't know.'

Which makes me think, *Fuck* and Surfman starts talking, double-quick in pleading speak to Stapp, so I whip into him, strike him down. '*You're on our side now. You made your decision.*' I step forward, formulate a gesture designed to hint that I am about to give Stapp an address: Waddenzee, c/o cousin Arnold.

'Please let me explain to him, tell him I have to do this . . . for my child, my wife,' says Surfman.

He could double-cross us, advise Stapp as to who we are and where we are from. But I think about what Burg might do, not to Surfman, but to his wife and child, innocent victims. So I motion to Wingnut, who explains in English to Stapp about the hold we have over Surfman. And we all suffer something when Stapp's face fails to register any decline in the contempt he is delivering to Surfman, even though he has no means of knowing that in all probability, in a lifetime of Sundays, we would never visit harm on a mother and son.

'You are a dead man and I fear for your family,' says Stapp to Surfman. He scans across us, dwelling one, by, one. 'I fear for you all.'

I cannot think clearly. All my judgements are clouded by the relative calm of a situation I had expected to be adrenalin driven. My anticipation was that we would have been fighting for our lives by now.

I message Wingnut, who addresses Stapp. 'We have to find Burg.' As he speaks, I unzip my Adidas jacket, take the fearsome blade in my not-so-steady hand and hitch up my sleeves one, by, one.

'I don't know,' says Stapp, in truth's rising pitch; an apple falling in his throat, fear being swallowed, indigestible. I place the blade between my teeth and go down onto my knees, unzip him. I look up into his eyes and try to read him. With one hand on the knife and the other on his failing, chrysalis cock, I exchange a deep look, extract his best gasp. 'He's always on the move.' I can feel him stir. 'He's gone south.'

'Where?' says Wingnut.

'I don't know.'

I brace myself and take a firmer grip, yank at his dick and put the blade against his balls. I can hear a collective flinch. I look down, check my bearings, take in a sight of what could be fowl Christmas carnage, then back into his eyes. I swallow and brace myself to do what is necessary. I will do it.

He sees that in me.

'No!' he screams. 'I'll tell you! I'll tell you what I know. Please!'

'Where is he?'

'Down across the chain ferry, near Rosenburg. That's all I know. I was blindfolded when they took me. They met me off the chain ferry. It was ten, fifteen minutes. He's got a place near the sea. I could smell the sea. There were dunes. That's all I know.'

I know.

I press the blade up against his balls one last time, one final reminder, and I let his cock slip out of my hand, uncut.

'*It's ten to six, Jimmy.*'

'*Ask him how we get into the roof. We've got to silence him.*'

We have bound Stapp and tied him tight to the joists in the loft. Roy has stuffed dusters in his mouth and sealed his silence with the knot of his tie.

'We'll call the tourist board in two, maybe three days and tell them you're here, if we have found Burg,' says Wingnut. 'If we can't find him, we don't make the call.' Stapp's eyes bulge, as if he is reconsidering something, so I unseal his silence.

'You must beat me. Please,' he pleads. 'In case he finds me. On my face, so it will last. Please.'

I nod to Roy, who looks around, picks up an onyx ashtray from an open box and wraps it carefully in one of the rags with no kind of relish. He looks away as he does his duty, not wanting to see the finery of his wielding, joyless charity.

OLD FOLKS' PARTY

The echo slam of the large front door still resounds as we walk away, steady and as suppressant of joy as we are able, over the bridge and far away to sunlit uplands. Bubbles of relief pop in my legs, chest and throat. Not only have we narrowed down the track that will lead us to Burg, but we have also made some amends with Flint and bagged booty to replace that which went up in flames.

This progress of a kind, and the fact that we have lived to tell the tale, makes me want to dance a jig, fizz myself until I am normal once more. There is a collective spring to our darksuit reservoir puppy-dog step. I want to scream past the rooftops that we are safe, still together and with one less cliff face to scale.

But I go flat, squashed by a re-cur echo of front doors slamming on a house that might seem empty. A house with a human silenced in its eaves; a house which on full reflection might not necessarily be a silent house, not as still as we might think it would be, creaking as it might under the veteran footfall of a forgotten frail-bone keeper who slipped through our fingers and out of our thoughts.

I grab Wingnut, represent bad image in nervous and messy tremble flutters. '*The woman. The old woman. We should have brought her with us.*'

'Christ! She'll get to Stapp. What do we do?' says Wingnut.

'Who will?' says Jessie.

'The old woman.'

'She'll set him free. Fucking Stapp!' says Roy.

'You were supposed to take her,' says Jessie.

'No, I fucking—'

I whip my arms at Wingnut. It is enough to shut them up, but it doesn't dispel the blame, which lies at my feet. I brought them here, across a bridge too far.

'She'll set Stapp free,' says Surfman, his voice cracking.

'*We've got to get her.*'

'We can't go back, Jimmy. It's nearly six,' says Wingnut. 'The others will arrive any minute. We've got to get that train and get out of here. Shit, Jimmy, we've got the bloody stuff, man.'

But his protestations fall on deaf and distracted ears. I know what must be done, am compelled to act by the plight of a relative stranger in my sights.

In the shoulder-slump and lip-sag of his desperate realizations, Surfman is the first by many miles to accurately measure the gravity of the situation. 'Stapp. He will get to my family,' he says.

'I'll go and get her,' says Roy, pulling the knife from his pocket.

'No!' shout three able-voiced as one.

'Someone has to go,' blubbers Surfman, extending a hand towards Roy in request of his blade, with which, in a simple and minimal malicious gesture of intent, he becomes one of us. Our interests being a perfect match for each other.

'*No. I'll go.*' I hand the sports-bag swag to Wingnut and tap out instructions for a rendezvous back at the beach house once I have done what is required to silence a harmless old lady. I tell them to be meticulous in their coverage of all possible tracks that lead them from here to the coast, I tell them to travel in two separate pairs by taxis to Haarlem, then onward by train to our temporary home.

I check around me for suits, and play codes in my head as I tap sharp steel through my shell suit. I prepare responses to the opening of a door by an old lady who has never in her life done me harm.

I tap the door . . .

Once.

Twice.

Thrice.

Nothing.

. . . make a left-right check along the street and take a step back to give the house a once up, once down, confirming to myself that there isn't so much as a prayer of gaining unassisted entry. Time ticks and I knock again . . .

Once.
Twice.
Thrice.

. . . and a creak. Which is enough. A glint of light in the opening dark. I kick out and the door swings away, knocking a frightened and aged keeper backwards, tottering against a wall, trying . . . failing to steady herself, and falling undainty to a wooden floor that would surely snap her bones. She warps in my sights, goes hall-of-mirrors as I dive into the doorway and throw myself on the floor to cushion her from the effects of my blow.

I can feel her, light as meringue on top of me. Her tremble thin lips and cloud yellow eyes have fallen big in my face.

'I am sorry,' I try to say.

She wails like Islam grief. The plates of her teeth fall against her tongue and her wail bubbles and bursts, spilling into the street. With the floor parquet on my back, I silence her sounds from the street with a kick of the door.

We lie on the floor, companions in horrific accident, and I search for alternative methods for the effective silencing of information she carries.

There is a knock at the door.

I put my hand on her mouth, feel her sounds go wet in the quantum condensation of a world occupied by lunatic elements.

Two.
Three.
Nothing. Then a shadow at the window. The

sequence repeats itself as we lie rigid, in desperate posture, and joined, no doubt, in quite different prayer. The door percusses three identical bars. A long, long rest.

The shadows disappear from the window, so I stand, put the blade between my teeth, as if in preparation for deep water, and haul her to her feet, straighten her cardigan. As we slowly climb the stairs I hear a rattle at a door. It comes from the back of the house, so I show her the blade. As we continue our climb, glass breaks. Voices come into the house.

In the eave heights of the house, Stapp's blood-crusting face is a picture when he sees me for the second time. It seems to age him – Dorian Gray. The old woman sits upon my knee as we listen to sounds of enemy passage through the house. You might think, looking at the console cradle of the way I am supporting her, that Time's arrow has shot itself in the foot during storytime.

The footfall through the house grows loud, gives way to the deep rumble of men's angry mumbles, which then fade back down through the house away from us. A door slams shut and the house goes dead quiet, beyond the muffled curse of Stapp's disappointment. I look at the old woman and plumb the depths of my imagination for humane mechanisms to engineer her silence, can think of only one safe place to buy time, in the camouflage of company.

★   ★   ★

'I thought you weren't coming,' says Elvira, casting her pale, pale eyes over the small, frail frame of the old woman who is looking around Kasbah with my tight grip on the tiny bone of her arm.

'*I'm sorry.*'

'It's no problem. Who is this?'

I take a piece of paper from my pocket and write, 'My grandmother. She is mute, too.'

'Aah,' says Elvira, puffing on her tiny pot pipe.

I grip the old woman's wrist tight in my hand, watch her face turn sad as she plays out her part in a mime we had quickly rehearsed – once she understood the mad demonstrations of my script.

'Can you not sign to each other?' says Elvira.

'*She is Dutch,*' I mouth.

'Shall we sit down?' She leads us to a table in the corner of the back room, where the Latinas had been hours earlier, and without even considering the bat of an eye, she offers her pipe to an old lady who is wholly unfazed. My supposed mute grandmother of three score years plus ten and then some, draws heavily on the resin and leans back as if to say, 'That's better; this has been one bitch of a day.' As she settles into the golden fabrics of the sofa, slow smiling, luxuriating in what you might think could be a second unleash of life, spun on mile upon mile of yarns of relief, I begin to hatch plans for her safe and secret custody.

I exchanged phone numbers and a kiss goodbye with Elvira, then watched her disappear, long legs shining black in thin velvet webs, the tiny leather refuge of her skirt, her hair blowing and bobbing and fading into the crowd. Then I took a frail arm in mine, as if I proposed no infliction of damage, and led her towards Spui, where we checked into a hotel – three stars and comfortable; safe but unlikely to pamper; interference nil.

She is settled in front of the TV, which I have moved so that she can see it from her position on the toilet. I have wrapped her up warm in knotted sheets, a neatly folded flannel secured in her de-dentured mouth. Her teeth are in a glass on the bedside table, so you can see I have tried to make life as good as possible for her, until, that is, I spoil her rotten with the administration of the finalities of her diet: the three tabs of acid which will trip her, by my calculations, deep into the heart of the day after tomorrow, by which time we will be long gone. Whichever way.

I am going to the railway station, getting a ticket for my destination, but first I pay the hotel manager for three nights, writing her that my grandmother is resting, that she should not be disturbed and has everything she needs until I return the day after tomorrow to collect her. I add, for good measure and the avoidance of any confusion, that she is an eccentric woman, given to fantasy, and I secure the pretty girl's unwavering belief with two fifty-guilder notes.

SOUNDS OF SILENCE

I have no Wingnut to assist me in the plotting of my passage back to Scheveningen, but I am less handicapped by my solitary state than you may think. I can sit in a quiet carriage, free from the whirr of shape formations in my head. Thoughts toss and turn in soundshapes for all of us. It is how we articulate ourselves; it is the wheat into chaff of what we say from what we think. For me, I have the further white noises of wordshapes behind my eyes, like a constant magician forever casting spells. Without Wingnut and his means of making me heard, I can lean my head heavy against the window, watch the flatlands glide by in a perfect cadent dusk, have my memory jogged.

Between the miniature villages of dolls' houses and manicure gardens, perfect painted along light-bulbed Disney waterlines, I am visited by patterns from the past, the shapes of things that formed me – and one particular act that did more than most to deliver me here. On a day when I have failed to exercise unrestrained infliction of harm upon adversaries, my First Act of Vengeance will soon be fourteen years old.

The morning after my bloody encounter with Lisa's lover outside the back entrance to Fischers, in the embers of the week of my enduring changes, Angela was led crying from the dining room of Newholme. Mrs Pinder took her under a wing, like a mother hen, and Angela looked daggers at me through her blood-shot eyes for two types of betrayal. What I did not then see, but can vividly imagine, worse in all probability than the truth of the matter, was Angela being taken to a slab in a cold room, occupied by deadpan men in bloodstain coats, to identify the alabaster face of her dead twin.

After I had left Lisa to tend to the bloody humiliations of Steve, I discovered that he was a trainee salesman for the local Ford dealership, who found raising his fists to women as easy as his forecourt patter. I also found out that he had soiled all of her available innocences. But I got to him too late. Lisa nursed him back to a strength sufficient to enable him to exact the weakest and most cowardly of his own vengeances. He did not mean to kill her, it was an accident. The evidence was compiled and he was defended in rooms, and within rules exempt of all morals, by shiny-shoed men more concerned with due process than truth. It was deemed that he merely slaughtered another human, and because he mixed in seemingly proper but actually rancid circles, because he kept the company of men considered by the law to pose a greater threat to us all than himself, and in reward of his intent to conduct betrayals in the interest of the state, Lisa's lover and killer was released back into the community.

I could not chill my blood.

Equally, and oppositely, I could not kill a man.

I plotted an arrival at a halfway house, and with the remembered taste of his filthy fingers in my mouth, with the bright burning image of the cower shape he made Lisa make with the single lift of an arm, I dwelt on my vengeance; I honed redraft formations of a perfect meting of justice.

I waited all day and into the night outside his flat; waited in the rain for someone to leave the building, then snook in through the closing door, made my way up to the first-floor landing and sat cross-legged on the floor.

I waited for his footfall, for him to catch sight of me, someone who didn't belong. I waited to see fear in his pig eyes, wanting to hear him beg, 'no', wanting to smell the shit in his pants, wanting to feel his tongue come away in my fingers. I wasn't sure that I had the strength to go through with it. There were flaws in the design of my vengeance. The more considered the draughtsmanship of my reprisal, the less certain I grew as to whether I had the moral infortitude to bear it. I touched the blade in my pocket, unsure if I could exact the vivid plan of the surgical swipe of it.

By the time I heard the familiar purr of his car, saw his shape walk to the entrance and make footsteps up the stairs, I had no idea what I would actually do. He walked towards me, slowing when he recognized me, making a hard smile that went soft as soon as I volleyed its return. He started back towards the lift, going slowly at first, to save face. I suppose, in retrospect, that even someone like him could have pride, esteem for himself, that he might have regretted his actions and endured all kinds of torment. But retrospect has no place in the mad pounding of an instant, which is all it took for me to get the jump on him, to tackle him down, drag him to the top of the stairs and then hear his dull thudding tumble, watch him stagger dazed to his feet as I made my slow descent towards him, with no idea what I would do to him until I did it.

In the end, I did nothing more calculated than beat him to within an inch of his life. The way he intended for Lisa, but with an exactness to the violence of my science. They saved him from sharing Lisa's fate, saving also my skin, because when the time came for Silverpiece to make two plus two equal four, the stakes were not so high that a custodian of the law could not, in an exchange of favours, concoct for me an alibi of watertight and false conviction that freed me to perform my second vengeant act, on the supposed behalf of another teenage girl, but for the actual benefit of her policeman father.

DIVIDE AND UNRULE

As soon as I walk into the beach house it is intangibly clear that all is not well. Wingnut bids a silent welcome with an unconvincing glance from between the turn of pages he is reading, looking quickly away as if he has something to be wary of in the return of a friend. The room is otherwise empty – no Jessie or Roy or Surfman – and I feel like a homecoming soldier whose generation bled for a cause his nation no longer believes in.

A moaning noise comes from the bathroom, fleecing Wingnut of the thin-veil indifference he tries and fails to sustain. Sheepishly and with his head still in his book, he says, 'Jimmy, you get it sorted?' not even looking up for a reply.

I sit opposite him, under the window with the sea's white horses silent through the glass. Taking the book from his lap, I make myself heard.

'*Where is everyone?*'

'Jessie's in the bathroom.'

'*The others?*'

'He's got a bad stomach.'

'*Where are the others?*'

'Out.'

'*Out where?*'

'Things got complicated, Jimmy.' He is avoiding my look, listening to me out of the corner of his eye like a shy princess.

'*Where's Roy? Where's Surfman? Did Roy have a go at him?*'

'No, nothing like that. Roy's cool. Him and the Surfman, they're . . . they're mates, Jimmy.'

'*So they've gone out.*'

'They've not exactly gone out.'

'*Where are they?*'

'We let him call his wife. He was so worried about whether Stapp had got free when you didn't show up. So we let him make a call. And when he called her, the cousin Arnold answered. He said there had been some men outside the house. It's right in the woods, Jimmy. Surfman said no-one ever goes up there. It was the right thing to do; we couldn't let him go on his own.'

'*They've gone to Waddenzee!*'

'They've gone to get Monique and Rudi.'

'*Monique? Rudi? What is this? The fucking Waltons!*'

'We thought it was the best thing, the most humane thing.'

'*Humane?*'

'He's one of us now, Jimmy. How did it go with the old woman?'

'*All right; she's safe.*'

'Where?'

'*In Amsterdam. In a hotel.*'

202

'But she'll talk. Shit, Jimmy.'

'*She won't talk.*'

'How do you know?'

'*She's out of it.*'

'She's what?'

'*She's out of her tree. She's tripping.*'

'The old woman?' Wingnut is laughing. His sheepish face has transformed into something quite mad. He howls like a wolf and Jessie comes out of the bathroom. 'Oh fuck. Jimmy's a fucking genius, man.'

'*What's wrong, Jess?*' I ask.

He looks away, sweating, shaking, muttering to himself.

'*What's wrong with him?*'

'Tell him, Jess,' says Wingnut, his laugh dead in its own tracks.

Jessie sits down on the edge of one of the sofas, head in his lap, shaking slowly. Jessie, who I have known since I was eight years old, who is part of the furniture of almost all my life, talks into his lap and avoids our exchange of looks as he unfurls the rotten core of his bad secret. He tells me he is a heroin addict, that he has been a smackhead for two years, until a month ago, when he got himself programmed into methadone. He says it like a true addict: as if the crime is in his ceasing to be able to deceive me.

'Sorry, Jimmy. I'm so sorry. I just need my tablets. I'm off it; I'm clean, you see; I just need my tablets.'

'*Tablets? What the fuck . . .*'

'He lost them. They were in a bag and—'

'*You knew about this?*'

Wingnut shrugs, doesn't need to say any more – that they were scared how I'd react, that maybe they thought I had enough on my plate with Angela.

Jessie pads back into the bedroom and curls up like a new kitten on the bed, shaking as though he has been plugged into some powerful source and saying over, over and over again, 'Please God, please God . . .'

For two whole years I have been living with not one, but two junkies.

I strip Jessie down. It's easy, once you know what you're looking for, to see him for what he is, and easier still to blame yourself for not noticing earlier. His arms and legs are still strong, with muscles like soft cable, close to the surface of his ravaged skin. I can see now that signs had been there all along. His skin blots up the oils as soon as I apply them. I turn him onto his stomach and rub his shoulders, down his ribs and into the small of his back, the way I have done a hundred times for Angela, to refer pain elsewhere, to displace it in time. And without demand or invitation, Jessie tells me the whyfores of where he is. In the sweat lavender balm of aromas working their therapies, he treats me as if I might swing incense. He treats himself to frank confession, talks swift until his chalice runneth over with words, bleeding poison from an unholy body.

'It was too good, you know, Jimmy. Too good. I loved it so much, those days. We'd get up, all larking about, and I'd cook breakfast and we'd eat together and Roy would make us laugh, spiking the food and watching our mouths burn. We'd chase him round the garden, get him in a corner and he'd turn on us, come at us with a stick or something, and we'd run away from him. And we'd have the whole day, down the arcade or the club, just dossing, and I'd get Anne-Marie to nick off work. Long afternoons. All shy, she was. We'd just lie there, drinking, naked under the sheets. Fuck, Jimmy, it was just too good. Better than I deserved, you know, and sometimes I'd wake up with this perfect day just waiting for me, and I'd shit myself. I'd think, it's got to end. I had to do something. You understand? The days, they just stretched out, right out to the sea, past you and the boys and Anne-Marie. I had to fill it with something else, tone it down. Like a noise in your head.'

I know exactly what he means, can fully understand how drugs can be a relief for winners as well as losers.

Wingnut comes in and I say, '*What about the gear? We could give him some of that.*'

Wingnut nods, the way a father can convince in crisis, giving me faith to clutch at, even though he actually knows nothing about how to improve

205

the situation. 'I thought about that, but he's been coming off. A month, he reckons. It'd be better if we could get him his tablets. Trouble is, it's lily white here, cleaner than England once you get out of Amsterdam.'

'*How much cash have you got?*'

'Don't know. About six hundred. Sterling.'

'*I want you to make a call.*'

CALL GIRL FOR VICE

'Yes. Yes, of course. Of course I remember Jimmy Mack. The mute one. And Jessie, too, his friend from Kasbah. He is ill? Methadone? *How* much? Yes, of course I can help. You'll pay for a cab? Two hours, then. But it's late. Can you fix me somewhere to stay?' This, Wingnut confirms, is the negative of the telephone conversation I saw and heard and otherwise witnessed, between him and Elvira.

An angel of mercy is bringing bad delights for our ailing Jessie, holding it above her head, out of danger and beyond the reaches of the murky waters of Cambodian border that lap up on her fatigue-T-shirt breasts. Hands high, as if in surrender, but carrying medicine – Crimean heroine – to save a wounded soul from burning bushels.

And you can gauge the seriousness of Jessie's plight for yourself from the way he reacts to news of his saviour.

'Jessie,' says Wingnut. 'That girl in the Kasbah; the one in black, with the long legs. You remember? She's coming up, staying the night. Maybe we'll take her to the casino.'

207

'Fuck that,' says Jessie.

'She's getting your tablets.'

'When? When! What's keeping the bitch.'

Which is simply not Jessie. Not the one we thought we knew.

Wingnut and I watch absolutely nothing happen on the deepening blackness of sea from the maple deck of this lonely house. Between the flick and fold of the cards in our absent play, deep within the liquor pourings, the clink and swallows of our plantation-style drinking, dim music drifts from the heart of the resort, comes lazy along the sand.

Jessie joins us with a blanket wrapped around him, knees tucked up and saying nothing until . . . until the sounding of an engine is followed by the sweeping beam of a parking car. He uncurls himself from the sofa, wheezing good news of the arrival of modern myrrh. Elvira joins us on the deck, taking a glass that Wingnut offers her as I pay the cab driver.

She looks different, with her Euro-flax hair piled into a slapdash clutch of clip. I sit opposite her, measure her easy smile, high-heeled and leg-fleshed. She leans forward to pour a wordless toast. And from these very first instants she is at home in a strange place.

'This is a wonderful house,' she says, and we sit in silence, hearing the 'hmm' and 'aahh' of all tensions draining slowly from Jessie's body. We hear the slow sluicing aquatics of Wingnut's bathroom preparations for sleep, until all is quiet. I motion to the beach, lift a lighter and rub my shoulders, and she says, 'A fire? On the beach. That would be lovely.'

The driftwood glow makes Elvira's features slow dance in never failing transformations of intricate change. Her face is high-boned and lived-in, full-lipped and occasionally coy. As she talks, there is a casual muscle to her technique for keeping the breeze from washing hair across her face. It enables me to see a whole life stretching out ahead of us. Naked mornings, wine afternoons.

All this on an opposite shore to where Angela is hostaged.

'What brings you here, Jimmy?'

I rub my finger and thumb in the universal sign of cash. '*Business*.' She smiles.

'Have you done what you came here for? Found what you wanted?'

I shake my head and indicate '*next*' with a curl of forefinger.

'Tomorrow? You are leaving?'

I shrug '*Maybe. If . . .*'

'If what?'

And with the faintest digit touch upon the side of my eye, I make myself understood.

'Who are you looking for?'

I recharge her glass and mine. I look out to sea, feel the tequila burning me with its delicate perfume. I look into her eyes, sparkling in the flame and glistening with good spirit, and I make a shape in the sand.

'Burg?' she says. 'An important man?' And even though she says nothing, even though she draws her knees into her breasts and clasps herself, sipping from her glass inthe lights of moon and fire, I have the certain impression that here on the shores of a shipless sea, two worlds might have briefly touched in the night.

TURNING TABLES

Jessie has recovered most of his appetites. He returned from the town laden with ingredients for breakfast, which we eat around the black-glassed kidney-shaped table of the dining room in this temporary but common-consent, magical home. There is a relative silence during preliminary tastings. For a minute or so Jessie has disarmed us. Then it is 'Pass me this pass me that,' and 'Where are the others?' 'They'll be here later; we're having some guests,' and all the time Wingnut looks warily at Elvira, wondering, When will you be going? We don't want you hanging around when the others get back; we are too many as it is.

'Jessie, this is wonderful,' she says.

As he replies, Wingnut and I share our own private exchange of proposals for the day.

'*I think*,' I sign, '*she might know Burg. See what you can get out of her.*'

Wingnut doubts the wisdom of printing our intentions upon space we share with a stranger. He eats and mulls, and finally he accepts his task.

'I wonder if you might be able to help us?' he says to Elvira, who nods with a full and masticating mouth. 'We have to deliver something, to some guy called Burg. Some big shot, apparently. We were just wondering if he's well known, famous, you know.'

She swallows, dabs her mouth and takes a drink. She doesn't need to say anything. It is clear to me, and probably to Wingnut, too, that she knows him. I track back through the mad blend of yesterday to see how, if someone was expecting us, they might turn a table or two and stalk the stalker.

'Burg? There is a Burg I know of. He used to live in Amsterdam, but he's not the sort you'd want to do business with. He's not a friend of yours, is he? A friend of your friend?' She puts her knife and fork down, sips at her drink and pushes her chair back as if to leave. 'Maybe I should go, you have things to do.'

I flick out a lightning gist to Wingnut, instruct him to ensure that she stays, make her feel at ease.

'He made his money in drugs, we heard. Have some pudding; there's some cake.'

'I'd better go.'

'No! You must stay. You've been so kind to us, to Jessie. The others will be back soon, and it's our last day; we're going back tomorrow.'

'After you have seen Burg?'

Wingnut looks at me, understands me immediately, and as I stand, as I go into my room to get the sports bag, I hear him reply. 'Yes. We have been given a package to give him, but we don't know where to find him. We . . .' – I throw one of the cellophane packs onto the table, then another and another – '. . . we'd appreciate it, really appreciate it, if you could help us track him down. You know him, don't you?'

She is calmer than the calm sea that swells wave-less beyond the beach. She leans into her handbag, emerges with a pack of cigarettes. She lights up, draws ruthless and inhales with purpose.

'If I were you, I would go back to England. Right now.'

'We have to deliver the package.'

'What is in the package?'

'We don't know. We can't know.'

Elvira looks at me, thinking in a thin cloud of smoke. She looks into me and leans forward, takes one of the heroin packs and casually drops it into her handbag. 'I'll help you find him. Just don't fuck with me.'

Wingnut and Jessie flinch in the corner of my vision. They look at each other, but before either can challenge the cementing smack of Elvira's involvement, a car comes motoring big and loud into our sound and vision. It screeches to a halt and Roy jumps out. My heart slows under the absence of threat, and Roy stops completely in his tracks the moment he sees Elvira.

Paradise has turned into Bedlam. Roy and Surfman, having returned from Waddenzee, are trying to assure us they were not followed here, that they had no option other than to bring Monique and Rudi, the rock-chick wife and hyperactive child of a man I could not kill, whose life it is easy to see now that I was right not to take in the middle of a night on the cold beach of the other side of this sea.

In the turmoil of Rudi's rampant discovery of all the rooms in this wondrous house and Monique's constant demands to be told what exactly is going on and who these people are, Roy gawps open-mouthed at Elvira. He traipses into the kitchen to help her make coffee. So it is no surprise that, after we have taken coffee on the deck, Roy follows Elvira back inside, taking the dirty cups with him and no doubt wiping dry with a tea towel as if he does so all the time. No surprise, either, that the next we see of them is in the shape of a couple paddling through shallow waters of sea, walking away from us, with Roy leaping around, showing off and burning energy before he bursts, ignorant as to the unquestioning way in which the apple of his eye had put a hundred thousand pounds worth of heroin into her handbag as if it were Clinique.

Sitting on the deck, nobody mentions Burg or the gear, whether Stapp has broken free or if the old woman has come down from bad Mammon. I snap my wrists but Wingnut can't see me, preoccupied as he is with talking to Surfman, Dutch style. Jessie is working his magic on Monique, getting her face to go serious then burst into laughter, and making her feel as if she is the only woman in the room, the centre of a universe. None of which is remotely connected to where we are really at.

I wave at Wingnut, but Rudi, who is seeking to hide, waves back, wide-grinning and impossible to dislike. I watch Surfman nodding at what Wingnut is saying, but also watching Monique from the corner of his eye as she hangs on Jessie's every word, unaware that her husband has seen me seeing him seeing her . . .

The noise of it all meshes in my head. It bangs in my drums. I am truly disabled, so I take my coat, resolve to take a grip on things and close the door on the chatter that forms a oneness hum from its different parts.

The seasound comes at me, but even with the sand scrunch under my shoes I can hear their goodtime noise, and I could swear that, as the waves come lapping up to trace a curve path for me to follow, I can hear the chink of glass on glass that precedes nonsense toasts between people, some of whom are strangers, some of whom know each other too well.

The constant shifting shape-fade shape-fade of the sea line spurs me to a dune peninsula. To my right is the north: Waddenzee and the sparse-homed lakes you might think would be safe. To my left is Rotterdam and everything you would be well advised to tread warily through. Soon we will advance left. And perhaps, with pictures forming as to what we will have to do there, it is a good

215

thing that, like Wellington's troops on a famous eve, they have their fun, and no bad thing that I am unheard.

'Jimmy! What are you doing out here?'

I turn and a gust of wind whips sand up in my face, draws a veil over the troubled image of the voice that has followed me when it seemed no-one cared. We blink at each other and Wingnut delves into the pocket of his overcoat, proffering a miniature bottle of duty-free Schnapps, which I take from him. The salt on my lips stings under the booze wash. My body hushes.

'It's gone mad in there. Surfman and Monique are having a row about her flirting with Jessie, so she brought it all up about the drug run, how he's ruined her life. Elvira's going to know everything soon.'

'*She already does.*'

'What do you mean?'

'*There's no such thing as a happy coincidence. Not with Flint. We have to stay one step ahead, that's all. First thing, we go to Rosenburg; find Burg's place. Me and you, Surfman and Elvira.*'

'I . . . I'm not sure it's a good thing to leave Roy and Jessie behind. Not at the moment.'

'*Why not?*'

'Just something they said.'

'*What did they say?*'

'They just need some reassurance. I just think they should be involved. You need to win them over.'

'*Win them over?*'

'I can see their point, I mean *I'd* rather we were just heading straight back to England. We've got the gear. We could tell Flint we couldn't find Burg. We could open the package, see what's in it.'

'*Flint has got Angela. That doesn't matter to you, but . . . I should have come on my own.*'

'This isn't about Angela. Not just her, or you. It's about all of us. Roy and Jessie would die for you, Jimmy. Fucking hell, we're here, aren't we? But it has to make sense. We've got the gear. Flint isn't going to harm Angela if we go back with the gear.'

'*You don't understand. It's not about the gear. Flint wants Burg to get the package. That's what it's all about. If they don't trust me, they can fuck off home . . . did you see that?*'

'See what?'

But it's too late. It came only briefly, for a second or two, onto the very limits of my sound and vision. With my back to the sea, I could swear that I see a grey Audi, tail lights fading, and gone.

217

BANG! BANG! THE MIGHTY FALL

Words that we all exchanged in anger repeat on me, as if I have indigestion, as if there is perhaps some poison trapped within me. I tried to bleed bad motive from myself, tried to rationalize why, for a few short seconds and for the first time in my life, I wished ill upon my friends.

In the privacy of my own room I am preparing for the seeking-out of Burg. But as I do, muffled sounds come from Elvira's room next door. Two giggles merging, different pitched, but the unlikeliest of perfect fits. Or so it sounds. She laughs, throaty now, an animal sound of base discovery, the kind of laugh that might encourage a man to advance to another base. I think to myself, what a wonderful world. Then I check myself. Much as Roy deserves a little love, or even a replica, there are more important things to attend to.

In the lounge, Wingnut is explaining to Monique that we must visit a man, and that if all goes well then there is every chance that she and her husband and son will soon be able to embrace a new life.

She is not convinced, but seems to take comfort from the adage turned reality of the sameness of the boat we are all in.

'You got the mobile, Wingnut?' says Jessie.

I shake my head to Wingnut who says, 'Sorry, Jess. We can't be too careful. It's for emergencies, you know that.'

'What happened to trust?'

I look at him as if to say, What in God's name has trust got to do with anything you do to Anne-Marie. But his disgruntlement is on a different plane.

'If you wanted to call Angela I bet we'd find a way,' says Jessie.

I shake my head and shrug *sorry*.

'Fuck you!'

He leaves, and I signal Wingnut to shout, which he does, 'You shouldn't call her, you shouldn't involve her.'

But he is gone.

'Where's Jess going?' says Roy, coming into the room, followed by Elvira, her hair in disarray, a smudge on the perfect bias of her cool. He sits down next to Monique and lights a cigarette, looks out to sea, placid, not as if something good has happened to him but as though something more potent has been taken away.

When Jessie returns, having decided against leaving a soundprint in a landscape inhabited by people who can only harm us, I signal Wingnut.

'Come on, boys, let's get some air, take a walk on the beach. No, Surfman, you stay here.'

'Call him Jan,' says Monique. 'It's his name.'

'We will call him', falters Wingnut, 'what the fuck we like. You stay here!'

We get down to the beach and Wingnut, not unquestioningly, transmits me. 'This is about the four of us. The others are here today, gone tomorrow.'

'You might think that,' says Roy.

'We've got to be on the same wavelength. We have to find Burg; we can't afford to waste any time. You and Jessie stay here. Me and Wingnut will take Surfman and Elvira down the coast.'

'Elvira?' says Roy. 'We've got the gear. You could go back or we go straight to Spain.'

'What about Angela?' Wingnut behalfs me.

'You don't care about Anne-Marie,' says Jessie.

'Or Elvira,' says Roy.

'*You've only just fucking met her,*' I sign, silent in the sea air. I tap Wingnut on the shoulder and he messages me, reluctantly.

'I love her,' says Roy, and no-one laughs.

The going is heavy. The sand is drying out in the outward passage of tide. Grains decompact, gain properties of freedom, make tiny movements for independence in conditions that once bound them together, when life was easier for people who wanted to walk upon them.

'Listen,' I message, stopping where the beach begins to shelve more steeply down towards the

220

sea. 'We came here to find Burg. If you don't want to do that, we had better go our separate ways. I will find him on my own.'

'Who gets to keep the gear?' says Jessie, at least one step ahead of Roy. 'We could split it. Flint doesn't even know we've got it.'

'Don't bank on it,' says Wingnut.

'We could go straight to Spain,' says Roy, 'Elvira wants to come.'

What?

'Fucking hell, Roy!' shout Jessie and Wingnut together.

And anything else which Roy might have to say is held tight in my grip. I have his stubble throat in my hands, pushing him down, and as I try to rein my temper, as we fall backwards together onto soft sand, I remind myself that we are family. But somewhere in flight he twists free; he turns tables so I land underneath him, and before I know anything at all about how I will finish what I have started, he has poked me in both eyes, has my arms pinned down with his knees and is pinching my nose. Blinded and speechless, I feel my mouth fill with foul taste. I breathe matter. Sand pits in my mouth and throat and I gag, choking soundless and trying to writhe free from his angry words that are big and strong. 'Don't, Jimmy. Don't! Don't treat me like that.'

A weight lifts from my chest and I roll onto my side, retching up sand and trying to blink vision back into my eyes, but I see only burning suns of yellow and purple in a starry black sky.

By the time I can breathe evenly through my emery mouth and open my eyes, there is only a single shadow between me and the bright horizon.

'We'd better hurry,' says Wingnut, 'they've gone to open Flint's package.'

He helps me back towards the house, holding my arm like one half of a pair of veteran promenade lovers. My senses of balance and perspective, proportion and reason are lost. Young Rudi is at the window, waving down at us from the arms of Monique. They watch us tramp up through thicker sand and Surfman comes up to her, puts arms around her waist, and she rests her head on his shoulder, as if she is reconciled to something.

Their body shapes warp in flexing glass, and in the fragment of a second that separates the speeds of light from sound, a sonic boom turns their faces animate. Surfman takes his family into his chest and, as the blast subsides, the sounds of a screaming woman and howling child drown all other noise.

With the instincts a father might have for an endangered son, I take the steps up from the beach two at a time and rush into the house. Jessie is stooping over Roy, who is on the floor with blood on his arm, curled into a foetal ball, unable to see Elvira returning a gun hurriedly to her handbag.

'I'm all right. I'm all right,' says Roy, jumping up, looking annoyed and ringing his arm, spattering blood like experimental art. 'What the hell was that?' he says, as if he has been cut up on a motorway. He looks around, watches our faces as we absorb the changes in him. Surreal; the colour of Picasso period.

With relief bursting like sunflowers, Elvira goes towards Roy, arms out to embrace him, but I dive across and tackle her to the floor, and Wingnut reads me, shouts, 'Don't touch him. It's indelible.'

Roy's face and arms are blue, painted like schoolroom numbers gone wrong; he looks like some Mister Man figure in a book that Rudi might read. With blinking white eyes in a face from a foreign galaxy, Roy looks at Elvira and smiles white teeth.

'Go to the bathroom, see if you can clean it off,' says Wingnut. 'Jessie, see if you can find him some bleach.'

'You can't use bleach,' says Elvira, 'his hand is bleeding.'

'Just get the bleach, Jessie. Quick!'

From many hundred miles away Flint has coloured us with her all-knowing stains. She has fired warning shots from a far-off galleon in a distant port, and with it she has assisted my cause in ways only she foresaw would probably be necessary.

Amongst the debris of the package is an A4-sized, blue-stained oblong tin. I take it into the kitchen, holding it between finger and thumb, and I open it, tentative and getting only the merest strokes of paint on each of two buff envelopes within. One addressed 'Jimmy Mack', the other 'Burg'.

I read mine.

'You should not choose to test my instructions, Jimmy,' I can hear her say it in measured tones through the unmoving letter-box purse of her lips. 'Heed me now. Deliver the other envelope to Burg. Be sure to do all the right things.'

Roy returns from his toilet with red-raw chest and arms. Red raw, that is, where they are not Braveheart blue. He trails a stinging waft of bleach, which has got into his eyes, shot through with blood. Tears stream down his smiling cheeks, as if he is a clown.

'Won't come off,' he says. 'Tried everything.'

'Come here. Let me look,' says Elvira, patting a space beside her on the sofa.

'Sorry, Jimmy. About before,' says Roy.

I shrug with fake-superior demeanour. There is sound sense in the notion that whilst I had been tunnelling my vision back to Angela, I had also been inadvertently discounting their welfare from my plans. But Flint, with explosive reminders from afar, has come to my aid, settled some of Roy and Jessie and even Wingnut's ash. She has re-established a kind of equilibrium.

I signal Wingnut. 'Me, Wingnut and Surfman are going down the coast to see if we can find Burg's place. You, too, Elvira.'

'She's not going,' says Roy. 'You can't make her go.'

224

'Don't worry, Roy,' she says. 'I'll be all right.' And she swings her handbag over her shoulder, fully loaded. She looks at me, and I know that she, at least, will be safe for sure.

LUCK AND JUDGEMENT

I have sped up away from a house, which is now full of mismatched pairs of other halves: Jessie and Monique; Roy and Rudi.

Once I am content that we form no part of secret convoy, Wingnut recites from a gambit script of ordained conversation I have prepared for his backseat companion.

'How do you know Burg?' he says.

'He used to live in Amsterdam,' says Elvira. 'He threw big parties. I was invited to some. That's all.'

'And when did he leave Amsterdam?'

'Not long ago, I think. He has children, wanted them to grow up away from the city. He's a family man.'

'*Oh yeah?*' I mirror.

'You'd better believe it. He dotes on them, and his wife. They've been together for twenty years. He could have anyone he wanted, anything. You know, all the trappings. But he doesn't want it. He gets rid of his . . . you know, his manthing . . .'

'Testosterone?' says Wingnut.

'Yes. In other ways.'

'Where has he moved to?'

'Across the estuary, near Oostvoorne, I heard.'

And now Wingnut plays a blinder. He lets it lie; he chits and chats about living in Holland and travel and then, 'Roy's a good lad, you know. He's not had much experience with girls, though.'

'I guessed that.'

'I wouldn't have thought . . . oh, never mind.'

'What?' she says.

'Well, I wouldn't have thought he was your type.'

'He is funny, has a good heart.' But she stops herself and I can see in her unmasked stripe of eyes that she knows our game. 'What is my type?' she asks, seeing the con behind the front.

The car falls silent, and I contemplate how strange it is that Roy has emerged from the wilderness at such a time, in circumstances as unlikely as you could possibly contrive. They could be fantastic enough to be beyond suspicion, but I backcomb through time, separating strand from strand, as if I am a nurse in search of fleas, and conclude that whilst Elvira could have followed us into Kasbah and met us by design, she could not have staged the events that led to Jessie's withdrawal and my impulsive, desperate call. Surely no-one could have planned that.

We have navigated half the sprawling circumference of monstrous Rotterdam, skirted its vast docks and weaved above inlet waterlines until the container canyons gave way to marsh and finally we arrived at the chain ferry, which is reassuringly smalltime in the distant shadows of a big city's trillion-guilder trade. A man in a wooden hut gave us a pink paper ticket from a roll, as if we were entering a raffle, and on the opposite shore of the estuary we drove into another world. It is market day in medieval Brielle and time to take stock.

In a restaurant that Elvira remembered from childhood, we order under the high-beamed vaults of a back room overlooking the canal. Even though it is summer, the room is thick with the smells of roasting game and rich sauce.

Elvira is quiet, sipping from her beer and looking out of the window, almost impassive, honing her indifference. Substrata, you can tell she is in tune with the bad reception our interference may yield. It is as if she can sniff something in the air, hear something in the ground beneath us.

Wingnut sits in sidelong awe of Elvira, who is dressed disarmingly demure in her woolly jumper and jeans. With her make-up worn and her scarfed hair in slight straggle, she looks as if some day soon she could become a person who might have a son whose friends would burst at imagined and domestic contortion sightings of her.

The food arrives on blue Delft platters – local beasts dead on ancient and foreign craft. I look across at Elvira, her deliciousness, and I hear the voice of a woman I love, words she spoke the first time we stayed at the beach house on a trip we made to pretty Delft. 'Mrs Van der Land told me about this pottery,' Angela had said, putting down a vase. 'The Mongols found old roof tiles in Morocco. They took them back with them, and then this company, this old company . . . what's it called?'

'*The East India?*' I had mouthed.

'That's right. They brought them back here. They should have brought some Temple Balls. I know what I'd prefer to decorate a room,' and she threw back her head and laughed. She turned on me, snuggled herself around my arm and said into my chest, 'You're so clever, Jimmy. How did you know it was the East India Company? Let's go back to the house, get out of it,' and with a lift of her head, 'fuck like rabbits.'

I catch myself smiling, like an idiot lost in simple thoughts.

Surfman picks at his food, looking as if he is beginning to face the harsh realities that will follow discovery of Burg, so I sign for the bill and we rise in silence, food largely untouched.

Oostvoorne is three miles along the coast, along a sand spit. We pass out of Brielle's chocolate-box strand, rattling along the cobble road and halting in traffic while a pleasure cruiser passes under the swinging iron bridge. Soon all traffic is behind us, just a leafy suburb glow of bungalows built along waterlines, no sign whatsoever of life. I wonder whether, once the lawns are mown, people simply sit inside, pride bursting from behind curtain chinks.

The strand loops us towards the sea and we tack back with marsh then dunes in a merger of land and sea to our right, the canal and then a flatscape of fields to our left. At a fork in the road we are signposted to Prins Willem, where the road soon peters to nothing, tyre tracks guiding us along the base of dunes. To our right a car is driving in shallow waters, coming back onto the beach and drawing figures of eight in the sand. As we get nearer I see a dog – a pit terrier with two flaring barrels of bull muzzle, romping in the sea then jumping up at the car, lowslung and sports, far too good to be suffering distress from sand and sea. The car halts and a woman climbs out, inelegant, struggling to stand in stiletto boots, leopardskin leggings and a short fur jacket that makes no effort at all to cover her swollen pear of a bottom. She looks like something you might find if you looked west for sex on a Blighty'd estuary.

'Ha! I don't believe it,' says Elvira, squinting. 'It is; it's her: Burg's wife.'

I look behind, as if to say, 'No. No, I don't believe it, either. This is too easy.' But I can see no way in which we could have arrived here to share shore with the spouse of our adversary by any means other than informed chance.

'Give me your scarf please,' Wingnut behalfs me.

'It was a gift,' says Elvira.

'Shouldn't we follow her?' says Wingnut, watching the sports car drive away, dog on board.

'*She might see us.*' I put my hand out to Elvira. '*Please.*'

She takes the scarf off and hands it to me.

The Prins Willem is like something from rural myth, told by weekending urban tellers. As we entered, the place fell silent and heads turned, fixing themselves in time for too long before drink and chat and games were resumed. The place harks to a distant past, with its glass-cased models of old galleons, nets on the ceiling, old oil lanterns and stuffed animals – crocodiles, otters and beavers. No fish, no birds, no game. Nothing that is exclusively of land or sea or air. The model ships are grander versions of the *Golden Hind* and *Santa Maria*, the like of which I built in happy childhood, fingers tacking together from the glue while rain pitter-pattered on the shack windows that looked out to sea. It feels as if I have somehow navigated the circumference of something unchartable to here and now.

Surfman engaged the bartender in chit-chat and Wingnut proffered Elvira's scarf which, of course, was being offered up by us as sacrifice, as something we found on the beach – such a beautiful scarf, and left, we think, by a well-dressed lady in a sports car. Who could that possibly be?

Our question was answered. It belonged to a

woman called Greta, whose house is only half a mile away and stands on the route taken by this bartending man and his dog on their evening walk. He will drop it off personally. I am sure he will, seeking future favour by sucking up to the new bourgeoisie, no doubt.

'No,' said Elvira, going to the bar with a sidle smile and jean-bursting hipsway. She took the scarf from the fingertip clutches of the barman, and said, 'Not Greta? Greta Burg?'

'No,' he says. 'Not Burg. Greta Nisteroy.'

'That's her. She is married now. I know her from Amsterdam. Does she still have her dog?'

'Yes,' says the barman. 'That's how I know her. I see her when I am walking mine in the evenings.'

'I must take it myself.' She leaned upon the bar, her face close to the barman, exerting all manner of persuasions that he is too weak to resist. 'She lives near here? Where?'

She received the requested information, like collecting essential juices from a gentle squeeze upon a willing-victim fat fruit, and in so doing she delivered me to the brink of belief that she may be on our side.

Suddenly nothing to fear in the whether or not of us surviving intact. It is as though I am able to do the Kipling thing: to face twin imposters and treat them both the same; the shit and bust of what has to be done.

I am neither humming the hymns of Dionysus in my inner head, nor quaking in ministries of fear. It

232

is simply the case that, after the torments of the last day, when friends have treated me as foe, and on the doorstep of the house in which our fortunes will be legislated, I feel ready. I am in tune once more with the forces that brought me here. I can look out to sea, watch a family preparing a barbecue for when the sun goes down and meantime frolic through the incoming sea, where only half an hour ago Mrs Burg – that Greta known to Elvira – drove in idle pursuit of her terrible dog. I can watch that family and re-engage my distant identities with the joy they are etching in the sand, the screams of delight they swirl on the breeze.

My far past was not always grim, my fates not ill from the inception of my infancy, though odds were stacked against me since the mad and gods-goading conception of me.

I can recall an early age when I was taken to a not-dissimilar beach, led down and reined in to save me from my own excitement. I screamed lungfuls against the strong wind in the latter days of my being able to sound myself and played in shallow sea with a bucket and spade and, gathering wet sand in every crevice of every cranny in my naked body, I would look up to check the progress of the advancing tide on my castle, see if my defences would be able to rebuff the forces of nature; and I would look the other way, too, to see if my twin mothers were kissing or fighting. The paradise they had built, and which had conspired me at its formation, was crumbling.

I can see clearly now, looking backwards, that they either kissed or fought; little in between those poles – love and hate being what happened in too much quantity around me then, and probably ever since.

Elvira directs us back along the dunes, with the sea now only ten, fifteen metres from the tracks we made on our way to the Prins Willem. We drive back up to the fork and hairpin back along the inland road with, once again, dunes and marshlands beside us. In the shotgun seat, she folds the scarf into measured quarters and eighths and sits tall, as if she might be the one at our helm. Iron-gated entrances stand like sentries at every quarter mile, steep-sloping roofs distant at the ends of drives that huddle luxury lives from sea winds.

'This is it; he said it was called Dunes.'

We drive past at normal speed and park the car once we are out of sight of the gates and house. I take the binoculars from the glove compartment and we climb up onto the dunes.

From our vantage in the tuft grass we can see that, unlike the other houses we have passed, which were mock baroque from the house of tack, Burg's place is a Bauhaus triumph. It is single-storey and subtle-levelled, with varied planes of roof in minor gradations, sediments of glass and steel sunk in the slow swoop of modest contour. There is a moat around the building, straight-lined, with Corbusier angles tracing the just of rooms. There is nothing remotely fairy tale about the place, save that it is the stuff that dreams *could* be made of.

Through the glasses, I watch a group of people sitting round the pool. In the water, children flock round the torso bulk of a late-thirties man. His shaven pate glints from water and sun, a helmet of a head which slopes neckless and strong into a broad brush back. He lifts one of the boys out of the water and throws him backwards with a great splash that makes the other children yelp on the very limit of my hearing. Some children leap at him, holding on; some dive, tugging at his legs, trying to topple him until he makes the shape of mock relent and falls backwards under the surface, coming back at them like a mythical beast from the deep, or something in a final cinema throe. The game continues until their heads turn as one, and I track the scope of my tunnelled vision to the source of their attention. It is a simple everyday thing: a father and his children being summoned for a meal.

They are summoned by an old woman, a woman I last saw twenty-four hours ago in a hotel room and stoned into another dimension.

Sea breeze on the back of my neck makes me shiver.

SINS OF THE FATHERS

Recollections of Burg and his family dining al fresco in the falling sun sting me like nettles from a past that is sometimes too harmful to grasp. I can remember playing with similar abandon to his children. Me, then, knowing no more about the atrocities about to be visited upon me than they know of the bad future we have plotted for their father, and therefore themselves. I try to remind myself that their idyll has been paid for in skin carnage: in pisspool subways in corners of this country and ours. I remind myself, too, that it cannot be right that they should escape with riches and privilege from the ricochet of destruction that other people's miseries have paid for.

As for my own childhood, I was also an innocent paying the price of elders' greed – to have something that was not, nor could rightly be, theirs – when my mother, to the unexpressed but burning chagrin of her lover, took herself off on a sweetheart reunion from adolescence to end all sweetheart childhood reunions from adolescence; when my mother, with my other mother waiting anxiously in their flat in Easport, sought out the man to whom she had once sacrificed her virginity, for the sole purpose of conceiving what turned out to be me. With her intentions unannounced, him blind to her secret purpose, she received the me-form of nostalgic sperm into her, when I swam from the sac of an unknown victim right up into the life-granting soul of her, when I breached something natural unnaturally. It was at that precise moment that three lives were, in various ways, ruined for ever. A fourth kept for ever in the dark.

I have seen photographs of reactions in nine-month delay at the conclusion of the gestation of me, shortly after I was of natural woman born, when I was given the subliminal and first of many bases for belief that nothing terrible would result from my contrivance. My mother and her lover beamed smiling into a private camera and then saved me, to their credit, from the glare of paparazzi, from the ridicule of peers. They took me up the coast to a safe place, where we lived in a splendid isolation, beyond any earshot of dissenting voices. In fairness, I was brought up in a kind of Eden. For three years, until the love of my one mother began to outstrip – as was inevitable, as would have been prophesied quite easily by any witch worth her salt, in drama or from life – the love of a lesser and passive mother. Things ceased to be rosy in the garden during my fourth summer, at the end of which my voice was struck from me. As the days grew shorter, my mother and I began to receive all kinds of messages, see many manifestations of the advancement of Birnam Wood.

My other mother sought distractions from the malfunct of our family way. She grew violent, returning to the house later and later from a different world she began to occupy. I would wake to hear arguments rage. Arguments about who should have received the spermtail me; about who should have borne me; about who, for all the other liberations they had granted each other, should have benefited from that single and irrefutable most unnatural gift to natural process. If Michelle, and not Frances, had been unsure of her persuasion at an early age; if she and not my mother could have engineered a chance staging – for one night only – with a long-expired flame, then things would be . . . things, as far as I am concerned, would not be at all. Such is life.

So I can look at Burg's children with their unearned good life and convince myself that I should assume no guilt for the dimming of lights on their immediate futures. I, more than anybody, have seen that while genes and environment might have much to answer for on the fringe and in the nuance of things, it is only parents who can fuck you over completely. Good and proper.

More immediately, I also feel undermined in the more serious echelon of confronting Burg. With the old woman not tripping and otherwise out of things in Amsterdam, she is on hand to brief Burg as to the threat we pose. Surprise has been wrested from us, our only solace that Burg is ignorant of our new-found knowledge that he is no longer in the dark as to our intentions.

To see him now, leaning back with his belly bursting from the glutton satiation of his appetite; he is not troubled by our prospect threat. He stands, kisses Greta on the forehead and sends the old woman scurrying inside. I hang on every individual shape his mouth makes, and from within the foreign palette of the pictures he paints I recognize the colour and shape of a universal word, 'ca-si-no', and another 'Kur-haus' – proper syllables that mean he is coming to meet us more than halfway, at the fantastic spa hotel that presides over Scheveningen's beach; a place to take tea or, depending on your tastes or state of desperation, gamble.

When we return, the beach house seems transformed, as if Hans Andersen might have dropped in on his way somewhere, delivering Christian influences. Or perhaps it is simply a woman's touch, with peace everywhere and flowers on the dining table, a vast array of tulip-shaped black petals that give me chills, as if Bad Omen has put a cold hand on my shoulder. Black on a growing life shape, death in a wrong place.

'Queen of the Night,' says Elvira.

'Where is everyone?' says Wingnut.

'Monique? Rudi? Where are they? Where are

they?' shouts Surfman, running through the house.

And while I motion for him not to panic, I know that something is most certainly not right. I hear a father's scream, which we follow into the dining room. Lashed to the table, bound and gagged, writhe Roy and Jessie and Monique. No Rudi.

'Rudi has been taken. There was only one of them. We could do nothing, he had a mask and a gun, a gun in Rudi's mouth. He went to play in the sand, I went inside for one minute. One minute. They'll kill him,' sobs Monique.

'The bastard!' shouts Roy as soon as the gag is released, jumping up and tearing out of the room, vaulting the deck railings and running fast across the surface of sand. Wingnut follows Roy; Surfman goes the other way with Jessie, and I look for Elvira to ensure there is someone who can comfort Monique, but Elvira is nowhere to be seen.

Roy is a hundred yards and more ahead of me as I catch up with Wingnut, running away from the resort towards the dunes and the dozen or so candied beach huts that stand unoccupied, like meerkats in natural habitat. We have no chance. They will be long gone. They . . .

A shot rings out. It rings loud, from somewhere untraceable. It echoes in the late afternoon sky, like gunpowder works of fire. Roy runs up to the dunes, away from the sea and kicking open the doors of the beach huts one by one, until . . . until he sinks to his knees and holds out his arms;

until . . . until, at the very same moment, I see a sign whose significance only I am receptive to. Grey and German-engineered, the bonnet of the Audi points straight at me, like the barrel of a gun. I walk slowly, limbs heavy from running in sand, heavy with the realization of my unweaponedness.

Rudi runs into Roy's arms. He screams, and Roy holds him, heedless of the danger he is in. Heedless, I think, until I tread warily to his side and crook my head, timid, looking inside the hut and seeing the face of Denny Lane, who will forever look scared to death, forever wear the uncosmetic scorch of a single bullet at the very centre of the coming together of his eyes.

Rudi is being buried alive by Roy and his father. He is smiling, enjoying this game, which is better than the last, which was too scary by far. Jessie stands next to them, looking out to sea. He has weakened under the toll of events, buckled and sought strength from his most reliable of sources. From the look of the dead expression on his face, as he stands barefoot, with sand between his toes, it will not be long before he seeks the fuller benefits of other fine grains, grains that transform from one state to another in a flamespoon morph to sweeten a molten mood. Sugar and butter, scratchy and cold, make caramel in a pan.

Elvira is tending to Monique, forcing herbal tea on her and whispering invented assurances that are rooted far from the truth of our situation. I tap

241

her shoulder, motion for her to come with me, and when we get into her room, I reach into her bag, take out the weapon and wonder what kind of happiness is a warm gun.

'Don't ask. You have to trust me. You have no choice.'

As Wingnut talks about Burg and the house with its gates and moat, tells them the old woman had been seen and that we must assume Burg knows all about us; as he brings the realities of tonight harsh into our visions, you can almost feel energy leaking through open doors and onto the beach.

'There is nothing to be afraid of with this man, with the situation.' Elvira is stepping forward, standing by the window with the sand and sea and sky behind her, wearing a short black skirt, heavy denier tights and knee boots that point at twenty past eight, twenty twenty in continental hours, and she talks slowly and certainly, as if she has perfect vision of our future. 'If you can get into this man's home, amongst his wife and children, he will not harm you. Not in his home. He will not commit violence amongst his family.'

'How do you know?' asks Roy, awe in his voice, reverence in the transfixed glaze of the look he gives her.

'Trust me.'

And I examine her as she says these things. I look for a twitch, a hesitation, a stutter or some other stumble. But it appears as if she believes that what she is saying is the truth. I signal Wingnut, who continues with his outline of what we have to do. He takes us through the arrangements for travel and rendezvous, and as he pinpoints the landing stages of our various departures, I ponder Elvira's jackboot stance on family values in the house of Burg.

Wingnut asks if anybody has any questions, and Surfman nods at Roy.

'Jimmy, we've been thinking; it's going to be difficult, for Surfman and Monique and Rudi, when it's over. We thought . . . we'd like him and Monique and Rudi . . . we think he should come with us, meet up in Spain. When everything's taken care of, you know, and . . . and so should anyone else, you know, who might want to, who's helped us.' For a nervous moment he looks at Elvira, then shies his eyes to the floor, takes a step back, not looking up for any rejection of his well-intended puppy-love proposals for the extension of family.

POST-NUCLEAR FAMILY VALUES

In the house where I was raised, Victorian values were to be seen only in tatters, trampled hopelessly underfoot by practically every step my parents ever took. As for my father, Michelle had to perform that function to the extent it was performed at all.

I knew both sides of my father-mother, my female dad, the man half of my twin mothers. Michelle suffered from the privy truth that clung to me like dried blood and broken waters from the moment I was born. I can remember Frances sitting me on her knee while Michelle was out beachcombing or up on the clifftops tending the allotment and grafting improbable growth from thin and infertile soil. She would tell me magical stories from her head, about mothers who loved their children. Soaring adventures where the hero was called Jack and was saved by the love of two strong women, each as strong as the other, each loving young Jack in equal measure. And when the story was finished, she would ruffle my hair and hold me into the berth of her chest and shoulder and neck. She would say in a sad voice,

244

'Your mothers love you. We both love you. Go to Michelle tonight. Tell her you love her.'

'I love *you*,' I said.

She put me down from her knee, took hold of my arms and, with tears coming onto her cheeks, she scolded me. She shouted, 'You must; you must love her. *She* is your mother, too!' Then she took me back into her breasts and cried, 'I'm sorry, I'm sorry,' and, this I remember as clear as bells sounding here and now, 'it's not your fault; it's not your fault; it's not your fault. It's my fault.'

Between what I estimate would have been the third and fourth anniversaries of the day I fought my way from the torn and bleeding loins of one mother, Frances and I had our lives infected by the ruining spirit of a relative outsider in a post nuclear domestic landscape of bliss turned blaze.

My toddling ventures up the cliff with Michelle were times designated as quality. Frances had initially said the path was dangerous and argued against my going, but that argument wasn't serious, and in the end Michelle said Frances was acting 'like a big girl', which made them laugh. I joined in and said, 'I'm a boy, so I can go up.'

Michelle carried me along the difficult stretches of path, held me tight and whispered kind words that made me lean, within myself, away from her. She told me stories as we dug the soil, sowed seeds and watered, made trips to and from the compost bin or across the horses' field with the manure bucket.

She pointed up and down the coast, told me how cliffs were made and how the coast was moving back because of the sea and silly men. I didn't understand; she didn't speak my language. She directed me to the oil tankers which still make infinitesimal progress on the horizon and said they were enormous ships. 'But they're tiny,' I said. 'Silly Jack,' she replied, and she told me how it was bad to use oil. With the wind in her hair and the salt blown from sea making our lips go dry, she talked about the power of things I didn't understand.

Sometimes, when I grew tired of the metal zzzipping rhythm from the to and fro of my mother's knitting machine, when I was bored with watching the colour patterns emerge, slowdripping and warped under the curving line from the weights she attached to the bottom of the piece she was working on, Frances allowed me onto the beach at low tide to get driftwood.

I would go to the edge of sea, look up at Michelle and shout, then wave. Sometimes she waved back and other times she didn't. Sometimes she wasn't there at all. In fact, she was there less and less as that summer passed.

One September afternoon I was sent outside, even though it was cold, because there was nowhere else to go. There was only one room in the shack. I could hear them shouting. My mother was complaining about harvest, saying there wasn't enough food for winter, that all her knitting money would go on food and still there wouldn't be enough because the allotment was a disaster. What had Michelle been doing? Where had she been going? There certainly wasn't any money coming in from the supposed fucking job, from the evening sorties into Whitby where she claimed to work in a pub. I wondered for a while what exactly a fucking job entailed, which, when you think about it, in my case and Michelle's, is not funny at all.

Michelle stormed out, and she shouted at me as she climbed up the cliff path, 'It's your fault. We were all right until you came. You freak!' As soon as she said it a sad look came on her face. She burst into tears and came back down the path to get me, but I ran in. I was scared of her and my mother bolted the door against Michelle's pounding. When I asked her what a 'freak' was, she put me on her knee and covered my ears so I couldn't hear what Michelle was shouting.

Later that week, my mother sent me out at low tide to see where Michelle was. I ran down to the sea and looked up to the allotment. There was no-one there so I ran back up the beach and took the cliff path, crawling on hands and knees along the difficult stretches, looking anxiously up all the way in case Michelle appeared at the top, like some ogre from fairy tale, standing guard to a secret kingdom.

But she wasn't there. When I got to the top I could see that the harvest had been taken in: dozens of bags in the hut. Like a hero, I took a bag of berries for jam and a bottle of pop from a crate at the back of the shed. Treasure to please my mother. I ran down the path, scooting down on my bottom along the difficult stretches and holding the berries and the bottle in my lap, feeling as if I would burst.

My mother took a tight hold of me, sobbing that she thought something terrible had happened. Where on earth had I been? I shook myself free from her and stood back, proud. I would make her life better. I felt like a changed man, as if I had a role, and I held the berries out to her like a trophy, then the bottle. 'Whisky?' she called it. Whisky which we didn't drink. 'Fucking whisky,' which was something we never had in the house. 'Stay here!' she screamed. 'Stay here and don't move!' I stood, rooted to the spot, holding berries like a tree.

That other me called Jack was as different as could be, stood perfectly still, like a mummy's boy, throughout the last remnants of the afternoon, and when evening came, splinters of the new real me began to stick in him. The old me was about to be visited and overwhelmed by the malformations of the new me.

I crept out onto the beach, down below the tideline. The sea was halfway in and I couldn't get out far enough to see the allotment. The sun had set itself below the cliff and I knew that if I didn't go soon it would be dark. As I made my way up the cliff path, I heard familiar voices

248

saying unfamiliar words. As I prepared to traverse a difficult section, my mother appeared at the cliff's edge. A shape blurred past me, then an explosion on the rock-slab pavement at the foot of the cliff. She bent down and threw another bottle, then another, until Michelle came rushing into view, cliff-edged and shouting. They pushed each other and I wanted to go to the aid of my mother – she would have no chance against Michelle – but I couldn't move.

Then she saw me and shouted, 'Jack!'

Michelle shouted, 'Jack! Go back!' But I couldn't move, simply watched a leaf-by-leaf document of my mother running towards me, her long skirt floating like flags of war, merging in the dusk with autumn shades of perennial flowers in the gorse. She shouted for me to stay where I was. She hesitated, looked back at Michelle, then came towards me, walking quickly with a scared face. Her skirt caught on the gorse and she leaned back to free herself. She tugged once, twice, and then fell, holding her skirt so that it couldn't billow as she sailed, slow motion and in a piercing silence onto the rock pavement, bleeding amongst the broken glass. My scream falling on deaf ears.

My final ever sound was 'MOTHER'.

KISS AND TELL

Kurhaus stands proud at the epicentre of all Scheveningen's beach-blanket fun, an elegant hark to a less hedon bathing past, with its chandeliered salon and its awesome glass cupola. It cusped away from its historic past thirty years ago, when the Stones rolled in to rock the joint, when guitars were unplugged after fifteen minutes because the locals were out of control in a place that was made for the taking of tea.

We are here in the best traditions of Kurhaus's reinvention, all together now, save Surfman and Monique, who keep home fires burning with young Rudi. Under a big and darkening sky we stand in shadows, waiting for the man.

Our intentions are plain: to hijack a car that might passport us into a militarized zone, to inflict a quick-passing coup upon a household; lie in wait for an unChristian dictator who we will message with manifestos for reform. And, if international laws permit, we will make a lightning exit into a different state to live out the remainder of our days to the tunes of a less malign legislature.

It is a simple and uncluttered plan that is surely

too simple, so I have volunteered myself to go into Kurhaus to reconnoitre a field of battle should our near future smudge its template.

The position I adopt is high above the infantry of ten-guilder tables, which are the cheapest and most patronized in the place. From my emplacement I can easily see that, in terms of the rules of the most serious, high-stake game any of us play, the cannon fodder of people on tiptoes are casualties. Mullet-haired men have come wearing Sunday best, glitter flecks in their box jackets, and stand in a thick swamp of low-budget cologne that makes noxious fusion with what the women have sprayed. Women who have done something unnatural, unflattering to their hair to look different, but feel better than they are – harsh lessons in a failing school of social mobility. It is a universal state the world over.

I move to the bar and drink from a frozen glass of vodka tonic while I wait and watch a moving image of high rollers in the mirror behind the bar being led to a fancy-chip table. Fat-face men with incredible tans light cigars. Nipped, tucked women shed fur onto the backs of chairs and giggle amongst themselves.

'Jimmy.' Elvira's face is big in my vision as she drags a bar stool next to me, climbing up high and crossing her legs between mine, with her knee practically . . . 'Jimmy, just behave normally. Everything is all right. Imagine we are together.' She leans forward, strokes my hair and kisses me softly on the mouth. Her lips are cold, moist like spring dew and, up close for the first time, I see her brand new. For a first time. She leans back, smiles, looks casually around and leans forward again. With a hand on the back of my neck, she comes to kiss me again, but says, 'These people behind us' – and she does, she kisses me – 'we have to go, Jimmy. Go somewhere else.' She pulls away, but not quite, whispering cold into my mouth, 'They are with Burg. He has arrived. The man behind me, I know him. Kiss me, Jimmy, put your hands on my face and kiss me.' And as I do, I see out of one eye, in the mirror behind the bar, one of the high rollers with a big cigar in his mouth ordering a drink, catching my eye and half turning, looking down at Elvira's legs and then back at me in the mirror with a lewd wink and a sly laugh.

For a brief eternity Elvira treated me like a lover, and for a brief eternity I betrayed a friend in ways beyond what he would have been appalled to see, so that by the time she rehinged us to our natural states, I feel as if I have been disloyal to myself as well as to a woman in another land.

Two staircases sweep up to the balcony. Downstairs, in the slow mingling lantern of people around tables, I see the steady, straightlined passage of an oiled and familiar pate glistening in entourage. Burg walks direct to the stairs, parting waters. We wait for him to curve away from us and set ourselves on a quick and gentle downward spiral.

It has been a fine day, but outside the salt is

wintry in the air. I watch the smoke with fire that comes from the cigarette fingers of Burg's liveried chauffeur and think how fine it would be to return to the beach house, to carry hot toddies out to burning hickory, where Rudi will be sitting in the lap of his father, listening to soft surf and the spit of barbecue, the last gulls and stories from the seas.

Burg's chauffeur sees us coming. At least he sees Elvira, watches every shimmer and slide of each kitten stride that closes the gap between the two of them. I stand back, watch her go into her handbag, bring out a cigarette and hear her purr, see him flick out in offer of Dutch fuck as both her hands clasp his, as if she were drinking from him. His smile is complete, lascivious and fixed. Fixed! In time. Fixed by a short-armed hooking venom swing to the temple from Roy that fells him like spuds in a sack dropped from the highest of tailgates.

'Bastard,' whispers Roy through grit teeth that mean what they say.

We lift the chauffeur into his own boot. He is a card we will need to play later. Elvira drives us away fast, speeding out of town on dead quiet streets. She smiles sedately across at me, sees her power reflected back at her in all kinds of ways.

'Are you all right, Roy?' she asks. Her smile comes and goes in the slowstrobe of cars coming against us. Her eyes are in caption from reflected glare, and she engages Roy with a hinting squint of appreciation, the merest flare of her nostrils, in exactly the same moment that she brings the limo back into third and piles on the revs, swinging the back end round to take us up onto the slip road to the motorway. I lose all kind of tracks as she drives with her feet on big pedals made for men, men who sit legs astride, occasionally scratching their balls, treating themselves to a fleeting cup of the power in their hands. She sits there in her denier and boots, skirt riding high on the curves that she's cutting through the map, with her legs wide apart like a trucker, gunning us down the barrel of the highway. She does all this, and still she catches me as I look up from a too-long fish-on-a-hook gawp.

'If Burg comes out of the casino and his car's not there, we have a problem. He will know,' says Elvira.

'He'll need his chauffeur as well as the car,' says Wingnut.

'Yeah,' says Jessie, lazily, as if he is rising from slumber.

'We'll stop soon, get him out of the boot. You can pour that booze in the cabinet down his throat. Chauffeurs drink all the time,' she says.

'Get him pissed?' says Wingnut.

'Really pissed,' says Elvira. 'So he can't talk.'

'She's good, isn't she,' says Roy. 'Isn't she great?'

The silence of my reply is augmented by Wingnut and Jessie, who like me are probably trying to predict what discord will result from the ways in which Elvira is diminishing my control.

'Jessie, you had better watch the route. You have to bring him back. Understand?' she says.

He nods as the car falls silent, caving in on itself in a vacuum of sound. The quiet noise of the aircon builds like timpani as I try to plot when I will step in. Bang! Start calling the tunes myself, but for the moment you cannot fault Elvira; she seems to know all the scores. As if by heart.

The chauffeur introduced himself as Gustav, speaking broken English that is thick clodded with Eastern European accents. Hungarian is my guess, but there is no time for getting-to-know-you nicety. We are too busy forcing our hospitality on him, pouring whisky down his throat as we drive south by southwest, insisting that he has several for the road, so that by the time we get to Oostvorne, pulling up alongside the gates to The Dunes, he doesn't even need to be asked to relinquish the remote control over the smoothflow glide of the iron gates, or to hand over the keys for the front door. He is like a baby, head lolling; like a teenage taxi homecoming from a first bad party, when your mouth is thick with the regurge taste of spirits you won't be able to smell without heaving, let alone taste or stomach for the next twenty years. He's not betraying anyone, just glad to be home, glad for the world to stop moving all around him, for the voices to stop. I dismiss a prelude of remorse as I help Roy to lift him and put him back in the boot before we make our way up the steps and into the house.

I signal to Jessie, who reaches down into his Chelsea boot and springs a blade of finest Sheffield which glints in the porch light as he gives it extravagant practice swipes to restore a kind of balance. Roy, too, springloads his weapon, his whole self, and I watch his smiling face furrow, like a frustrated child in rigorous examination.

The guard shouts out as soon as he registers the unfamiliarity of the face beneath the chauffeur's cap in the narrow jar of the opening door. He reaches to his hip to fight blade with fire, but Roy stuns him to the floor, rushes into the hall and poleaxes a manservant as he dashes towards us.

I raise a finger to my lips and a death hush falls like a slab.

Groans from the floor emerge, but through them I can hear a fast-advancing beat of cavalry along the floor of upstairs rooms.

'Jimmy, what the hell is . . . ?'

The verberations of Wingnut's panic are drowned in the clatter and bound of a dog. The beast we had seen on the beach comes leaping downstairs towards us.

Jessie withdraws the threat of his blade from the guard's throat, prioritizing dangers and diverting his resources towards the dog. He stands crouching, poised, posturing himself to draw fire, invite attack, until I dive at him in what might seem to be a turncoat ambush. I knock him to the ground and, like a wunderkid celebrating goal, I kneel on the floor with my arms wide and my hands open to

256

the heavens. I find a pico-moment of peace in the madness and, just as the dog has flexed himself to pounce, with slaver foaming cloudburst above the tight coils of the musculature of his flanks, I engage his mad eyes. I feel his rank breath on me in the fraction of time before he strikes me backwards to the ground. He is heavy on me, with his drool tacky on my face and the bleeding flesh of dead meat rich in the taste of his kiss.

I draw on the subtle language my own dogs taught me and use my all-bar-one senses to tell him what I am at. He licks me with eyes open and beyond the grotesque of his distorted muzzle, I can see that he understands the subtlety of conflict, what generals for hundreds of generations knew before him: that there is no difference between peace and war. They are simply different kinds of games. He turns me over with his weapon head. I roll with it and he comes at me again, tossing me around the room, and if I could I surely would: bawl out laughing the laugh of helter-skelter.

He stops, sits erect next to me, knowing the rules. He rolls away under my first touch, like a kitten. I roll him round and round, and when we have finished we lie on the floor next to each other. I stroke his belly and he purrs.

'That was very impressive,' says Elvira.

The old woman is in a chair by the fireplace and the guard is tied to the manservant, back to back in the centre of the room. The engine of a car ignites outside, and I watch Roy begin a journey back to the casino, a journey he makes at his own insistence for all our benefits, seeing that Jessie has changed since he has been outed, that he is not the man to be entrusted with a fast and disciplined return. He volunteered in whispering confidential, referred to his best ever friend as 'that fucking junkie', as if Jessie had a leper sign on his back saying 'bloodtype: H'.

I harbour unexpressed doubts as to whether Burg will walk unsuspectingly through the circumstances we have constructed. But in the absence of superior alternative, I wish Roy Godspeed, like something from Shakespeare, allow myself to sink back into the luxurious leather of Burg's sprawling sofa as the limo spins away to Kurhaus, where Roy will ply the chauffeur with yet more drink and prop him up in the driver's seat to drunkenly await the return of his lord and master.

Elvira sits next to me. Her boot jags nervously, triptrip-tripletime, up and down in her long . . . thigh . . . leg-cross, and I give myself severe reminders of why I am here. Holding captive the guardians of sweet-dreaming children, I reaffirm the goodness of my motives.

'Jessie, would you get me a drink? A beer, please,' says Elvira. The dog twitches at my feet as Jessie walks past on his lapdog way into the kitchen. 'So tell me, Jimmy, about this girl of yours.'

I shrug, as if to say, '*What can I say*,' and she laughs.

'Oh, you could tell me if you wanted,' and she leans across, whispers with a breaking husk. 'It didn't stop you. Before. In the casino,' and she puts a single finger on my thigh, 'when you kissed me.'

I get my message across to her, see that she understands when she says, in all seriousness, 'I will never hurt Roy. Never.'

I lean down, stroke the dog and Elvira says, 'She must be quite a girl.'

'Here you go,' says Jessie, handing Elvira her drink and standing over us. 'So, Jimmy. What happens when Burg gets here?' Which is enough to vanquish any thoughts I was having of Angela.

What we will do when Burg arrives depends, of course, on what Burg does when he gets here. But in the rules of war we have the uppermost of hands; we have the most coveted benefit of surprise. So we may as well maximize these resources. As if in wait for Indians that come in the night across prairie; and like those once-pilgrim forefathers sitting in trespass on someone else's land, we prepare for battle.

In what I assume is Burg's study, there is a walnut and unalarmed gun cabinet. What good could Burg make of police interventions? Shotguns, rifles and pistols hang in idle threat, looking more like ornaments than the instruments of grief they actually are, until we smash the glass, take them out and pass them among us, bringing them to life. We have guns at home, used purely for sport, but

259

these are completely different kettles of fish. They feel somehow pure in the hand, perfectly balanced, with carved butts and gleaming barrels and, in the case of the pistol I have taken a particular shine to, with chambers that roll almost soundlessly across a hundred precisely engineered clicks.

We retire to the lounge, take nightcaps and wait with guns on our laps and our captives looking at each other thinking, Oh Christ! What's going to happen next.

SHOTS IN THE DARK

Headlights come panning across the windows, like a scene from air raids or prison camps. We take up positions in the hallway, more than half-cocked, but not knowing whether, when a push comes to being shoved, our fingers will freeze on triggers.

A car door opens and shuts. Then silence, for what seems like e-ter-ni-ty, until a shout rings from the driveway, a familiar voice that shouts in unfamiliar desperation. I leap out into the blinding flood of car lights. Squinting into the shining squad, I follow the familiar voice until I see him.

Blood spills lusciously from Roy's bowed head. He is kneeling on the full-beam driveway with his hands tied behind his back, like a deer-hunting victim of senseless battle, waiting to be used as a pawn in an even more senseless game within war. Burg stands next to him, looks me straight in the eye. He takes hold of Roy's hair, wrenches him back and flips open the chambers of his pistol, theatrically loads one, two, three bullets and snaps it back again, rolls it like shaking dice and puts the barrel into Roy's mouth.

I walk towards him slowly, throwing my weapon onto the driveway and raising my hands high.

'Jimmy! What the hell . . .' Behind me I can hear Wingnut as he sees Burg's finger cocking steel of his own. And into an endless moment comes the hollow sound of metal on metal merging with the quiet laugh of Burg.

'Lucky day,' he says, pushing Roy's still breathing face into the driveway. 'Now the rest of them. Outside!'

Wingnut and Jessie come slowly onto the drive, surrendering arms.

'Where's the other one, the Dutch guy. Where is he? Answer me!' he shouts.

'He can't talk,' says Wingnut. 'He's mute.'

'Aah,' says Burg, walking towards me. 'So it's true. You're the one,' and he whips his pistol into me. I see his sly smile lost in the fat of his face as I take my tumble, limit my losses.

He turns to the car, to his three henches who stand against the limo holding guns. He instructs them in Dutch and they advance towards us. I can hear their tread, like slow thunder. But their stealth advance halts as I hear the voice of another Dutch-speaking individual, stopping her countrymen dead in their tracks, persuading them to unconditionally surrender.

Elvira steps out of the shadows with a babe in one arm and a gun in the other, held against the heart of the small child. She voices quick-fire demands that wipe all the smiles from all their

262

faces and the still night is broken once more, this time by guns clattering onto the ground in a metal, unsweet melody of Burg's world collapsing.

'Roy, are you all right?' she says tenderly, pressing the gun deeper into the flesh of the child.

Roy nods, dripping blood and smiling as wide as the night. He slowly stands and Elvira smiles back, looking as if she should be going on a hot date, not giving the slightest hint that, if she was presented with just or unjust cause, she would unhesitatingly brandish the power in her hands.

Elvira is steadfast, declining all appeals to relinquish her stepmother hold of Burg's infant. She stands over the master of this house and much wider domains as he reads the contents of the blue-smeared surviving letter from Flint, flicking through the pages and slowly gathering pace. His face is appalled and he looks for a moment as if he might heave. We all watch, open-mouthed, as the colour drains from his tan face, as he stands like a foal and walks, unsure of foot, slowly out of the room posing no more threat than his gunpoint captive son.

I follow him into his ceasefire and decommissioned study, watch him remove a painting from the wall to reveal a safe that he dials entry to. I watch him take eight cellophane lookalike packages. He hands them to me, one by one, as if he is a Third-World coffee grower.

We return to the lounge, me with my booty,

him with absolutely nothing, and Wingnut complies with my instruction, asking to see the communication from Flint. But it seems only proper, as guests in his house, and seeing him crumple into something quite powerless, that we accept his refusal. He has suffered enough for one day, and Elvira returns his child as if it is something official at the end of worry-making absence, sins forgiven.

We leave his house in several one pieces, knowing nothing of the long-distance puppetry of one woman's hold over a man. We also leave with, in quick estimation, a further one million pound's worth of heroin and a bootful of armaments.

I am in the driving seat now, firing the engine, but as we are about to glide away at journey's end, Elvira leans forward, says, 'Wait,' and walks slowly towards the house with her handbag over her shoulder, as if she is returning to a restaurant to reclaim a forgotten and valued personal possession.

Two rounds shatter the night, turn the interior of our borrowed car perfectly quiet until we see her emerge onto the driveway with spilt and bad blood spattered on her face and fine clothes. Roy breaks his silence and shouts out. He runs to her and goes giddy as he realizes that the two dead sounds in the North Sea night were Burg becoming a thing of all our pasts.

I drive in silent shellshock around the estuary and north towards our temporary home, with only the imagined wailing echo sounds of a dying man and the tittle-tattle of orphan children to invade the luxury of our kid leather. It did not seem strange in the least, at the end of this most abnormal of nights, that none of us felt the compunction to ask Elvira why on earth she had done what she did.

PLOTTING CLEAR PASSAGE: ABSENT BLUE WATER

Back at the house, we sit on the deck passing tequila along the line. I lean back and hear the bathroom sound of Elvira scrubbing down like a flourishing surgeon at the end of operations of heartless precision. Wingnut is shuffling the heroin on his lap, and I wish it were less. If only you could split it into a four-year-old Cosworth, a fortnight in Florida and a diamond for your gal. But it's not. We have come too far, and I think that perhaps things were better in the lesser leagues of our recent past. These are big denominations, these grains of powder, and it is time to consider the reality of our options for delivery, how to get the stuff across borders and waters, through customs.

Roy leaps up like salmon on speed and grabs the tequila from Jess. He drinks it like lemonade, as if quenching his thirst. He stares ahead, looking manic, and drinks again.

'We can take the gear. To Spain. Now!'

Elvira comes out of the bathroom, looking like millions of dollars and asking what is going on.

'It makes sense, Jimmy,' says Roy. 'Easier to get it through France than into England.'

'I can bury it – in a board. It worked the last time,' says Surfman.

We pass the tequila round until it's empty, all standing now, looking out of the window at the night waves in the light of a silvery moon, and we break out a fast-catching smile collective.

It is, actually, a fucking good idea.

Irons must be struck, and with a body going cold on the other side of the estuary, we have to make hotfoot our escape before the steady plod of heavy boots advance on the house. But there is much to be decided in the scheme of who goes where and when with whom. The only thing I know for certain is that I must return to England. I have to see Flint to negotiate the terms for retrieval of Angela, and also to explain the reasons for my emptiness of hand, to give assurances that the gear can be collected, and to personally comply with the as and when of what Flint wants.

Roy is trying to persuade Elvira to join him in Spain. He is selling Almeria like a new recruit on a sales training course, resorting finally to desperation. 'But it's going to be brilliant. I guarantee it.'

In truth, whilst I appreciate the addition of all the new dimensions to Roy's outlook that have resulted from Elvira entering our lives, I hope that she will grant him a clean and violent separation. Not simply for the sake of Roy, but because, with two million of heroin for luggage, I have a preference for a convoy that does not include the resounding silence of her history of motivation.

She has business to attend to in Amsterdam, and although she says nothing to commence the tiny taps that will eventually cause cracks and rip Roy's heart seam from seam, I see their union as one of convenience, on her part, at least.

The plan, hatched by Wingnut and Surfman, is simple and as inconspicuous, risk-free as you could get, given the excess of all the baggage we carry with us.

They have concocted an exchange of value to link us all in a many self-interested chain of commands, within which Rudi will ride shotgun with substances of lesser value.

The boy will travel across the entire length of France, driven by Wingnut and distracted by Monique. For additional company they will share the journey with fifteen bags of heroin and a surfboard, all the attendants which that kind of luggage brings with it. They will cross that most careless border between France and Spain at La Jonquera and will then drive east, into the peninsula that spits back at France, and rendezvous on a station platform for a lasting encounter. Surfman – father, husand and secreter of fine powders – will be there, flanked by Jessie and Roy, just three more beard-growing packers edging a hedon way, with cheese melting and wine boiling, into the land of Dali.

It is a fine plan, and polished to its very edges by the sight of Surfman, for a second time, secreting one variety of recreational release within another. On the driveway, he straps his freshly customized and barely dry sailboard to the roof of the car, dragging further dirt across our tracks.

'I should come with you, Jimmy,' says Wingnut.

'*I need you to take Monique. And you have to sort things out at the place. You have the language.*'

'But you don't.'

And without meaning to, I hurt him. '*I managed all my life, before we met.*'

I bid my farewells to Roy and Jessie, who assure me with conviction that they will be fine, that it's been ages since they have been on a train. It's going to be great, which makes me more happy than sad, but a little sad, nonetheless, as I listen to them plan the journey, try to calculate whether or not they will be temporary peseta billionaires. Elvira catches me watching them, nods towards the kitchen and I follow her.

'They'll be all right,' she says.

I shrug.

She pretends to be distracted, looking out of the window, up the coast towards the pier. I wait for her to turn, fix a look on her, an unambiguous questioning of why she has done the things she has done for and on behalf of us.

'You think I would have killed the child, don't you?'

I shrug again, lacking the resource to tell a lie, and I choose not to write one upon the expressions of my face and demeanour.

'Look at me, Jimmy. What do you see? My breasts, my legs. These hips.' She slaps them playfully, with serious intent coming faststream in her face. 'I can't have children, Jimmy. Not ever.'

She turns away from me, looks back towards the pier. 'I have done things I shouldn't have. I felt I had no choice. I did, of course. We all do. One night . . .' She turns back towards me, face impassive. '. . . There were two of them; friends of Burg. I didn't want to do it, not two of them, but I needed Burg, at least I thought I did. One of them was big. Rough. The other one held me down.'

Her voice cracks. I can see her sad face in a shallow-water reflection of the window, white horses scrolling across her image. I take her shoulders in my hands. She goes tense, slowly unflinches.

'I suppose he used the money he made from pimping me to buy presents for his wife, his children. When I complained about what happened, he gave me five hundred guilders and told me I was finished. So I don't know, Jimmy. I don't know if I would have killed that child. What I thought when I had the gun, when I had my finger on the trigger, that barrel pressed right into his fat belly . . . what I felt . . . It felt as if it was an evil belly of a bastard. It wasn't just a child, it was the son of him, and all I could think about was where he had come from, what made him.'

There is a knock at the door and Wingnut comes in.

I kiss Elvira, on the cheek, and she pulls me close to her, holds me and whispers, 'Don't tell Roy what I said. He wouldn't understand. I don't want to hurt him. Goodbye, Jimmy.' She turns her back, spins on the lethal heels of her boots and walks away.

'*So*,' I say to Wingnut. '*This is it.*'

'Not for long, though. You'll get Angela to call us? Let us know you're all right.'

'*I'll be all right. We've done everything.*'

'What about the gear?'

'*Flint will pick it up. Don't worry. She'll be in touch with you once I get over there.*'

'Are you worried?'

'*We've done what she asked, delivered the package.*'

He shuffles from foot to foot, looking at the ground like a little boy. Outside, Jessie and Surfman are loading up the car, arguing about who gets to sit in the front, about who is going to drive the first stint. And somewhere unseen, Roy will be squeezing a last drop from Elvira, holding on to something that slips through his fingers – faster, the tighter he squeezes.

PART 3

BACK IN BLIGHTY

It is not even a week since I last saw Angela, which is less time than you might think would be necessary to forget what she looks like, to almost have lost track of why we came here in the first place, on the last legs of ricochet percussions from the actions set in train by the abortive saving of her.

The hostess hands me a Bloody Mary, semiclad in a triangle napkin in the way that only happens in belted, airline mollycoddle, and I try to reconstruct the parts that form the sum of Angela. In the thin air of flight, I let my thoughts take their own fancy, into a world in which we are no longer tethered to old habits and debts. A wedding, perhaps, in the autumn throes of a new Iberian bliss. A child to set us on our way, to rule a line on an old life and mark a new beginning in a land from where new worlds have been discovered.

I take the magazine from the pocket on the back of the seat in front and flick through the pages until I get to the map of Europe. Looking down on clouds that patrol the North Sea, I picture Roy and Jessie with Surfman on the train; and in the car, Wingnut and Monique, young Rudi asking if he's nearly there. By the time I have come to terms with the wholly legal baggage with which I return to Easport, they will all be deep into France, travelling south, with kilometres to Lyon dropping like ninepins. I order another Bloody Mary, and the lady in the next seat gets me all wrong with the thousand condemnations of her sub-breath tut. I don't want to get high; I just need to plane down, reach a level of normality before I come to earth with what I pray will not be a bang.

It feels as if it is a new me – something distilled, simply an essence of the real me – walking up the gangplank, holding a rope to steady my rickety steps, about to re-engage a part of umbilical past.

And then the sight of her stabs me in the guts, in my eyes; assaults me from an early history of the hardening of me. Lisa looks down on me, scraping blond hair from her face, putting it behind her ears the way she always used to.

'Jimmy! Oh, Jimmy,' she calls, her voice deeper than my memory had banked and making the sound of a thousand impressions of life having got to her.

Of course it isn't Lisa, nor am I hallucinating or waking from sleep or simply deluding myself. Angela has changed the colour of her hair, and, getting closer as we advance upon each other, the way she has applied the substances intended to alter appearance. No lipstick, a pale foundation and a light lustre upon the lids of her eyes; there is new candescence in the whole of her. She even seems to have changed the way she stands, the nature of the heat she issues.

'*You look different.*'

'I missed you, Jimmy. Thank God it's over.'

'*You look different.*'

'So do you. You've had your hair cut,' says Angela, rubbing her palm up and down on the tight bristle of my nape and skull.

'*It's over? How do you know?*'

'Mrs Flint did it. Made me over. I'm glad you like it.'

You don't look like you, I think. But I mouthshape, slow so she understands me, '*You look beautiful.*' She kisses me, and with my eyes closed, a whispering breeze bringing familiar smells and sounds into full focus, I transport myself back into a land I know too well. It is an instant between the return from a foreign land and a departure to a different one. In this moment, nothing and everything is real.

'Ah. Love's young dream.'

Beyond the blur of Angela's face, my lord and master climbs imperious to the deck.

'What do you think, Jimmy? What do you think of our brand-new girl?'

I smile. Which is all I can do. I let her read what she wants from the open book I pretend to be, and I watch her skip across pages to the heart of the truth of the matter. With a single backward nod of her head she indicates, behind Angela's back, that I should keep my thoughts to myself.

'You've done well, Jimmy. I'm very pleased.'

'*Well?*'

'News travels fast. It's a shame you had to do what you had to do. Never mind, when you deal with that sort . . . you know. Come on down; Angela's just done some lunch. Nice to have another girl around the place.'

Angela links me, makes me feel like a weak part of chain as we follow Flint into the salon. She reaches up on tiptoes, falling into me as we walk, and whispers in my ear, 'She says we can stay. Here. On our own. She has to go away.'

'I was saying to Angela, I have to go away for a few days. You can stay here if you want, have the run of the place,' says Flint.

'*No.*'

'Jimmy!' says Angela.

'*No!*'

'Well, it's up to you. You're very welcome.'

None of this is real. It has nothing to do with Elvira holding a gun to a babe in her arms or with Jessie's habit of quiet desperation or Denny Lane dead in a beach hut, so I am cutting to the chase, putting my hand on the cold flesh of the worked-out tan musculature of Mrs June Flint's arm, and nodding to the stern, from where we telescoped into the miserable lives of the users of magic powders from across the waters. And the minute we are out of Angela's eyeshot I am

278

in the company, once more, of Flint. The skin of Mrs June has been shed; it lies, silken carapace, in the finery of her salon.

'You have something for me, Jimmy?'

I shake my head.

'Where is it?'

I mouth, '*In Spain.*'

'How much?' she says, matter of fact and betraying no kind of surprise in the expression of her face or words that I have arrived empty handed. She must see or hear or otherwise sense a calculation of which I am barely aware myself, because she immediately says, 'You know there's no point in lying, Jimmy. Not after all the good you have done. You see, I must have it all. Wait there.'

I stand on the poop deck, holding on to the rail and looking across at the old fish docks, where polystyrene cases are being loaded onto wagons. The morning catch. Fish that would have been lifted from life source at more or less the moment Burg was falling to a floor on the other side of this sea, with the image of his son fading to black, as if someone had turned a light on during photographic process. I was not there, but I can picture it, as clear as day. It is something I have been trying all day to black out from the screens in my head.

'I wasn't sure you could do it. Kill a man,' says Flint, leaning against the rail, broadsides. 'Two, if you count Lane. I'm sorry about him, Jimmy. He was there to watch, that's all. Temptation – a terrible thing.'

'*You sent him?*'

'Oh, Jimmy.' And as she explains that she overestimated the hold she had over Denny Lane, underestimated his propensity to steal quick bucks, I piece together a full jigsaw image of the many strings of her puppetry, the perfection of her enforcements, the seamless fit of me into her plan and how unaccidental was the fullness of Elvira's flesh contact with our world.

She presses a button on the frame of the door that leads down into the salon. We stand close to each other and I can smell the luxury of her. Her breasts rise and fall, slow, long, lemon on her breath, strains of vermouth. She smiles at me, soft, and a heavy tread comes up towards us from the salon. Stapp gives me a quick sidelong look through the almost-closed purple peaches of his eyes. He hands Flint a cellophane package of similar dimension to others which are too familiar.

'You know Jan. Jan Stapp?'

I nod and Stapp leaves as I turn to Flint, quizzing her with my face.

'Chancey? Yes, I'm afraid he had to go. Didn't you see the letter? The photographs you gave to Burg? I am impressed, Jimmy. But you should have seen them. Jan is quite an artist – with a knife. Chancey not such a worthy canvas. But I'm sure you would have approved. Open that. Here,' she hands me a knife and gestures towards the cellophane package. 'Go on, cut it open. That's right, all the way down. Now throw it overboard. Go on. Give the fish a treat. Go on!'

'*Is this real?*'

'Oh, yes. It's the best stuff. Do it.'

And I do. I take a hundred thousand pounds and more and feed it to the ducks.

For the first time since . . . I don't know, I feel at peace with my circumstances. We eat lunch and I drink too much fine claret too eagerly and listen to Angela and June chitter chatter the way I feel sure only women can. At the table of my rich and powerful, arguably benign and villainous, host, I find a deep sleep.

STATELESS

Perfect strangers are now benefiting from a new lease of life in the windmill we made home, but which we always knew was never for keeps. So Angela and I have booked into a low-rise sprawling hotel built for travelling salespersons on the edge of Easport, marooned by a ring road. The room is small and steeped in an unshiftable staleness of cigarette smoke; it is deck-accessed, with shower caps, a remote control that doesn't work and full tea and coffee-making facilities to occupy the hours that the dial on the trouser press counts down. Irrespective of whatever lilies or candlelight you might use to adorn the place, which is exactly what Angela has done, it is most definitely not the kind of place you could make home. A woman would be advised to reserve her touch for a different location or activity – the kind of activity more in keeping with the kind of place. But I am tired, and Angela has gone shopping.

Somewhere between afternoon and evening, I shower and shave, plan and prioritize to the other-hemisphere sounds of soap in the room next door.

I write a note to Angela, saying I will be back by nine and that if she likes we can go out for a meal. Leaving the key at reception, I feel Engeland pack itself in the treat of my shoes. I take purchase on the island nuance that separates us from the continent: the way the receptionist dances a disco cameo to the infectious beat of a boy band as she goes from the key hooks to the register; the way she tends to residents as if they have been granted an outlandish favour.

I walk past the happy hour wine bars and not-open discos. It is dead time in the centre of town, so I make my way up Dockroad towards the marina, but staying on the right side of the dual carriageway, not getting sucked into Flint's forcefield, which has done its worst in my absence, extending across a sea, recruiting Stapp in a shuffle of the deck. Stacking everything in her favour. Leaving nothing to chance.

Office workers are drinking outside the bars, leaning on polished capstans and, two hours since five, sailing three sheets to the wind.

'Hi, Jimmy,' comes a voice from the half-hearted shadows of the Earl de Grey. The Earl de Grey is a public house which is temporary home to an elder profession and mentioned in signs on the walls of the modernmost temple in all of Easport, the Marriott Hotel, where residents are implored to 'Please note that the Earl de Grey is not a normal pub'.

I know the woman from the early days in Easport,

from the brief time I spent here after leaving Newholme, before I established an imperfect legitimacy of operation. I don't know what to call her, am saved from embarrassment by the fact that she knows the state I am in. So I nod, break my stride long enough to notice that she has a big belly now, that her neck sags and twenty years of chemicals have taken their toll on her hair.

'Still with Ange?'

I nod, slowing out of politeness, but falling into misinterpretation. She lifts her skirt, which is double-take short in the first place. The tiny elastic of her knickers runs like a black blade into her white fat, like meat flesh cut with cheesewire, that kind of mismatch of something not fitting the bill. But she has had a bad lot, is above blame and simply cutting her cloth accordingly by lying in beds other people have made for her. But she does something to make me dislike her, to banish qualm from my onward progress. She holds her skirt up and runs her tongue around her mouth, smiling as she does it. I know this girl, and I would recognize pathos if it was where it should be. Which it isn't. She actually means it.

'Fifteen, Jimmy. For French. You can feel me.'

It seems, in the compression of time, the expansion of space that has been dictated by the events of the past week, as if I am a million light years from the paradise whereabout of the boys, from where even Surfman and Monique and Rudi, who we didn't know from Adam or Eve or Cain or Abel ten

284

days ago, are lazing in a house built for and against the sun. They will be there now, together, making home whilst I am held here, stateless, unable to pass from port.

Flint had my lack of movements secured even before I told her where the bounty was havened. She had known about the heroin we acquired from Stapp and Burg, had made preparations for its recovery and was even able to tell me that Wingnut and Monique, smokescreened by Rudi, had made it safely into France and through La Jonquera. She told me that she would personally oversee its collection and wholesale destruction. With Angela below decks in the gentle clatter of the setting of table, she had whispered to me her good intent, that she could not trust Wingnut or Roy to destroy it, and certainly not Jessie.

'*Jessie? How . . .*'

'It's my job to know,' she had said, smiling, going on to tell me that I should message Wingnut, advise him that she will be there before he knows it and to do exactly as she instructed.

'You'll be stuck here without a passport, with me watching every step you make until every gram of that shit has been accounted for and taken out of circulation. And remember, your prints are all over that stuff. You'd be looking at ten to fifteen, Jimmy. That would be a shame with you on the verge of a new beginning.' She went on to tell me how she had taken a shine to Angela, how she doesn't usually get things wrong or change her opinion about people, but in this case she had. 'Keep an eye on her, though, Jimmy. Once a junkie . . . Even if she's not taking it, she's still a junkie.'

Almost by accident I have meandered my way to the Whalebone, standing small, proud-chested in the dusk amongst grain silos, final embers from the west glowing on the dull steel of the conveyor casings that jag the skyline like teeth in a broken saw. The Whalebone beckons me, it whispers at me, invites me for a final drink in a place that could only be England. And as I go in through the saloon doors, I feel as if I am doing something for the first time. It is all around me, the round-vowel voices and the foulmouth banter of domino clatter, the etched glass windows of tap room and lounge, the big-frame curve of the polished bar in the stalactite glisten of glasses and optics, the smells of gravy and peas and a hundred years of nicotine. Wax and bleach are somewhere unseen.

'Jimmy, lad.' Tommy Curl nods, reluctantly it seems to me, from the bar in the back room. He takes his pint and sits down without offering to buy me a drink, not waving me through or asking how's it going. And now I come to think of it, he didn't even look me in the eye when he said, 'Jimmy, lad.' He gave me no encouragement to stay. He shied from me.

But I do stay, on my own and by the bar, drinking warm beer too fast. I buy cigarettes and chainsmoke to enter a spirit that spurns me. I

286

receive trailer-info preview snippets of a lonely future: private screenings of a soundless wakening, one teabag in a cup, an unopposed schedule of the day; the spastic bliss of doing what you want when you want it, the joylessness of that. And I feel a waft of the possibility of being alone, like an essence smell of something quite perfect in a foreign street, something that excites and disappoints, expresses richness of life, poverty of prospect.

I am a willing victim of drink, offering myself up to it and letting it mottle the Victorian photographs, the panorama of proud sportsmen. And all the time, from pint to pint, I feel the flit of Tommy's eyes, looking at me and away, from his safe place. I flip back through recent events, pass from present into past, backward in album, and it becomes clear to me what part he has played in the setting of me on my marks, the readying of me to go in pursuit of people who have delivered me to the here and now.

I slip away from the Whalebone, leaving a space that somebody will fill, not saying goodbye to Tommy Curl. It is dark and I am in no mood for the compilation retrospective of night walking, so set off towards the heavier traffic of the ring road to seek a cab.

'Jimmy!'

Tommy walks up to me, is about to say something grave that is heavy on his insides, but I stop him in his tracks.

'*No!*' I message him. I save him an unnecessary

confession and see a burden drop to the pavement. He gives me as kind a smile as his kind of good man can deliver, says thanks and goes with a shake of the hand. I don't dwell on the depths of shit that Tommy had got himself into, that left him with no option other than to set me up for Flint: to drip-feed me with morsels of a big one-off – a lighthouseman and a windsurfer in the dead of a night – that was always too good to be true. I wonder what part he played in the fuelling of Angela's debt, that irresistible flamepull that sent me reeling into Flint's world. I watch him go and, despite it all, the sight of his stooped and shamed back going through the saloon doors of the Whalebone makes me think that maybe it would not be the greater of evils to have a bad and ruinous father than no father at all.

The carriageway was cabless and, as is ever the case, the walk back is longer, deigning too much time to think; so much so that I have decided that when I get back to the hotel, I will ask Angela to call my mother. If I can forgive Tommy Curl, bid him an unbloody farewell, then the time has surely come to commence the ruling of a line under a more deeply rooted part of what seems now to have been a former life.

I see the light in our hotel room, can see Angela moving across the window high above me, making me anxious to feel her touch, so I run across the carpark, take the steps two at a time, stride

288

out along the deck towards our door and, with my hand upon the handle, I hear her laugh. I peer through a chink in the curtains, watch her sprawled on the bed. In a cheap motel, amongst the flowers and candles she has used to forge a makeshift home, she looks many million dollars. She is wearing just her pants and a short cropped T-shirt, and I watch her giggle in the TV white light. She has balanced a glass on her flat stomach and, as she laughs, wineglow shadows make psychedelic crimson pools on the wisp line of hair that runs almost to her navel. She laughs again and spills some wine, drags a finger up along her belly and licks it. But her face goes straight and she sits up, turns the alarm clock towards her. She is sad and I see her say to herself, 'Come on, Jimmy,' then curl up on the bed with her back to me, not watching the TV any more.

I love every inch of her.

HOME FROM HOME

Weatherwise it's such a lovely day, and driving north from Easport towards Warnsea, we pass the windmill tower of a place that was once home.

We are on our way to another of my homes, the most distant in terms of both time and space. Frances had told Angela that, yes, she would love to come with us, to form a part of the bidding of farewells. She had added that she had wanted to go back for a long time, that isn't it strange, the serendipity of things, because she had actually planned a trip up to the north coast. It would be nice. The way Angela related it, the tone of my mother's voice, which I pictured as she told me, unbalanced me. Like a song that doesn't quite pick up the beat, like a crescendo that doesn't quite burst, I was left wanting more, feeling that something remained unsaid.

Angela puts a consoling hand on my thigh and squeezes. She turns in her seat, curls a leg under her bottom and says, side-saddle, to Frances sitting in the back, 'Was Jimmy a good boy when he was young?'

'He was a real gem. Full of energy, always out on the beach, making things, exploring. Do you remember?' I look at her in the rear-view. She forces a fragile smile that slumps under its own load. She looks away, coughs into a handkerchief and watches the roadside blur by.

'It sounds idyllic, where you lived. I can't wait.' Angela jigs up and down, turns half circle to face Frances again, resting her chin on arms that are crossed on the back of the seat, but unwitted as to the truth that she has already been in my infant home. She has lived there, used it in convalescence and for the same purpose my mothers chose it in the first place: for privacy.

'What was Jimmy's father like?' says Angela, casual but in for a penny.

Although she is silent, my mother is, in partial reflection, unfazed. She says, eventually and in even metre, without looking away from window gaze, 'People change. There was nothing so terrible that can't be forgiven. I was ill, you see. That's when Jimmy went into care.'

'It must have been awful.'

'It was.'

'Well, you've survived. Both of you. It must be in the blood.' She puts her head on my shoulder.

The car falls silent and we are welcomed to Warnsea. I change gear: once, up; twice, down. And we are thanked for visiting Warnsea, travelling west and away from the sea towards a red road that will whisk us quickly north.

'I think you'll be happy, the two of you,' says Frances. Her voice is sad, as if she doesn't believe it. She is altogether less composed than she has been at any of our meetings. The jaunt is gone from the way she sits, the way she talks, the movement and gesture of her. She is leaden.

I can feel Angela's head turn on my shoulder and see half a honeymoon exchange of kindness reflected in the mirror image of Frances's eyes, and I remind myself in the cocoon of travel that there is nothing real going on in the getting-to-know-you vestments of the first meeting of mother and lover.

Much as it discomforts us all, it is only right that we make this folly of a trip into the past. Indeed, it is only fair to Angela that I do so, given that we are now on the verge of something new. It is time to wipe a slate clean. What harm can come of it? Tomorrow we finalize matters with Flint. If all has gone well, we will receive our passports back and whatever happens today will be of no consequence.

'You remember,' says Frances. 'It's been twenty years – more – and you remember,' she says, easily pleased by a simple manoeuvre, a right turn off one road onto another. Then a left, and a precarious descent along a road that is announced as dangerous, liable to subsidence, a dead end.

'*I have been back*,' I gesture. '*Just once*,' looking across at Angela, who is summing two plus two and getting four.

I park the car in a clearing in the trees a hundred yards from the cliff. A storm is brewing over the sea and the wind has turned nasty, gusting us off balance as we make our way towards the edge.

'No!' shouts Frances through the wind. I turn and see that she has an arm linked through Angela's. She has lagged behind, going her own sweet way, and is now steering Angela away from the beginning of the path that leads down towards the cove. 'This way.'

She sets off along the cliff top, towards the allotment and the more difficult path, with its two precarious sections that have become even worse with age, as if they might be paying a price for harmful deeds their edges have precipitated.

I cannot protest, of course. So I tramp along behind them, the way a child would if he was not getting his own way. They are huddled tightly together against the wind, walking slowly in unsuitable shoes, treading carefully through the gorse. The path forks: right, towards where we kept our allotment on the extremity of land's horizon with sky or distant sea; left for the marked trail that goes on to Whitby. They go right and, as we walk straight towards the sea which appears in a thin seam that gets fatter with every step, the wind whips up danger. You can hear the bedlam chorus of gulls swirling up from the cliffs. Each step takes us many miles further away from madding crowds.

Except we are not alone. Stood by the ram-shackle shed, with a half-cocked leg resting its

293

foot on the blade of a spade, is the rear plane of a shape so familiar to me twenty-five years on that I struggle to catch my breath, feel something trap itself within me.

Frances stops by the side of the figure, as if in casual conversation, and then turns, still linked with Angela and huddling against the wind, coughing into her handkerchief, then beckoning me to join them.

The wind is stronger now, funnelling up from the cove beneath, and I set myself at an angle, walk on, head down for the final twenty yards or so. By the time I can hear voices through the wind, by the time I look up, I can see quite clearly the features of a mother of mine who looks nothing like me, and nor is there any reason why she should. Of that I have not a single seed of doubt. Stood, as I am, on the thin scratched grass where once we grew things together against laws of nature, where we fertilized growth that had no right to ever fruit, I can be certain of this one thing in a widespan, big-sky world full of doubt.

'Angela,' says Frances, 'this is Michelle.' And then, speaking to Michelle, she says, 'There you are. I've done my bit. I will speak to you later. Jimmy, could I have the keys, please. It's cold. I'll wait for you there.'

My mother hooks her arm through Angela's and they walk away, unlike any kind of relative strangers you would ever have seen, swept along by the wind, which they allow to take them like kites. Michelle ushers me into the shed.

'I've got some tea going,' she says. 'Come on, the wind's bitter. It's a bit, you know, a bit scruffy, but I've tidied up. It's nothing like it was when we used to come up, but at least it's warm.' She opens the door. 'So you're called Jimmy now, eh? We've all changed. Except Frances. She hasn't changed at all.'

I go into the shed. I sit and watch her make tea on the edge of a cliff where I uttered my last call of 'mother'. Her hands are small and her weathered face and thinning hair stick out from her coat like a dying flower.

There is a broken bottle behind the calor fire. I stand, bend down and pick it up, and with all the venom I can summon, I resurrect clear vision of my mother crying by a fire with knitted ruin on the floor. I hold it up.

'*Remember?*'

'Is there any point in me saying I am sorry?' she says, 'I loved you. I loved your mother. You can choose to disbelieve me if you want. But if you want the truth, that is the truth.' She hands me a mug of tea, which I take. 'It was you who didn't love me. I was so alone. Do you know how that feels? Of course you do. You blame me for that, don't you? For putting you in that home, for making Frances go mad. But if it wasn't for me, Jimmy; if it wasn't for me, there wouldn't be a you. She wouldn't have done it, not without me.

Have you ever thought what it took to do what we did then? How we agonized? Who would be left on the outside? You lost your voice in an accident that nobody ever intended.' She drinks her tea and looks through a cracked pane of glass out to sea.

'I used to believe that anything is possible, if you believe it is right. But now I know there can be no such thing as perfection.' She looks down at her feet and kicks the broken neck of the whisky bottle. 'We grew things here. We grew things in salt air on top of a dying cliff. That wasn't real, that was a trick.'

I haven't sipped from my tea. I hold it in my hands, less hot than it was when she gave it to me. She puts a finger soft upon my chin and lifts my head up to see her. She is crying and I am not. She takes the mug from my hand, places it on top of the stove and opens the door. 'Goodbye, Jimmy. I just wanted you to know, you're not the victim.'

'I . . .'

'Tell it to your mother.' She holds out her hand and I take it. It is hot, firm and surprisingly strong in its grip. 'And do me a favour, please. Would you?'

I nod.

'Tell her I love her. If you believe it, tell her. She might accept it coming from you.'

FOREIGN HAULAGE

I go out of my way to make life as easy as I can for my mother, on whom the day has taken great tolls. For my part, the events on the cliff are unreal, like a dreamcall in the last fragments of sleep.

As I wait for thunderbolt realizations of the gravity of recent declarations, we drive my mother home to York. It is out of our way, but there is nothing to be read into what I do, nor is there any significance in the fact that I accept her offer for us to stay the night. It has been a long day, and . . . well, it gives us time to walk round the old town, and we can dine and drink without worrying about the drive back.

Angela, who has unfumblingly grasped, without so much as a grumble, the improbabilities of the making of me, puts her head on my shoulder in that road-movie coupling I have always envied in the swift passings of others. She lowers her voice into a whisper that brushes my neck and says, 'You should have told me. But I know now. I'm glad about that.'

Tomorrow, if all has gone well, we can leave –

for Spain. Red tail lights kissing all kinds of things goodbye.

Furthermore, I have Michelle's message for my mother. I give houseroom to the vast baggage of doubt that riddles me, as to whether or not I should tell her. I have to reach forward into the future, grapple with the ricochet damage that can be wrought by the good intentions of ordinary truths. But for now Frances is a sleeping rear-view image, pale and restless, breathing heavily. Angela, too, is in the early stages of sleep on my shoulder, so I turn the music on low and watch the North York Moors glide towards us, as if we were in a slow passage through the highest-tech arcade of the next millennium.

As we edge closer and closer to York, I ease off the gas still further, not wanting the journey, its safeness, to end. Angela twitches, falling down stairs in her dream, and I watch her reverberate back into peace, watch my hand lift the sleeve of her blouse in an act of treachery. She twitches and I let the sleeve fall, but not before I see a not-so faded blemish that wasn't there last night when I traced my tongue over practically every inch of her.

Frances introduces us to Sam and Lydia and Holly, half a brother and two halves of sister who are going to a party. Angela listens in wonder to the in-their-stride politeness of my step family. She listens and then endorses my polite decline of dinner. Frances doesn't counter our argument that it might be better if Angela and I take a walk rather than intrude. One step at a time. So we leave the hubbub confine of my mother's home, halting briefly with a backward look when we get to the end of the gravel path. It is a grand house, with a lusciously unkempt jungle garden and rickety cars parked in a weeded clot. It is a mayhem house of free spirits, the kind of house in which you would imagine there would be an ascendancy of happy over sad, more truth than lies in the revelation of one occupant to another. Which has nothing at all to do with the whether or not of my telling Frances that she is still loved by a lover from a previous life. Truth has more to do with what is at stake than morality.

Don't you think?

There is a different American couple sat at the identical table as the last time I came here, and just as on that previous occasion, when I failed to execute the simple task of dining, this new couple observe me with as identical and unknowing a New World rudeness as their compatriots.

The waiter chooses to hide the truth of his recognition of me, tends to us with polite and sympathetic regard for my limitations. As he observes Angela's instructions and brings aperitifs, he jolts the voyeur silence of that other table with a disapproving slight of look that snaps the Americans into a plate-stare, a call for settlement of bill with half a bottle of wine not drunk, no pudding or coffee.

We sit in a silence that is neither awkward nor strained, deliberating over the eating of plump seared flesh in delicate sauce with tiny vegetables on fine china plates the size of long-playing records. I have a fillet steak, Angela a trio of monkfish, mullet and sea bass. We finish with a board of cheese, another bottle of rich wine. We pick slowly without exchange, and as the restaurant slowly empties I see stretching glimpses of a future life, when children have left home, when two people know each other too well on the wrong side of discovery.

And after all that has happened today, when she does speak, Angela proffers a last remaining slither of Camembert and says, 'Go on. You have it.' She stands, smiles and says, 'I won't be a moment,' and I watch her as she walks towards the toilet, where I know she will spend a little too long, do something which has to stop. I think about everything we have all risked and I want to hate her, but I can't.

Better than your own bed, better than the finest hotel, is the uncommon luxury of guesting in someone else's home – some good host you know well enough to be invited, not so well that the first sounds you hear are dream-lingering alien, not so well that everything you scroll amongst, advancing into an ordinary day, performing everyday tasks, surprises you. Different lotions on different shelves; the peculiar fashioning of tea and coffee and toast and jam; the unfamiliar pattern of the spines of books and records. New smells; old smells in new cocktail. Faces you can recognize from unseen spoken history. What is most uncommon this particular morning is that all these things are true, and that the stranger who hosts me is my mother – my real mother, my earth mother, the particular mother of mine who is the woman of whom I was natural born.

I sit and eat and drink amongst the come-day, go-day transit of family. Sam slaps my back, playfully convivial. Asks me, 'How's it going, Jimmy,' between his bites at toast, his hangover attack on juice. 'Good meal last night?' And no sooner have I nodded than Lydia comes in and shouts, 'Hi, Jimmy,' from the echo delve into fridge. And they discuss, with me in their midst, their simple tasks of how to fill the summer remainder now that school is out. Holly comes in last with big uncombed hair and her face still puffy from sleep. She turns the TV off, flicks the radio on, shouts, 'Ha!' and opens the window, hurls the remote control for the TV onto the lawn, and an episode from ritual recommences. Frances comes in with morning post, holding aloft a card from Australia where the children's father is canoeing sabbatical down the Murray.

And then, in the recharging of a teapot, with the hurried buttering of more toast, the room slowly empties as sisters and a brother go their separate ways into a day, leaving me attempting to eke traces of family resemblance: in the angles of brow, the juts of nose, the purses of lip, pallor, mood. Nothing that I can see, of me in them.

Sam is the last to leave. He asks me to come along, see what it's like down at the museum where he's got a summer job, but I decline and he rushes out of the house, without offence and slamming the door, sending a signal to Angela for emergence from the safe hiding of her toilet. I have no difficulty in understanding why she might prefer not to endure such a family scenario, when she, my lover, is more sister of mine than they could ever be.

Frances puts toast down in front of Angela and asks me as she goes back to the stove, not would I like some more, but, 'What did Michelle . . . What did she have to say to you?'

'*This and that*,' I indicate with shoulders and open tilting hands, the jut of a fat bottom lip.

She laughs. 'After twenty-five years?'

'Jimmy,' says Angela, reaching across and imploring me with a squeeze of my arm.

'*No*.' I shake my head, unseen by my mother.

'It's all right, Angela. He'll tell me when he's ready.' She says it as if she is a mother who might claim she knows me better than I know myself.

It is quite natural that Angela should want to do what, by some consent, comes naturally to women, even if the circumstances in which she persuades

302

me to spend a morning in York shopping are by no means normal. She is, after all, about to spend the summer in Mediterranean climes, for which she will require a new wardrobe.

I do not wish to generalize, to compose a fallacious rule from the specifics of my own limited experience, but you could posit that sometimes women shop to renew, to rule lines in time and seasons, to establish references against which to plot a path from somewhere bad to somewhere better. Which is why I consent, because I can see where she might be coming from. So for an hour and a half I attend her perusals like a well-trained courtier, until I am granted reprieve. When she suggests that I go for a drink – 'Go and read the paper or something, I'll be all right on my own' – I know it is an unreal parole and, of course, I mistrust her motives for wanting to be alone. But I play the game, for a last time, allowing her to think that I believe she is either buying something expensive for herself, or something for me.

I do not go for a drink but buy a paper, some magazines, too, for the flight and for empty afternoons in the sun, and I find myself a spot on the grass beneath the minster, from where I watch a small fraction of the world go by. A small fraction which, after half an hour or so, becomes the greater part of my own small world when Angela makes the familiar linking shape I last saw yesterday, walking along a cliff top enjoined to my mother. They go into the restaurant and I watch Angela take, for the second time, the table I myself have recently twice taken.

It is lunchtime and the grass is becoming crowded with picnickers. I feel encroached upon, so I stand and leave to take my place at a bar the way Angela knew would have been for the best from the start.

I have the devil's own job to find a den of pure iniquity, untampered by uberbrewers, but eventually I find my kind of place beyond the city walls, where you have to go to avoid the plastercast of history reinvented. I order a pint, drawing hostile looks from the barmaid, who considers me rude. Steve Ryder is on the television, wordlessly linking yesterday's Wimbledon highlights with the treats today might later have in store. Heavy juke metal drowns him. It pounds for the entertainment of bikers playing pool with their molls.

At one o'clock, halfway down my second pint, Steve Ryder fades to bulletin. His image is replaced by a female newsreader I cannot name, and in turn her pretty face is cut to that of an altogether more familiar figure. Silverpiece is staring into camera. He is proud as he talks, holding aloft a plastic bag of white powder. On the desk in front of him, from which he holds court as the nation waits for a Russian darling to take centre stage, are fourteen similar bags which, if dusted, would be printed with the contour maps of my unique fingers. I reach across the bar and grab the remote control for the TV from the shelf where dirty glasses are queuing to be washed. I take aim and pump up the volume until the TV on the wall practically shudders to be heard above the anthem metal chorus of jukebox.

'Oi!' shouts a biker, then another and another in disharmony.

'Give me that,' says the barmaid.

'This is just the first of many hauls, I can assure you,' says Silverpiece. 'It is our aim to completely halt the passage of narcotics into the eastern ports.'

'Oi, I said.' A heavy hand is on my arm, a metal-fingered fist upon my tailoring. I look around, see the augmentation of doubt taint him. I smile and hold up one finger to him, turn back to the screen and hear a call from the manager, who is coming through from the other bar.

'Hit the fucking mute,' he shouts.

'This latest coup was achieved with the full cooperation of the Spanish authorities,' says the pretty girl. I have heard enough. So, in the interests of quick departure, obeying instinct for the bloodless preservation of self, I do as the man asked. I hit the fucking mute myself. I hand back the remote control and do my best to apologize as I make swift departure without staying to finish my drink. I have better things to do.

Summertime York on Saturday afternoon is no place to make swift progress, so I reconcile myself to the impossibility of running to the restaurant. I walk with the flow, tossing as I do the possibilities of something terribly wrong having occurred in the Spanish sun to the heroin claims of Mrs June

Flint, to the freedom and well-being of my adopted family.

'Jimmy?' says Angela. I see her say it through the window of the restaurant. 'What? I've not finished.' But she leaves anyway. I can see from my mother's expression that she misunderstands my reasons for breaking up the party. I gesture that I have to go, that I will write. And my heart goes out to her when I see her battered resignation. In an instant, I fully understand that in the lottery of life I am, relatively speaking, no victim.

Angela thinks it peculiar that I am driving as fast as I can towards a voluntary meeting with a man of the law. Given her understanding of the situation, she thinks it strange that I should wish to present myself to Silverpiece. And as she expresses doubt, as she pleads with me to not turn right onto Dockroad, I am fully aware that what I am doing carries considerable risk. The nature of my relationship with Silverpiece changed when I did what I did to save Angela, when Flint entered the field of our dubious friendship. But the way I see it, if I want to know exactly what the fuck is going on I can either turn to Silverpiece or I can turn to Flint. In the making of this choice, Angela and I do not see eye to eye.

Looking up, I can see Silverpiece's office from where I stand. Behind me are the cranes of dock, points of departure and arrival.

'Let's go, Jimmy. Please.'

I stoop, lean into the car and kiss her on the mouth. She tastes the same as she ever did.

'Jimmy,' comes a voice from behind me, 'what in God's name are you doing here. Come on, get back in the car. Quick,' says Silverpiece, looking nervously behind him. 'I'll meet you at the hotel.'

'*How do you . . . ?*'

'I know everything,' he says.

And he does. He knows everything. He tells me that what he knows is a danger to himself and a greater danger to me. He returns to me my passport to a different life, placing it on the table next to the tea and coffee-making facility, then hands me a perforated piece of paper, tissue thin. It is a remittance advice from a royal bank, advising that twenty million pesetas now belong to me, in the care of the Banco Bilbao Vizcaya, Paseo de la Castellana, Madrid.

'She owns you now, Jimmy.'

'*No way.*'

'Just wait, son. You just wait.' He says it with a carefree smile, as if there might be worse fates than being owned by Flint.

PARADISE OR PROXIMATE

I wake slowly into a complete stillness of dark and I am truly blinkered from any hint as to whether it is day or night, other than the whispering splash of body on water that comes shimmering through the shutters, so I pad with tiny steps towards the window and brace myself for harsh and blinding light.

The big sky is brilliant blue, speckled with sunspots that I blink and blink away until they have faded completely. The figure standing by the pool is Ramon, here to cook tonight's feast. It is our first anniversary and we will celebrate long into the night. Ramon is here, I should tell you, because Jessie is not, and even if he was, he would be in no fit state to be relied upon for the preparation of any kind of food.

The shutters and thick walls, the stone floors and ceiling fan do well in their efforts to fend heat, but still I am sheened with restless sweat. I shower, dress and move slowly through the quiet house. Snippets of lemon grove, grey jaggy mountains, a distant white village come at me as I go round and down the stairs, hear the house echo with my lonesome progress.

The clock on the kitchen wall tells me that it is two fifteen. Time for siesta. I pour myself an orange juice, drink it quickly and pour another, reconstructing as I hydrate the chronicle of late night and early morning. It is fiesta, and though we did not open the club last night, in deference to the passage of Virgin and the revelry of penitents, Surfman and Monique took us on a customary dawn cruise along the coast and into caves.

I can hear Wingnut as soon as I open the door to the garden. He is sat at a table by the pool, in citrus shade with Roy and Ollie in earnest study, repeating after him, '*Buenos dias. Que tal?*'

As soon as he sees me, Ollie jumps down from his seat, ignoring his father's urges that he finish his lesson. Ollie bounds across the lawn, running open-armed through the sprinkler spray and launching himself at me. I catch him, spin him ritually round and he bellows, 'Buenos dias, Jimmy! Que tal?'

'*Muy bien*,' I smile. '*Y tu?*' I nod.

'*Muy bien*,' he shouts, jumping up and down just like his father, with a muscle-ripping smile and understanding my every unspoken word of foreign tongue.

I carry him towards the table and Wingnut disapprovingly folds the books closed.

'*Where's Angela?*'

'Riding,' he says. 'With the Americans.'

Roy takes Ollie from me. 'Come on, let's go for a swim, then you've got to get some sleep before tonight.'

'I want to go with you,' says Ollie.

'I've told you, you can't,' says Roy.

'I want to see the planes.'

'No.'

'When will you be back?'

'I'll wake you, don't worry.'

Ollie, who has been with us since the spring, for reasons more bad than good, has never met Elvira. He has seen photographs, heard endless stories and watched video footage of Roy's trips to Amsterdam with her. And, never having met her, he has the perfect basis for false expectation that she will be everything his father also hopes. What Ollie does not know is that, if Roy's wildest dream comes true, then he will be the closest his new mother could ever get to having a child of her own. This knowledge of mine is, as far as I know, secret from Roy.

'Are you going to see Jessie?' asks Wingnut when Roy and Ollie have gone. Discussion of Jessie's plight is *non grata* in the company of Roy, as has been the case for several months.

I nod.

'Do you want me to come?'

I shake my head. '*I need you here for tonight. We've got to open the club. We can't afford to close it again.*'

The club has to make us sufficient money between May and October to last all year. I have got an MC over from England costing five hundred quid a day whether or not he magnets in and shouts out to the Eurotrash from the costa. For us, it is a good number, but there are many other not quite so good numbers breathing down our necks, so we have to be on our mettle. It's not like Warnsea here. This is *sol*, in the mountains and not far from Med, but it is work. *Mañana* is the preserve of our competition.

I take the mountain road to Granada, going north of the beach hordes and winding my way spaghetti western through foothills. It occurs to me, driving through another dusty white village that greets and bids farewell with roadside animal carnages, that on the drive back I will be making eastward progress through Eastwood country.

Jessie has been in Granada since winter. He is beyond the point of return, and the only thing remaining in my compass is to visit him occasionally to monitor the soundness of his impurity, and to pay his rent so at least there is only one purpose to his stealing. We thought for a while that he had made it. He came off the methadone and returned to the seeming heart of our fold. He asked us to treat him normally, so I put the door of the club in his charge. Can you imagine that! In the shit or bustness of that scenario, bust wins ten out of ten. I know now.

Today is the first birthday of our second life together, which means that, with some sugarcoated diva holding silver aloft in the centre of an English court, it is three hundred and sixty-four days since

Angela and I made our tormented flight from Easport, not knowing the slightest iota of what fate had befallen Roy, Jessie and Wingnut at the drug-hauling hands of English and Spanish officials.

I had driven Angela through the night along the coast road, which I can see now, down the mountain to my left. We drove nervously on the wrong side of right through promenading villages. I listened to Angela's Spanglais pleas for direction at the outside tables of bars where young children played on midnight's morning slopes. And we finally arrived at a vaguely familiar unmarked road that led to our hacienda.

We drove slowly, parked the car at one of the entrances to the lemon grove a hundred yards from the house and inched our way towards the flickering lights of garden chatter. We crouched by the fence and singled out, one by one, Wingnut, Monique, Surfman, Jessie, Roy and Rudi.

'Who the hell are they?' Angela had whispered.

They laughed at something Roy had said. Surfman patted him on the back and Roy repeated whatever it was, making them laugh louder, giving me grounds to stand up and walk through the gate towards them, with Angela following me, saying, 'Who is that girl? Jimmy! I want to know!'

Monique introduced herself and Angela came to see that there was no cause for that kind of concern. I soon learned there was no cause for any concern.

Wingnut read to us from that day's local paper,

telling me that five hundred million pesetas' worth of heroin had been captured on a Spanish boat in English waters. It was a triumph, even though none of the crew had been captured. And he added further flesh to those newsprint bones by telling me that there had been a reception committee to greet their arrival, arranged by Flint. A concert party dancing to the tune of a score that shantied to Flint's baton. She had extended her arms across the Biscay Bay, was working in league with the English authorities to seal off the passage of drugs into England's eastern ports, providing them with information in exchange for heaven knows what.

Granada glistens beneath me now, sudden in a mountain sky, as if by simply driving over a final summit I have lifted a sheet and found treasure. I stop at the Buenavista, as I always do, and order a *licor de Manzana*. I drink it slowly, taste its boozed apples and let the day's edge bevel until I can build some kind of hope that this afternoon, perhaps, Jessie will say that he wants to return. But by the time I let the car freewheel down towards the hazing gardens of the Generalife, the delusion turns to its rightful vapour in a second fermentation.

Jessie is living student-quartered in a one-room apartment in a corner of a clean and respectable old house. He has to cross a corridor for hot water and the toilet, but it is comfortable, with a rocking chair and a bed, a small table and a two-ring electric hob. The air is unconditioned, but a window opens on to a view of the old town, and for most of the year there is the pleasant chill of altitude in the offing.

He greets me in the usual way, an exchanged shake of hands, more formal than either of us deserves, but a realistic measure of the disappointments with which we both have to cope. I drive us up to the Parador in the first stage of an ordained procedure which we follow like the pulpit numbering of hymns. He tells me what he has done since we last met: about the friends he has made; about how he is coping on two hits a day and that he isn't mixing with bad sorts, not dealing; that he thinks he can ween himself off, maybe get a job; he tells me how he hates the tourists, especially the English. And I cannot answer him, for every reason imaginable, when he poses his ritual enquiry as to the welfare of Anne-Marie and Roy. He is quite lonely enough without knowing how the tiny parts of the world he loves the most have spurned him.

I accompany him down the hill, with the jewel glaze of Alhambra coming in and out of our scope as we pass through the garden glades. Our communion ends as it always does, with an uneasy embrace, a demonstration of flimsy hope. My shirt uncreases from the union and I watch him walk back towards the town, all alone. His progress today is slower than usual, his tread less steady. He moves like an old man expecting trouble in paradise. And I know, from what he once told me, that this is the only way he can cope with any kind of situation that could be deemed to be paradise or proximate.

CE-LE-BRA-TION TIME . . .
TONIGHT!

At midnight the torches begin to weave up the hill and voices soon follow. Ollie runs across the lawn shouting, 'Dad, dad! They're coming; they're coming.' Wingnut leaps up to help Ramon with the food, Monique and Angela bring the glasses to the table.

'Get away. Ollie, I've told you this is dangerous,' says Roy, lighting blue touch paper, retiring with Ollie in his arms as the first giant rocket scorches the warm night, and before the first powder burns glittering to the ground, a roar comes from the beacon village cortège.

Gathered round, we each take a glass of cava, drink to absent friends, and Wingnut flicks a switch to the DJ, who kickstarts the party as we watch old ladies and young children advance, two steps forward and one step back in the rhythms of another continent to the electric beat of 'Macarena', pop's freak hijacking of the Andalucian virgin.

From my room, I watch the village making merry,

316

dancing on the lawn like a thousand leaves slow blowing. Wingnut is rushing to and from the barbecue carrying ribs for Ramon, and the smell of charcoal and crackling fat comes up to the balcony on succulent breeze.

Angela is dancing with the Americans. They are here for the summer and have taken to calling unannounced on horseback, trailing a spare for Angela. They have a place on the other side of the valley, and at night, when we sit out and wait for the perfect stillness, it is the resound of their distant voices that stands between us and perfection, connecting me, as they do, to my most recent disappointments.

Angela's absences have become not longer, but more regular since the beginning of summer. I have checked for traces of the obvious, scrutinizing her bloodlines in the dead of sheetless sleep. Even if it is not apparent in tapestries on her skin, the pattern of something is emerging in the escalation of heat and tempers. And this evening, when I returned from Granada and she, supposedly, from the back of a horse, I smelt the absence of beast on every strain of her regalia.

It may pass, prove itself to be something lacking in me, the securities I yearn. Or it may announce itself, which might be something I could live with, something I can process into becoming an insignificant thing, because what we have accomplished here is too close to everything I have wished for to risk ruining it with a violence of whim. But in the

317

meantime it takes its toll, both shrivelling the ego of me and making me love her more.

Earlier this evening I had pushed open the bathroom door, watched her bathe and knelt beside her, put my head on her wet shoulder.

'Tomorrow, Jimmy. Can we go to the Meson for lunch. Celebrate, just the two of us. I want us to be alone. Talk.'

'*Of course*,' I had motioned, drowning in dread, airless in the heavy steam.

Some of the village children have jumped into the pool and Roy's voice comes loud through the music, countering to the scolds of proud parents, eager that their offspring should not abuse hospitality.

'*No problema. No problema.*' He fends off the gesticulate censures of mothers, volunteers to go in the pool himself to ensure the children are safe, which brings on fresh rounds of beration from the mothers, now blaming their children for ruining poor Roy's night. How little they know.

I sip my way through a bottle of cava, with a steady building calmness coming at me from below, as if osmosis works for mood. Days of visiting Jessie are invariably downcast, and I try to reflect that there has been more positive than negative in the slow emergence of result from the game of escape we have played and seemingly won. Jessie was, in any event, relegating himself to inevitable decline long before we left.

At the barbecue, Ramon ceremonially serves the last ribs, a giant xylophone of flesh on bone, and pours a jug of water on the coals. Smoke billows high into the trees, and when it has lifted he takes another jug, chases Wingnut across the lawn with it, catching him and pouring it over his head, then Wingnut chases Ramon towards the pool, Ramon jumping in before he can be pushed and Wingnut, fully clothed, following him in to a round of applause. More music. More drink. More dancing.

'Hi, Jimmy.'

Elvira walks towards me and the breeze catches her trousers, low and tight across the hips, loose silk rippling like a river along her legs. She stands next to me for a moment, looks down on the party and drinks lustily from my glass.

'I like Angela,' she says, 'and the Americans. They're fun, aren't they?'

I turn towards her. The cava has made her lips wet in the lights of moon and torches. I watch her mouth move, watch the insides of her in a thousand-movement synchronicity of teeth and tongue and lips in speech.

'Are you happy here, Jimmy?'

I want to put my glass down, touch her. She looks as if she would be cold; her shapes look firm as they fleet in the breeze. I want to find the warmness of her, the inside of her, but I look away. Angela is still dancing with the Americans. Roy is playing with Ollie and the other children in the pool.

'Roy has asked me to marry him,' she says. 'I haven't told him yes or no, yet. I wanted to speak to you. I will only say yes if you think it is the right thing for him. I don't want to spoil things between Roy and you, the others. It's not that I don't love him. There are all sorts of love, but I think it would be better to be here, together. He needs his friends, I know that. So, Jimmy,' she says, taking the glass from me once more, drinking it empty, 'what do you say?'

What can I say? Where is the win in this situation? Unless, of course, you believe in make-believe. Which I have to.

'Thanks. I'll never hurt him, I can promise that. It might not be enough, but it's more than most people have.'

She dwells by my side, and I sense that she is waiting for something, but I lean on the iron balustrade, resist myself and wait for her to go, which she does, with a lingering hand on my shoulder, two slight taps of 'thank you' with her fingers.

I finish the cava, let it make me drowsy, wanting it to take me. I lie on the bed, listen to the merriment and music of the party and, if I strain, I can hear cicadas rubbing their knees together out of time to the music. Their ancient white noise is the last thing I hear before I drift into sleep.

The party is waning when I am woken, not by the long-broken dawn, but by a tugging hand on my arm, a shaking from dreamless sleep and the portent voice of Angela. Bad news is in the air, I see it before I hear it.

'Jimmy, Jimmy. There's been a phone call from England. It's Frances. She's ill.'

Angela is helping me pack. She folds my suits neatly and creaseless while I look down from the balcony for the dust signals of the taxi. It is a perfect cloudless day again. On the verge of leaving, I can see how terrible it would be to wake one day and take such things for granted. There are, of course, more complex ingredients than mere climate in the making of perfection, but with the heat-softened sounds of the setting of table, of bodies climbing from the pool, you might think that it would help.

Ramon is preparing a barbecue lunch on the terrace. He calls up to me.

'Jaime. You want to eat?'

I shake my head.

'Good journey,' he calls, bright as a button.

'Jimmy?' says Angela.

I turn around. She closes the suitcase, looking peeved, nodding towards the door where Elvira is standing.

'I was wondering,' says Elvira, to Angela as much as me, 'if I could talk.'

I nod and Angela shifts her weight from one foot to the other.

'With Jimmy,' says Elvira.

321

Angela walks towards me. 'I'll wait for you downstairs. The table is booked for three o'clock. We can't be late. Your flight is at six.' She tiptoes, kisses me and leaves.

'Are you sure it's right for you to go to England, Jimmy?' says Elvira.

'*Of course. Why not?*'

'It's only a year since we did what we did. You should be careful. Those people, Jimmy; it's never over for them. The enemies you make are for ever, and the friends you have, or think you have, people like Flint, they're not friends for so long.'

'*Everything was OK*,' I say with a splay of arms, an 'O' shape of finger and thumb.

'That kind of money never passes from one to another without some bad happening. It doesn't go away, it passes along a line. Even if she did destroy all that heroin, it has an effect. Be careful. Not everything is as it seems.'

'*What do you mean?*'

'Think about what happened. Think about who has gained.'

The *mesón* spills red-clothed onto the Plaza Mayor, but we go inside, into the cool interior of hanging hams and the growling dead heads of game. We walk past the long teak bar and the photographs of Dona Maria shaking hands with bullfighters and singers, King Juan Carlos, too, and we are led by Dona Maria herself up the stairs, through the empty dark-wooded dining room that only opens in the evenings, to a table set for two on the balcony. From here we can see the whole of the plaza, less mayor than most, but a wonderful square of many levels which spans architectural style, centuries and cultures. The prints of Africa and reconquest are everywhere.

'You want the card?' says Dona Maria.

I shake my head.

'Bring us what you think,' says Angela, and Dona Maria, who is eighty if she is a day, pads away quickly, muttering approval of our trust in the wisdom of her choice.

Angela fidgets, as if she might be nervous, a quality she has never displayed in all our years of being together on all our various terms. She drinks water and pours me wine from the earthenware jug.

'I'm going to miss you,' she says, offering once more to come back to England, but unable to withstand the quickflood onset of relief when I repeat my insistences that I travel alone.

'It's been a year. It seems longer, as if we hadn't really led that other life,' she says, articulating my very thought at the precise moment I was unable to give it voice. She looks scared that something might be about to change. 'Things won't change, will they, Jimmy? We can stay like this, the way we are.'

I nod, forcing false assurance, square-pegged and with all my might.

Dona Maria brings us a tortilla to share, the first of many first courses. She puts the plate down and a palm on Angela's cheek, presses it and says, full of joy and sincerity, '*Guapa, guapa. Salud, dinero, y amor.*' Good health, money and love.

'No,' says Angela. '*Amor, amor, amor,*' and she looks at me as she says it, answering the quizzical gait of the features in my face. 'I've been learning. Wingnut found me a tutor, in Almeria.'

We eat the tortilla, sharing the single fork that Dona Maria left us.

'Do you remember when you told me what it was going to be like here? It was true, Jimmy. But don't you think that no matter how good things get, there's always something more, something not there?'

She passes me the fork, dabs her face with the red napkin, painting fast-fading pink on her white face which she shields constantly from the sun. She stops talking, leans back and takes a deep breath, about to tell me something. She passes the tortilla slowly round her sealed mouth, and she does. With her lips together, she talks to me . . .

'*I am not good at this. I want to be. I want to hear everything you say and think. I love you, Jimmy. I really do.*' And she signs it with tears coming down her face, without the slightest crack in the voice of her message to me. Angela doesn't cry, never has. It is something that has always and most definitely been absent from her nature. Until I realize. I realize that something else, until now, has always been absent from her.

'*I am pregnant, Jimmy.*'

She is happy.

STANDING ON THE BANKS, WAITING FOR BODIES TO COME FLOATING BY

I heard someone say that once.

In the recess of past I strain to retrieve the moment, like an outreach of hands in darkness. 'Don't get angry,' the voice had said. 'If people are unkind, leave them. Stand on the bank of the river and wait for their bodies to come floating by.'

It is an optimistic kind of thing to say, that brand of belief in the prevailing strength of good over bad. Just deserts in a benign order where God is good and the meek are not of necessity trodden underfoot. And given that the first familiar face I see when disembarking from the flight is that of Flint, I have more cause to disbelieve the axiom than otherwise have faith.

'Jimmy. It's been a long time. Welcome back,' says Flint.

It was my mother who said it, on the beach at Spurn Head, when Michelle had wished ill on people who were calling at us from the dunes. My mother had said, 'Don't get angry. Just stand on the banks.' What good did it do her? That kind of mentality. What good had it served her when the person to whom she had said it was looking down on her after she had fallen from the steep bank of sea.

'I have a car outside. I thought you might appreciate a lift,' says Flint. 'How is Angela? Has she settled?'

I force a smile, not daring to wonder what brand of omniscience had prompted her to receive me, and knowing only that charity is not why she has met me from a plane, having set me on courses of all kinds of action whose culminus was flight in the first place. Elvira's words repeat on me, words that implored me to consider everything that stood to be gained as a result of our journey through the Netherlands.

I follow her towards the limousine and climb into the considerable lengths she has gone to in order that I should feel at home. And more; she has enabled me to voice my opinions to the contrary. In the back of the limousine, she introduces me to a young man, fresh-faced and horn-spectacled. 'Jimmy, this is Julian. He is a signer.'

But I don't look at Julian. I look at a more familiar face from my not-so-distant past. Stapp smiles awkwardly, fidgets and looks away, still bearing the marks of our meeting in the Herengracht eaves.

I am reminded that I am in Flint's game, a more complex game than I could ever have suspected.

'*Hello, Jimmy*,' says Julian with a sanctimonious

smile straight from college and thinking he is doing someone a favour.

'*I'm the mute. You can talk and I can hear,*' I sign.

'Fine. Just let me know when you want to say anything,' says Julian.

Flint looks across as the car moves off, quizzing, concerned at the lop-side half of our interchange.

'*I want to get out. Stop the car.*'

'He says he wants to get out. Stop the car.'

Flint looks at me, knowingness in every muscle of the expression of her face. She shakes her head and says, 'Jimmy, I wish I could get through to you, or at least hear what you want to get through to me. I was only trying to help. No, you can't get out. You're coming with me. You have no choice.'

'*All right,*' I say to my horn-rim helper. '*Ask her what exactly it is she wants me to do.*'

Which he does.

'I want to know you are all right, Jimmy.'

'*We can cut to the chase,*' I say, in the champagne comfort of the limo, in a car made for everything but chase and city-centre parking.

Flint smiles at me. 'I want this to be pleasant, Jimmy. I have done you no harm, and you have done everything I have asked. So far. There is no accident in those two facts, Jimmy. I don't believe in accidents.'

'*Neither do I.*' Accidents can occur at birth, they say. People might say that of me, and they would be right, perhaps, but not in ways they could

328

possibly imagine. '*Was it an accident that I came into your web?*' I look at her as I sign, as horn-rim Julian drops his penny.

'I don't know what made you do that. All I know is that you had a cause to save. I thought it was a hopeless cause.'

'*Even hopeless causes don't happen by accident, do they?*'

'Angela was ill. She was an addict; that is all I know.'

'*It was easy for her. Too easy to get in so deep.*'

Flint shrugs, uneasy.

I remember words once delivered by Silverpiece, a message he gave me as to how Flint treats her own. And I am one of her own, I know now. Denny Lane was one of her own; Silverpiece told me that. He got Angela into the state she was in, and was then sacrificed by Flint to ease my path to Amsterdam and ensure that I stayed on it. Chancey too.

'*How is Tommy Curl?*' I ask. As I wait for the time delay of messaging to make its way to her, I remember the time I last went to the Whalebone, bore witness to his unconfessed contrition.

'Tommy Curl? I don't know.'

'*Let's go to the Whalebone. Ask Tommy about friendship, how much it takes to betray a friend. Ask him what it costs to buy a lighthouseman these days.*'

'You wanted a quick way out, Jimmy. There's no such thing.'

'*Always a price to pay.*'

'Basic economics, I'm afraid, Jimmy.'

'*What's my price?*'

'You have never killed a man, have you, Jimmy?'

I shake my head.

'And nor shall you.'

'*What then?*'

I think of other recent words of warning spoken to me, spoken by a woman whose hand I held while walking along a path. A woman who killed men I might have been suspected of having killed, men Flint knows I did not kill, which simple fact could only have made its way to her from select candidature.

'A woman? You want me . . . you want me to kill a woman. You want me to . . .' says Julian, stumbling over his words, the meanings of the message he carries, the gravity of the to and fro of the pulls on him. 'You want me to kill Elvira,' says Julian on my behalf.

'Very good, Jimmy. Very good.'

'*Why did you do it? Why did you want the heroin? Just to destroy it? You're no Samaritan.*'

We are approaching the ring road. Flint leans forward and says to the driver, 'Take us to the flats.'

'I have to see my mother.'

'Elvira would kill *you*, you know. If she had to.'

'She's ill. She has pneumonia; she could—'

'This won't take long, then you can go.'

I am owned.

SELLING ENGLAND BY THE GRAM

We are driving into an estate I last visited a year ago with Flint, down longscope lines. But now I can almost smell it, reach out and touch it. With leather upon my seat there is only tinted glass to stop it tainting me.

Men stand with dogs at the entrance to the estate. They flex, then relax as the driver's window glides down. They are vicious, powerless gate-keepers to an insignificant empire that you might think nobody would bother fighting for, on the fringe of a margin of a small corner in the field of real battle.

'You might wonder why I do this, Jimmy,' says Flint.

We make a slow, purring passage through the high, towering pink blocks. Drying clothes flap in the breeze on the tiny balconies of makeweight gardens. And the commune fields designed for bonding and leisure by men safe-distanced in civic grandeur are no-go; no-go for all but the desper-ado lounging clusters on the dogshit grass. There are many dozens of them, lying down, done-in, fidgeting. As we get closer, I can see that they are not fidgeting, they are writhing, slo-mo and hopeless.

'If I didn't do it, others would. The problem wouldn't go away. I've saved hundreds of people from themselves, maybe thousands. A year ago they would all be inside their flats now, shooting up for the price of a packet of Bensons.'

'*You did it to raise the price!*' But Julian has switched off. He's in a navel-gazing hunch, thinking that if he can't see it then maybe it will go away.

Some of the junkies are standing, fragile and unsteady, walking slowly towards the car, thinking our visit might be something it is not.

'Now they know it comes once a week. I can control it. They have to really want it, need it. They're coming to learn the value of it, the risks that everyone has to take to provide it. If they really want it, this is how it should be. The price is critical, you can understand that.'

One young boy, thirteen or fourteen I would guess from his lanky, ungrown gait, comes up to the car. He is covered in sweat and holding his stomach. I watch him through the window, slow approaching with an open palm outstretched, like something from another culture, a world with a higher number. I can see his mouthshapes of 'Please. Please. Please.' His face is dead and the 'please' grimaces of his silent pleas get smaller and smaller until he runs out of steam. He loses his will and sinks to his knees. I expect him to sob, but he hasn't got the strength.

'It has to be done. We sealed off the coasts; we had to. You must understand, Jimmy, that it's not a bad thing we have done. But we still have our enemies. There's a new generation over there. It doesn't go away, and now they have a problem: their prices are falling. They're coming after me, Jimmy. I have to protect myself, you see.'

Sat opposite, she looks at me. Fixes me with her cold eyes, strong legs crossed in a tight skirt and rock breasts pointing like warheads.

'You're on my side, Jimmy. Do you understand me?'

I nod. I understand completely.

'I'm sorry about your mother. I have a car for you. Come and see me after you've seen her.'

I point at Julian and indicate that I want him.

'Go with him, Julian,' says Flint.

And poor Julian practically shits himself, he really does. You can almost see the shudder of his sphincter failing him. But he comes with me anyway, making me wonder what kind of a hold she has over him or someone dear to him.

I will jettison Julian before making the drive to see my mother, but for now he is needed to make sense of me to a part of my past that might help me more fully understand the present I am in; acquire pointers to a better future, for me and the few people I care about.

Silverpiece is not surprised to hear my Julian voice requesting a meeting from the payphone opposite the lighthouse. He tells Julian that he will be with us as soon as he can and he also tells Julian to ask if I know what the fuck I am up to.

We walk leisurely to the shore where Jessie's petrol touch unwittingly broke a bottle on the hull of Flint's strategy of squeezing supply. When we get to the edge of river meeting sea, on the brown flats between marsh and the income of cargo, Julian's troubled thoughts burst into the seashell rush of tide and breeze.

'I don't know what's going on. I don't want to hear these things, the things you ask me to say.'

He says this not because he can trust me to hear it, but because he cannot bear not saying it. He doesn't look at me as he talks, chooses to avoid the answer he might receive, so I take him by the arm.

'*I cannot let you go back to Flint, let her hear things you have said and heard. And it is about to get worse. You are on my side now.*'

He looks away. I see the rise and fall of swallowed fear in his silent throat. It is a warm day, even in the breeze of being almost at sea. But still he shivers.

'*You have no choice. You have to trust me. I almost killed a man here. He was stood just there a year ago in the dead of night. I have never killed anyone, but soon I will. I have to. You heard what Flint said.*'

He looks at the point on the beach that I gestured to, and I can read him well enough to see that he is visited by outline imaginings of how he might encounter the ending of his own self. He is fresh-faced, has led no kind of life at all yet, nothing that might approach what is required for the meaningful contemplation of death.

'*The question you must ask yourself is who will survive. Me or Flint. And even if you think it is Flint, you are here.*' With that, and with my hand reluctantly clasping his throat, I have him – in the nine tenths of my possession.

'You,' he says. 'I choose you. I do. Honestly I do.'

'*Of course you do.*'

Silverpiece is pulling up in an unmarked car, walking down the jetty steps to join us. He is alone, stooping into the breeze, looking as if he might be blown away.

'Jimmy.'

'*Silverpiece.*'

'*How are you?*' he signs.

I make the silent face shape of laughter and watch him also see the not-so-funny side of the got-to-laugh of what he has said.

'This is Julian,' says Julian. 'He's a signer. He's on my side.' Words of confirmation to choke the voice that speaks them. 'I know everything. I know about Denny Lane feeding Angela's habit to suck me in. I know about Tommy Curl setting me up, and Stapp, too. How they needed a mug to do their dirty work. And I know why Flint wanted Burg killed. I know about fixing the supply to jack the price up. And I know that you are in it up to

335

your neck. But you have to switch sides. You have to do that, or you have to kill me.'

'Why don't you do as she asks? It's a simple thing,' says Silverpiece.

'A simple thing until the next less simple thing.'

'That's the world we've chosen to live in,' he says.

But what I don't tell Silverpiece is the real reason that I am doing what I must do. I do not confide the genius protection that Elvira has garnered for herself from her knowledge of me and the thing I consider to be of most value in the imperfect paradise of this life we have manufactured.

What she knows, what I did not know myself until today, is that she is prepared to mould herself to marriage and otherwise impossible motherhood, fully aware of what value I would attach to that. And if that is not enough, I have a mother's interest to protect. A new child also.

All I ask of Silverpiece is that he goes radio silent until tomorrow night. That and the imprisonment remand of Julian for a breach of the peace that he is neither capable of committing, nor able to resist confessing.

And for the want of any kind of alternative, I have to believe him when he nods his rueful agreement.

CLOSING A CIRCLE

I have seen my mother, staked out on a hospital bed and drip-fed with morsel lifelines which enter her in plastic tubes, like a meeting of the worst of medieval trials and the best of modern science. There was nothing I could say to her, no available means for her hearing me, in any event, just the rolling undulation of barely a life being graphed on a screen.

I held her hand, whispered in my own way that I love her and always have. I said goodbye to the cancer of my capacity to blame, the will to do it. And in so doing I lost a defining essence of myself. In the chemical warmth of a side ward from a place to die, I received a vision of where to begin afresh. I also saw a way forward.

That starting place which I have chosen to finalize my plans for squaring up to the future is the good and bad beachcombing shack of my happiest and saddest days.

It is a perfect evening and I have lit a fire in the shack for when the sun goes down. The chill comes thick and fast then, even in summer. Before that, I will swim out to see if I can catch the last glitter spawn of sun in the cove from the shadows of beach. It is a game I used to play with Michelle, who was strong in the risings and fallings of sea. My mother would do as I am now: fan the flames of barbecue so we had something to warm us from inside and out when we came running, dripping, shivering back to the homestead of shore.

I have created a good fire, a well-rooted glow of driftwood entrenched in a dry rock pool. But I have cheated, artificially aided by several lavish squirts of the wood with my plastic-containered, superstore-branded liquid fire. I have seasoned the haddock and constructed a grill from coathanger wire. The sun traces a slow curve behind me to the west and well north of a different beach, where I have performed a similar task, but with sardines wrapped in foil, with the heat of the sun remaining long after the light had gone, ice chinking in sangria, the music chatter of friends. Those evenings were holiday happenings, not the stuff of real life. What kind of a reality is it when you lay your head down for dreams, safe in the knowledge that the sun will rise blistering, for sure, on the other side of sleep.

I must wait for the fire to almost die, to glow embers, so I stroll up the beach, trace the retreating line of sea and sand. With Roy and Wingnut, Jessie, too, far away, there seems to be no great stake in what I have planned for tomorrow, no domino fall to affect others in the aftermath of failure.

Other than the fact that, if she survives, Flint will simply engage some other body to enact the widowering of Roy; ensure the motherlessness of young Ollie.

I turn and look up at the cliff, scanning along to the allotment and back down the cliff to the rock pavement, reliving the steep decline of many lives.

The chill of the sea takes my breath away, and uncontrollable engines pump blood to compensate. I flail my arms and legs in no kind of methodology until I am beyond the breakline of waves. Looking ahead, the sun is painting its glitter pools twenty yards away, receding further as I swim. I force myself to swim faster, making three or four strokes between breaths and seeing the sea open its arms, welcoming me into the uncoved outreach of its mass. It opens its horizons to me, but still the sun's light advances, out of reach. It is cold beneath me, cold in the deeper waters, in the outstretch shadow from the fast-sinking sun. Finally I give up and watch the sunlight line swim away from me. I have swallowed water and it glues like tar in my nose and throat, dulls my hearing. I am too cold. My hands are numb, my feet, too, and I can feel my heart shrivel, cold as ice, so it hurts to breathe. I turn around, but all I can see beyond the adverse camber of the swell of sea is cliff. The beach and shack have disappeared.

I lie back and regather my energies, feel my pulse

lull. And all I can see or hear or touch or smell as I bob to something else's rhythm with my eyes closed is the salt of the sea and the red buds of funeral flowers under a perfect aqua sky.

The tide is on its ebb, taking me from shore. I realize that unlike the growing spawn of me in a faraway belly, resting and close to the shores of an almost landlocked sea, I am in waters that are far from safe. I swim back towards the beach steadily, measuring my progress. But I am getting nowhere and the edge of sea is a constant, unmoving calibration against the horizontal of cliff. My legs are stiff from the cold, my arms are heavy, but I force myself to swim faster, not caring that I am swallowing sea, that there is no science to this displacement of water. I count myself down, set targets. Fifty strokes and I will be safe. But I am not. A hundred strokes and the sea's line falls everso slightly against the cliff. Another hundred strokes and my lungs begin to burn, but I can see the shack now. I force myself over the breakline of waves, and the waters are less frozen. I ride in on surf that doesn't actually aid my progress but makes me feel as if I might be travelling down some kind of slope. I reach down with my toes, ballerina, to feel land beneath me, wanting to scream. I want to sing. I am not about to die, feel my lungs slowly fill, feel my flailings turn surrender, giving myself to the deep in a careless sacrifice.

I fall to the sand. It grits on my chest and face, clods in my hair. Sea is in my mouth and throat and belly. I have it in my lungs; sand in every cranny of me. It laps at me, still claiming with occasional surges, so I stand. My legs are weak. I can smell fish, the charred skin of fish, and alongside the dry rock of fire, I see a familiar figure tending to barbecue.

'I thought you were in trouble for a moment there. I hope you don't mind, but I started the fish,' shouts Flint. She has tongs in one hand, a handgun in the other.

'I never had you down as being naive, Jimmy.' She looks up, smiles and steps away from the fire. 'You'll be better than me at this, I'm sure,' she says, motioning me towards the fire. She sits on a rock nearby with the gun resting against her thigh. 'It's a shame about Denis. He was always one of mine, you know, but I suppose loyalty is something you have to stay on top of, keep encouraging. At least Julian is someone I can rely on. And the sergeant. You and Silverpiece forgot, you see, forgot about the phone call any sergeant knows that everyone is entitled to.' There is no pleasure in the words of what she says.

I take the tongs from her, turn the fish over. It has cooked too quickly because the fire is too strong, so I lift the makeshift grill higher, away from the flames. 'Have I spoiled it for you?' she asks.

I shake my head, slowly, smiling at her, and I am sure, if you viewed us from afar, that I would not seem to be facing my killer, or exchanging a kind

341

of discourse with a woman who has, in the past few hours, killed a man who has shown me little other than kindness in my life. But, if you were watching us, you would also see my hand upon liquid fire, see that I have shielded this from June Flint with my freezing and naked torso.

'Do you want to eat your fish? Before I do it,' she asks, raising the angle of her handgun. And I could swear she feels genuine regret at what she must do. She looks kindly upon me.

I, however, feel no remorse at what is about to happen. It is, indisputably, for the better, for the enrichment of everything that is dear to me. So I look kindly back at her, look long and deep into her eyes and step back, putting fire between us. My chest is warm, but my heart feels quite, quite frozen as I quickdraw the plastic bottle from behind my back, feed fire with fire and hit Mrs June Flint with a perfect flaming parabola in the dusk.

And in her burning mad shapes, she does not scream or plead or beg. She is as silent and stoic as a good Saint Joan, save for the shots she fires blindly into the rocks. She throws herself to the sand, rolls over and over, but I take aim once more, ordealing her with fire, basting her with lashings from war. Time and again.

Until she is done.

EPILOGUE

The priest nods at me and I hand my son to Angela in order that he can be named before God in the ivory silk gown I never wore, but which Frances had brought with her in order that I am the last generation to be skipped.

After thirty years of me never having entered church, this is the second service that I have attended within the last year, the first having taken place in Granada last week, when we bade our final farewell to Jessie. Although this is a happy occasion, I can hear Frances's sobs in the echo stone, and I look around as the priest takes young Jack from the arms of his mother.

The priest makes a cross with holy water on the head of my son, incanting in an ancient tongue that is joined by the screams of a soul who is recognized by God and the Church, and out of this fusion of voices comes a terrible sound. A stone-cracking shot rings out in the church, echoes and spills from the darkness, through the open door and onto the promontory of cliff.

Elvira flinches, reaches quickly and surely into her handbag, as if this is something she has been waiting for. Outside, screams rise from the sea like the mad soundings of flocks of gulls and a ripple ebbs then flows through the church as friends and family laugh hysterical relief.

Through the arch doorway of the church I can see a thin strip of land and then sea, a boat bobbing in the swell, full of waving villagers under the falling fire of gunpowder. Into a big sky, my son's countrymen have launched a firework commemoration of the soundings of baptism.

THE END